TANISHA POLLARD

Secrets On Ice
Wintercrest Series Book 1

First published by Tanisha Pollard 2026

Copyright © 2026 by Tanisha Pollard

All rights reserved. No part of this publication may be reproduced, stored, or transmitted in any form or by any means, electronic, mechanical, photocopying, recording, scanning, or otherwise without written permission from the publisher. It is illegal to copy this book, post it to a website, or distribute it by any other means without permission.

This novel is entirely a work of fiction. The names, characters, and incidents portrayed in it are the work of the author's imagination. Any resemblance to actual persons, living or dead, events, or localities is entirely coincidental.

Tanisha Pollard asserts the moral right to be identified as the author of this work.

First edition

ISBN (paperback): 979-8-9935159-6-0
ISBN (hardcover): 979-8-9935159-7-7

This book was professionally typeset on Reedsy.
Find out more at reedsy.com

*For the ones who love deeply, set boundaries anyway,
and refuse to shrink for anyone who isn't ready to stand beside
them.*

Contents

Prologue	1
Chapter 1	5
Chapter 2	16
Chapter 3	25
Chapter 4	31
Chapter 5	41
Chapter 6	55
Chapter 7	63
Chapter 8	69
Chapter 9	77
Chapter 10	82
Chapter 11	88
Chapter 12	92
Chapter 13	96
Chapter 14	101
Chapter 15	106
Chapter 16	114
Chapter 17	119
Chapter 18	123
Chapter 19	128
Chapter 20	135
Chapter 21	140
Chapter 22	147
Chapter 23	151

Chapter 24	154
Chapter 25	159
Chapter 26	165
Chapter 27	169
Chapter 28	174
Chapter 29	180
Chapter 30	185
Chapter 31	190
Chapter 32	198
Chapter 33	203
Chapter 34	208
Chapter 35	212
Chapter 36	232
Chapter 37	243
Chapter 38	255
Chapter 39	264
Chapter 40	270
Chapter 41	283
Chapter 42	306
Chapter 43	313
Chapter 44	324
Chapter 45	329
Epilogue 1	335
Epilogue 2	340
WINTERCREST WOLVES — OFFICIAL TEAM ROSTER + PLAYER CARDS	346
LOCKER ROOM CONFESSIONS	349
WHAT KIND OF WINTERCREST GIRLFRIEND ARE YOU?	353
Acknowledgements	357
Book 2 Teaser	359

Prologue

Anonymous Chat — 1:12 a.m.
   He shouldn't be awake right now.
   Not with practice in the morning.
   Not with the noise in his chest refusing to quiet.
   But the app is open again, glowing in his darkroom. And before he can stop himself, he types the truth he's never said out loud.
   FrozenFire:
   You ever want something you're not supposed to want?
   She stares at the message, thumb hovering over the screen.
   It's stupid how easily his words get to her — how familiar he feels without a name or face. How he somehow says the things she's never admitted to anyone.
   She pulls her blanket tighter around her shoulders and types back:
   PaperHeart:
   More than I should. Why?

❅❅❅

   The blinking cursor taunts him.
   He could lie.

He could delete it.

He could pretend he doesn't think about her more than he should.

But he's tired of pretending.

FrozenFire:

There's someone in my life I can't shake. Someone I'm not allowed to want.

But every day it gets harder to pretend I felt nothing.

❄❄❄

Her heart clenches.

God… she knows that feeling. Loving someone quietly. Wanting someone you shouldn't want. Hoping no one can see it on your face.

PaperHeart:

What makes them off-limits?

❄❄❄

Why is she off-limits?

Because choosing her risks everything.

Because she's too close.

Because he's wanted her longer than he should admit.

He exhales, fingers tightening around the phone.

FrozenFire:

She's the one person I could ruin everything for.

And the one person I can't stop thinking about.

❄❄❄

Her breath catches.

It's ridiculous to feel connected to someone she doesn't even know.

Ridiculous to imagine he feels remotely like she does — not about him, but about the one person she's never stopped loving.

Prologue

Still, she answers honestly:
PaperHeart:
Does she know?

❄❄❄

A humorless laugh slips out of him.
If she knew...
God, if she knew.
FrozenFire:
She used to look at me like she does. Now I'm not so sure.
Maybe I missed my chance.
Maybe it's too late.

❄❄❄

She swallows hard.
It's never been too late in the books she reads.
Maybe real life deserves the same kind of hope.
PaperHeart:
It's never too late for the right person.

❄❄❄

He stares at her words longer than he should.
Why does she sound like someone he already knows?
Why does she feel like home?
FrozenFire:
What about you? Anyone you shouldn't want?

❄❄❄

She inhales sharply.
She should lie. But she doesn't.
PaperHeart:
Yes, someone I've wanted for a long time.
Someone everyone tells me I shouldn't touch.
But I can't help it.

❄❄❄

His chest tightens.

Whoever she is, this girl understands him — the ache, the longing, the fear.

FrozenFire:
Sounds like we're both in trouble.

❄❄❄

A small smile warms her lips.

PaperHeart:
The best kind.

❄❄❄

He hesitates before typing again, letting himself be honest in the only place he feels safe doing so.

FrozenFire:
Maybe one day we'll say it out loud.
To the right person.
At the right time.
Neither of them knows how close they already are.
In just a few days, they'll walk into the same bookstore —
At the same hour —
Waiting for the same stranger…
And finally, see the faces they've been falling for in the dark.

Chapter 1

Lizzie

The first rule of surviving a Wintercrest Wolves hockey game?

Always bring a book.

Not because I don't love hockey—I do. I grew up in this arena. I know the chants, the stats, the way the ice smells before the puck even drops.

But because I refuse to give Ethan Walker the satisfaction of seeing exactly how much space he still takes up in my head.

"Are you seriously reading?" Sasha drops into the seat beside me, the crowd roaring around us. "Lizzie, this is not book time. This is Ethan Walker ice-god time."

I don't look up right away. Not because I'm nervous.

Because I'm stubborn.

"It's a hockey game," I say calmly, turning the page. "I can multitask."

Sasha snorts. "You're multitasking your feelings."

I finally glance at her. "I'm managing them."

She studies me like I've personally offended her. "You know, one day you're going to admit you're into him."

I arch a brow. "I've never denied being into him."

Her mouth drops open. "Wait—what?"

"I've denied doing anything about it," I clarify. "Different thing."

She blinks. Then grins. "Ohhh. Growth."

Below us, the arena lights blaze as the players skate out onto the ice, the Wintercrest Wolves jerseys sharp against the white. The sound system blasts something aggressive enough to rattle my bones.

The entire town breathes hockey.

The ice gleams under the arena lights, freshly cut and waiting, the surface so smooth it almost looks unreal. Players circle lazily during warmups, sticks tapping, skates whispering as they carve shallow lines that will disappear the second the puck drops.

This part always feels like a held breath.

I settle back into my seat, adjusting the book on my lap even though I'm not really reading anymore. Habit, mostly. Armor, if I'm being honest. I've perfected the art of looking unaffected here—of blending into the crowd like I'm just another fan instead of someone whose entire childhood is stitched into these walls.

Game nights are familiar. Comfortable. Predictable.

I know how this goes. I know the rhythm of the periods, the way the crowd swells and falls, the exact moments when hope sharpens into something dangerous. I know how to keep myself steady through all of it.

Especially when Ethan Walker is on the ice.

I tell myself I'm prepared. That tonight will be no different

Chapter 1

from the hundreds of games before it. That I can sit here, turn pages, cheer at the right moments, and leave without carrying anything extra home with me.

The puck drops.

And just like that, the breath I didn't realize I was holding releases.

Not shocking, considering my dad, David Harper, co-owns the arena with Ethan's dad, Michael Walker. Their pride and joy. Their legacy.

Which means yes—I grew up here.

Yes—I know every crack in the concrete, every echo in the hallways.

And yes—I know Ethan.

Too well.

And somehow... not well enough.

When the announcer calls his name—"Number 17, co-captain Ethan Walker!"—the arena explodes.

I don't look up immediately.

I don't need to.

I already know what I'll see.

When I finally do glance down, he's skating like the ice was built for him—smooth, controlled, lethal. Dark hair curling at the nape of his neck under his helmet, shoulders broad, posture easy and confident.

He taps sticks with Ryan—my brother, the other co-captain—and Ryan grins like the game already belongs to them.

They look unstoppable.

Sasha whistles. "Your almost-boyfriend looks good tonight."

"Almost-boyfriend is a stretch," I say dryly.

"Future husband, then."

"Also incorrect."

She leans closer. "You know he always looks over here."

"He looks everywhere," I reply. "He's reading the crowd."

She gives me a look. "Uh-huh. And somehow always finds you."

I shrug. "We've sat in the same section since we were kids. He's probably checking for Ryan's family."

"Or," she says sweetly, "he's checking for you, Lizzie Harper."

I don't deny it.

I just don't indulge it.

Because here's the truth I don't say out loud:

Ethan Walker knows exactly what he's doing.

And I'm done pretending I don't see it.

**

The Wolves don't ease into the game.

They attack.

From the opening face-off, bodies crash into the boards with bone-rattling force. Skates carve sharp lines into the ice. Sticks clash. The puck snaps back and forth so fast it's hard to track unless you know the game the way I do.

And I do.

Because this isn't just hockey.

This is Wintercrest's religion.

By the end of the first period, the score is tight and tempers are tighter. A Wolves defenseman takes a hard hit along the boards and doesn't get up right away. The crowd roars, half-

Chapter 1

angry, half-feral.

Sasha is on her feet, shouting things that would definitely get her escorted out if anyone official heard her.

I close my book.

There's no hiding now.

The second period turns ugly.

The opposing team starts chirping—cheap shots after the whistle, elbows a second too late. Ryan takes a hit that sends him sliding across the ice, and my stomach drops even though I know he'll pop right back up.

He always does.

Ethan skates straight toward the guy who did it.

Not fast.

Not reckless.

Controlled.

Dangerous.

The ref steps in before anything explodes, but I see it—the way Ethan's jaw tightens, the way his shoulders square like he's cataloging every insult for later.

That's the version of him that scares other teams.

The third period starts with Wintercrest down by one.

The energy in the arena shifts from celebration to something sharper. Desperate. Hungry.

People stop sitting.

They lean forward instead, gripping railings, clutching drinks, holding breath.

The Wolves press harder, cycling the puck relentlessly. Ryan drives the play like a general, barking commands, taking hits, dishing them right back.

And Ethan—

Ethan is everywhere.

He backchecks hard, strips the puck clean from an opposing forward, then explodes down the ice. His skating is effortless but aggressive, like he's daring someone to stop him.

I feel it then.

That pull in my chest.

That familiar ache.

Because when Ethan plays like this, it's not just skill.

It's intention.

With three minutes left, Ryan intercepts a sloppy pass and launches the puck toward the net.

Time stretches.

The shot is perfect.

The goal horn screams.

Tie game.

The arena detonates.

I'm on my feet without realizing it, screaming my brother's name as the Wolves crash into him at the glass. Helmets knock together, gloves slap shoulders, sticks lift in victory.

But no one relaxes.

Wintercrest doesn't do ties at home.

The final minute is pure chaos.

The opposing team scrambles, dumping the puck deep, trying to force overtime. The Wolves refuse.

They trap.

They pressure.

They dominate.

Ten seconds left.

Ryan steals the puck near the boards and sends it flying toward the slot.

Ethan is already there.

Waiting.

Chapter 1

He catches it on his stick like it belongs to him.

A defender slams into him from the side. Another crashes from behind.

He doesn't fall.

He shifts his weight, muscles flexing, balance unshakable. He spins just enough to create space—just enough.

I swear the entire arena stops breathing.

Ethan lifts the puck.

It arcs clean and deadly over the goalie's shoulder.

Goal.

The horn howls so loud it feels like it rattles my bones.

People scream. Jump. Cry. Hug strangers. Beer sloshes everywhere. Sasha grabs my arm like she might rip it off.

And I don't even notice any of it.

Because I'm looking at Ethan.

He skates to the glass, slamming his glove against it, grin wild and victorious. His chest rises hard, breath fogging his visor.

For one brief, electric second, his gaze lifts.

And finds me.

Not the crowd.

Not the chaos.

Me.

Something sharp and knowing flashes in his eyes.

Like he meant that goal.

Like he always does.

My heart is still racing when the horn finally dies down, the sound echoing through my chest long after the crowd begins to move again. I barely register Sasha tugging me toward the aisle, barely hear the overlapping voices and laughter spilling into the walkways.

Because something about that moment won't let go of me.

The way Ethan didn't hesitate. The way he absorbed the hit, adjusted, created space where there shouldn't have been any. The way he waited—patient, controlled—until the exact second everything aligned.

That wasn't luck.

That wasn't instinct.

That was choice.

I've seen Ethan score goals before. I've seen him win games, celebrate championships, skate through pressure like it was nothing more than a mild inconvenience. But this felt different. Sharper. Intentional in a way that makes my chest ache now that the adrenaline is fading.

Like he wanted that moment.

Like he claimed it.

And the worst part—the part I don't want to examine too closely—is the certainty curling low in my stomach that he didn't do it just for the team. Not entirely. He plays like someone who knows exactly what he's capable of when he decides to stop holding back.

I tell myself I'm overthinking it. That the lingering buzz in my veins is just leftover excitement from the win.

Chapter 1

But even as we move toward the family lounge, even as the night shifts forward like it always does, I can't shake the uncomfortable truth settling into place.

This isn't the boy I grew up with.

This is a man who knows how to take what he wants.

And I'm no longer sure I'm prepared for what that realization means.

As the crowd pours toward the exits, Sasha and I slip down the private hallway to the family lounge. The air smells like hot chocolate and nachos and victory.

Ryan bursts in first, helmet under his arm. "Lizard!" He pulls me into a sweaty hug.

"Ryan, you're gross."

"That's championship energy."

Then Ethan walks in.

And the room shifts.

He's fresh from the shower, hair damp and curling, wearing the Wolves' black hoodie with the sleeves pushed up. His forearms are distracting in a way that should be illegal.

When his eyes meet mine, something soft flickers there. Familiar. Warm.

"Hey, Lizzie," he says.

My name sounds different in his voice.

"Hey," I reply easily.

He nods at my book. "Good one?"

"Yeah," I say. "Kept me entertained."

He smirks. "Did you watch any of the game?"

He's closer than I expect—close enough that I catch the

faint, clean scent of soap and something sharper underneath. Heat radiates from him, leftover from the ice and the effort and the win, and suddenly the room feels smaller.

I'm acutely aware of everything at once. The brush of his sleeve. The way his voice drops when he talks to me. The familiar ease of standing this close without anyone questioning it.

I force myself to stay casual, to keep my expression light. To not lean in.

Because this—this quiet, unguarded proximity—is more dangerous than the chaos of the game. It's where lines blur without anyone meaning for them to.

And I've spent years pretending I don't notice when that happens.
"Enough."
"Enough?" He steps closer, lowering his voice. "If we printed your name on the ice, would that help?"
I laugh, shaking my head. "You're ridiculous."
"And yet," he says lightly, bumping my shoulder, "here you are."
The touch lingers longer than it should.
Sasha is absolutely vibrating beside me.
When Ethan turns back to Ryan, she leans in. "You two have chemistry."
"We do not."
"Lizzie."
"That's just Ethan," I say calmly. "He's always been like that."

Chapter 1

She raises a brow. "And you've always reacted."

I don't answer.

Because she's not wrong.

As the night winds down, Ethan swings his duffel over his shoulder.

"See you around," he says casually.

"Yeah," I reply.

He leaves.

Sasha watches him go, then looks at me. "You're not fooling anyone."

"Maybe not," I say quietly.

This isn't a love story.

Not yet.

But if Ethan Walker ever decides to stop skating around the edges and actually come for me?

I won't be hiding behind a book.

And I won't be waiting forever.

Chapter 2

Ethan

I know exactly where Lizzie Harper is sitting before my skates even hit the ice.

Section 104. Fourth row. Left side.

I don't look for her. Not consciously. I don't scan the stands like some lovesick idiot, pretending I don't already know where she'll be. My eyes just go there—automatically, the way muscle memory takes over when you've done something a thousand times before.

She's curled into her seat tonight, book resting against her knees like armor. Even from the ice, I can picture the way she's pretending to read, pretending she isn't watching every shift, every line change, every risky play like it matters more to her than she'll ever admit.

I tell myself it's habit. Familiarity. The same reason I know which boards rattle the loudest and where the ice chips up fastest near the blue line.

Not interest.

Chapter 2

Definitely not want.

* * *

The whistle blows and I lock in. I'm co-captain. I have a job to do. The Wolves don't win because I'm distracted by my best friend's sister hiding behind a paperback.

But between shifts, when I hit the bench and cold air burns my lungs, I glance up anyway.

Just once.

Just enough to make sure she's still there.

Just enough to see if she's watching.

She is.

And something tightens low in my chest before I can stop it.

I don't remember when I started noticing that look on her face — focused, intent, like she's tracking me instead of the puck. Or when that started meaning something different than it used to.

I only know I don't let myself linger on it.

Because wanting Lizzie Harper is a line I don't cross.

* * *

Winning on a last-second goal should drown out everything else.

The noise.

The adrenaline.

The satisfaction that comes from doing exactly what you're trained to do under pressure.

It doesn't.

All I can see is the way Lizzie froze when the puck went in. No jumping. No screaming. Just her hands gripping the railing, eyes locked on me like she felt it too—like something shifted that neither of us was prepared for.

That image follows me even as my teammates crash into me, shouting and laughing, gloves slamming into my shoulders hard enough to knock the air from my lungs. I grin. I raise my stick. I play the part.

But something in my chest feels wrong.

Because when instinct pulled my gaze upward after the goal—when the horn was still screaming and the crowd was losing its mind—it wasn't the stands I searched.

It was her.

I didn't mean to do that. I didn't plan it. But the second our eyes met, the rush twisted into something sharper, heavier. Awareness cutting straight through the high.

I shouldn't notice her like that.

I shouldn't care whether she's watching, or what she sees when she looks at me.

And yet, even as the celebration spills around me, the truth settles in, uncomfortable and undeniable.

That goal wasn't just about the game.

And the part of me that understands that doesn't know what to do with it.

＊

The locker room is loud—music blasting, voices overlapping, gear clattering against concrete—but the noise barely reaches me. I peel off my pads on autopilot, movements efficient,

Chapter 2

practiced, my mind lagging somewhere behind my body.

I should feel satisfied.

Invincible.

Like the win erased everything else.

Instead, there's a pressure sitting behind my ribs, heavy and unwelcome, like the adrenaline burned too fast and left something exposed underneath. I sit longer than I need to, elbows on my knees, staring at the scuffed floor while sweat cools against my skin.

This is the part no one talks about.

The moment after the celebration, when the noise fades just enough for your thoughts to get loud.

Lizzie's face flashes in my mind again—focused, intent, feeling everything without ever demanding space for it. It hits me how much I've memorized without meaning to. Her reactions. Her silences. The way she watches like it matters.

I scrub a hand over my face and stand abruptly.

Lingering here is a mistake.

And I don't let myself do mistakes where she's concerned.

There's a line I don't cross.

I've known exactly where it is for years—clear and immovable, drawn the moment Lizzie stopped being a kid trailing after her brother and started being someone I noticed for all the wrong reasons.

Ryan's sister.

Off-limits.

Untouchable.

I repeat it to myself whenever my thoughts drift too close, whenever I catch myself wondering what would happen if I didn't step back when she steps forward. Wanting her isn't the problem. I can handle wanting.

It's acting on it that would ruin everything.

So I keep my distance. I keep my smiles easy and my hands to myself. I make sure no one ever suspects how easily she could dismantle me if I let her. I don't linger. I don't push. I don't take the risks I take everywhere else.

That's the rule.

The boundary.

The thing that's kept me steady for years.

And tonight—standing here with my heart still racing and her face burned into my mind—it feels thinner than it ever has before.

* * *

I finish toweling off and pull on my hoodie, the locker room mostly cleared out now. The music's been cut, the noise reduced to distant laughter and the low hum of vents overhead. I sling my duffel over my shoulder, already shifting into the version of myself that leaves the rink behind.

The win is done. The night should be winding down.

I plan to stop by the family lounge on my way out—quickly meet up with Ryan. Then I'll head home and let everything settle where it belongs.

I take a breath, grounding myself in routine. In exits and timelines and the comfort of knowing what comes next.

I step into the hallway.

And that's when I see her.

Madison Tate is waiting.

Of course she is.

Chapter 2

She's leaning against the wall like she belongs there — glossy smile, perfect posture, confidence sharpened to a blade.

"Ethan," she says, voice sweet and practiced. "You disappeared."

"I showered," I reply flatly. "Like a person."

She laughs, undeterred. "Most guys would stick around to celebrate."

"I'm not most guys."

She steps closer anyway, nails grazing my sleeve like she's reminding me of history.

"I need a quick clip for socials," she says. "Walk me through the goal. One-on-one."

"No," I say.

The word lands heavy.

Her smile flickers. "Excuse me?"

"Ask Ryan," I repeat. "He set it up."

She studies my face, irritation slipping through the cracks.

"Busy tonight?" she asks, pointed.

"Yes."

Her gaze sharpens — not because I said no, but because she knows that no means someone else.

She doesn't know who yet.

But she's close.

* * *

The second I step into the family lounge, the tension drains from my shoulders.

Because Lizzie is there.

She and Sasha are on the couch, mugs of hot chocolate

in hand, mid-laugh. Lizzie throws her head back, curls bouncing, laughter spilling from her like it's effortless.
Real.
Unfiltered.
It hits me harder than the win.
That sound used to follow us everywhere when we were kids — basement hockey games, late-night movie marathons, summers that felt endless.
Back then, I thought she was just Ryan's annoying little sister who refused to stay on the sidelines.
Now?
Now I don't let myself finish that thought.
"Hey," Ryan says behind me.
I barely register him.
Because Lizzie's laugh just faded, and the absence of it feels wrong.
She looks up when she notices me.
Her smile changes — softer, more careful.
Something pulls tight in my chest.
"Hey, Lizzie," I say.
"Hi," she replies — easy, but not unaffected.
Good.
She shouldn't be unaffected.
I sit beside Ryan to give myself distance I don't want.
"Madison was looking for you," Ryan mutters. "Again."
"Yeah," I say. "She'll survive."
Sasha snorts. "Bold of you to assume that."
Lizzie elbows her. "Stop."
Sasha doesn't. "What? She's exhausting."
I almost smile.
Almost.

Chapter 2

Then Madison walks in.

Perfect timing.

Her eyes lock on me instantly, then flick to Lizzie.

Something dark and calculating sharpens her expression.

"There you are," she says brightly. "I thought you left."

"Not yet," I reply.

She steps closer — too close — like she's reclaiming space.

"I still need that interview," she says. "Tonight would be perfect."

"I'm not doing it tonight."

The finality in my voice surprises even me.

Madison stiffens.

Her gaze slides back to Lizzie.

Recognition dawns.

Ah.

There it is.

"Well," she says coolly, "I'll find someone else."

She leaves without another word.

Sasha mutters, "Tragic."

Lizzie doesn't look at me.

That's what bothers me.

When she and Sasha step into the hallway, Ryan turns to me slowly.

"What's going on with you?" Ryan asks, low and sharp.

I turn. "What do you mean?"

"I mean you've been acting weird around my sister lately." His jaw tightens. "And before you say you haven't—don't. I've known you too long."

I scoff lightly. "You're reading into nothing."

"Am I?" He crosses his arms. "Because Madison walks in and suddenly Lizzie goes quiet. You show up and she changes.

That's not nothing."

I exhale slowly. "Ryan, she's like my little sister."

The words come out automatic. Practiced.

Ryan stares at me for a long beat. "Good," he says finally. "Then keep it that way."

There's no humor in his voice. No teasing.

"She's family," he continues. "She doesn't need mixed signals, and she definitely doesn't need you being... whatever this is."

"I'm not doing anything," I say.

"Make sure of it," he replies. "Because if Lizzie gets hurt, I won't care what you meant. I'll care what happened."

He grabs his bag and walks out without another word.

I stand there longer than necessary, staring at the door Lizzie walked through.

Snow is falling when I finally step outside — quiet, relentless.

I shove my hands into my pockets and tell myself the same lie I always do.

That I'm focused on hockey.

On the season.

On my dad's expectations.

On not crossing lines that would blow up my life.

Lizzie is just Lizzie.

Smart. Beautiful. Untouchable.

And the problem is—

I don't think I can keep pretending she is.

Chapter 3

Lizzie

Sunday after a Wolves win is supposed to be calm.

Recovery day. Groceries. Laundry. Pretending I'm not replaying the way Ethan Walker looked on the ice like it's burned into my retinas.

I tell myself it's leftover adrenaline. That the images looping through my head will fade once the day settles into something ordinary.

But the truth is, my body hasn't caught up with the calendar yet.

Every quiet moment brings it back—the sound of the goal horn, the way my breath caught when Ethan didn't go down, the instant recognition that bloomed sharp and undeniable in my chest. Not nostalgia. Not habit.

Awareness.

I hate that part the most. The way my body reacts before I can talk it down. Before logic steps in with reminders about boundaries and history and all the reasons I've spent years being careful.

I've always been good at restraint. At waiting. At telling myself patience is the same thing as strength.

Today, it feels more like avoidance.

And I don't know what to do with that yet.

Unfortunately, Sasha doesn't believe in peace.

At exactly 6:14 p.m., she kicks open my apartment door like she's storming a crime scene.

"I bring offerings," she announces, tossing cookies, iced coffee, and a fuzzy blanket onto my couch. "And a solution."

I peer at her over the rim of my mug. "To what problem?"

She points at me. "Your nonexistent love life."

I sigh. "We've discussed this."

"Yes," she says, settling beside me. "And I've decided you're being dramatic."

"I am not—"

"You flinch when Ethan breathes near you," she cuts in. "That's not normal behavior for a grown woman with a master's degree and excellent skincare."

I roll my eyes. "He's my brother's best friend. And a professional hockey player. And emotionally unavailable."

"Allegedly," she says. "Which is why you need an outlet."

I narrow my eyes. "I don't like where this is going."

She grins and pulls out her phone. "Heartstring."

I stare at the screen. A soft blue heart. Clean. Minimal. Intentionally anonymous.

"No photos," she continues. "No names. Just conversation. You control the pace. You control the exit."

That... gives me pause.

What surprises me isn't the idea of talking to someone new.

Chapter 3

It's how steady I feel considering it.

I've spent so long navigating spaces where my role is already defined—Ryan's sister, David Harper's daughter, the girl who grew up in the arena and learned how to take up less room when things got complicated.

Heartstring feels different.

It isn't about distraction or rebellion or proving anything to anyone else. It's about stepping into a space where I don't have to carry history on my back.

Where curiosity doesn't come with consequences.

The thought doesn't make my chest tighten.

It loosens something instead.

Not because it scares me.

Because it doesn't.

"I don't need a distraction," I say slowly.

Sasha tilts her head. "You don't need one. You want one."

And she's right.

I want something that belongs to me.

Not Ethan's orbit. Not Ryan's shadow. Not the Wolves' ecosystem.

Just mine.

"Fine," I say. "But I'm choosing everything."

Sasha beams. "That's my girl."

I type my username without hesitation.

Paperheart.

Soft doesn't mean weak. It means open.

The prompts feel easy.

Hobbies: reading, writing

Personality: introspective, romantic

Topics: books, connection, humor

Sasha tries to add bad jokes. I let her.

The screen refreshes.

✧ Match Found: Frozenfire ✧

"Okay," Sasha says. "That is hot."

"It's a username," I reply, but my pulse jumps anyway.

I open the chat.

Frozenfire:

So you're a reader. That's rare. Or maybe just rare around here. Either way... hi.

I smile before I can stop myself.

Paperheart:

Hi. Reading is how I stay sane. My best friend says I hide in books.

Frozenfire:

That's not hiding. That's choosing where you put your attention.

I inhale slowly.

That lands.

The reaction is immediate and inconvenient.

My shoulders ease. My grip on the phone loosens. It's the same physical response I had in the arena, when everything inside me leaned forward before I could stop it.

I don't like the comparison.

But I don't ignore it either.

Because this feels different in a way that matters. There's no performance here. No expectations layered over the words. Just curiosity meeting honesty without either of us rushing to define it.

I hadn't realized how rare that was until now.

Sasha watches my face. "Oh."

"What?"

"He's not flirting," she says. "He's observing."

We keep talking.

Chapter 3

Books turn into childhood. Childhood turns into fear.

He tells me he's surrounded by people but rarely feels understood.

That one hits too close.

Paperheart:

Sometimes I feel like people see what they expect to see, not what's actually there.

He takes his time responding.

Frozenfire:

That makes sense. Expectations can be heavier than silence. But I like how you think. It feels... real.

Real.

No one ever uses that word for me.

By the time Sasha leaves, I'm curled into bed, lights off, phone warm in my hands.

He asks what I want most.

I don't dodge it.

Paperheart:

A love that feels steady and electric at the same time. Like home—but bigger.

The pause stretches.

Then:

Frozenfire:

That sounds worth waiting for.

My chest tightens.

Then:

Frozenfire:

Same time tomorrow?

I don't hesitate.

Paperheart:

Yes.

Frozenfire:
Goodnight, Paperheart.

The screen goes dark, but I don't move.

Because in a few hours—with no face, no history, no complications—

I feel more seen than I have in a long time.

And that scares me.

Not because it's wrong.

But because it feels like the beginning of something I didn't plan for.

Chapter 4

Lizzie

I've never looked forward to nighttime so much.

It's ridiculous. A little embarrassing. And still—here I am, choosing it anyway. But I can't deny it: I spend all day waiting for that moment when the sun goes down, my bedroom gets quiet, and my phone lights up with a message from **Frozenfire.**

A week ago, my evenings were peaceful and predictable — books, tea, maybe a candle if I was feeling whimsical. Now?

Now I'm a grown woman curling into bed early like I'm thirteen with a crush.

I build my evenings around it now without meaning to.

Shower later than usual. Pajamas chosen with care even though no one can see them. Phone placed face-down on my nightstand like it might betray me if I stare too hard.

I tell myself I'm not waiting.

But I am.

I wait for the quiet to settle, for the world to shrink down to my bedroom and the soft glow of my lamp. I wait for the version of myself that feels less guarded to show up—the one who answers honestly instead of carefully.

There's comfort in the predictability of it. In knowing that somewhere, someone else is also ending their day the same way.

Thinking of me.

The thought makes my chest warm and unsettled all at once.

I don't examine it too closely.

I just reach for my phone.

Which... I guess I am.

On a man I've never met.

On a voice made of text messages.

On someone who doesn't know my real name.

And that's insane.

Because deep, deep down, some traitorous part of me still aches for a man who does know my name — the one who's been in my life forever, the one who smiles at me without meaning anything by it, the one who would never see me as the girl he could fall for.

Ethan Walker.

I sigh into my pillow. It's stupid to still think about him like that. Ethan has never given me any reason to hope. I hate that my mind still goes there.

That even now, wrapped up in something new and fragile and entirely my own, Ethan's presence lingers like unfinished business.

But wanting doesn't mean expecting.

I've learned that lesson the hard way.

Ethan exists in the part of my life that's familiar and

Chapter 4

complicated and carefully contained. Frozenfire exists in the part that feels open—unwritten.

And I refuse to let nostalgia sabotage something that's actually giving me space to breathe.

I don't want to keep choosing what's safe just because it's known.

Tonight, I choose what feels real.

My phone buzzes. My heart flips.

Frozenfire:
Long day. Been thinking about talking to you since noon. That's weird?

I stare at the message longer than necessary, my thumb hovering over the keyboard.

Noon.

That means I crossed his mind in the middle of his day, during whatever real life he has outside of this quiet, shared space we keep returning to.

Paperheart:
I don't think it's weird. I think it means you're honest.

The typing bubble appears. Disappears.

Appears again.

Frozenfire:
Honesty feels risky lately. But talking to you makes it feel... safer.

My breath catches.

I sit up, pulling the blanket closer around my shoulders like it might ground me.

Paperheart:
I get that. Sometimes it's easier to be real with someone who doesn't already have expectations of you.

There's a longer pause this time.

Long enough that I wonder if I said too much.

Then:
Frozenfire:
Exactly. You don't ask me to be anything. You just let me exist.
Something in my chest softens, unfamiliar and dangerous.
Because I didn't realize how much I needed to hear that.
Paperheart:
No. I... kind of feel the same.
The little typing bubbles appear instantly.
Frozenfire:
Good. I thought I was losing it.
I hug the pillow closer.
This is dangerous.
This is fast.
This is more emotion than I've felt in years.
And I can't stop.

* * *

Ethan

This app was supposed to be a joke.

Ryan dared me to try something "emotionally mature," and I rolled my eyes and downloaded Heartstring to shut him up.

And now here I am a week later, sitting in my truck like a fool, waiting for Paperheart to message me back.

It's pathetic.

But she... she makes it impossible not to care.

She listens. She understands things I've never said out loud. She doesn't expect anything from me — not leadership, not perfection, not winning.

Just honesty.

Chapter 4

I didn't know I needed that.
My phone dings.
Paperheart:
I feel kind of the same.
I reread it three times, a slow warmth spreading through my chest.
She feels it too.
This strange pull between us.
This ease.
This… connection.
Frozenfire:
You have no idea what that means to me.
And it's true.
Talking to her makes me feel lighter. Steadier. Like I'm not carrying everything alone.
But I can't let myself get too lost in this. I don't let myself wonder what it would mean if she were someone I already knew.
I don't even know her name, and she doesn't know mine. That's the whole point of the app.
Still… I can't help it.
I'm falling.

* * *

Lizzie

The next afternoon, Sasha convinces me to go with her to the arena to drop off a form Ryan forgot.

"Babe," she says as we walk in, "you need to practice interacting with real humans before your first date with

Frozenfire."

"It's not a date," I mutter.

"It's an emotional date," she corrects. "Worse. Way worse."

I elbowed her, but she isn't wrong.

We turn the corner — and there he is.

Ethan.

Leaning against the vending machine, head tipped back, hair falling over his forehead, Wolves shirt clinging to muscles I have no business staring at. He looks tired. And good. Too good.

My stomach drops.

And then he looks up... and that small, warm smile he only does with people he likes spreads across his face.

"Hey, Lizzie." His voice is soft in a way that feels dangerous. "I didn't expect to see you today."

I choke on air. "Yeah—I—um, same."

Beautiful. Stunning performance.

"You good?" he asks, stepping closer. "You seem jumpy."

"I'm fine. Just—alive."

He laughs. Actually laughs.

It hits me like lightning.

"Good," he says. "I like when you're alive."

My whole soul malfunctions. Sasha wheezes into her iced coffee. Ethan looks like he regrets saying it the second the words leave his mouth.

We stand there, staring at each other a little too long.

Then my phone buzzes.

A message from **Frozenfire**.

My heart flutters.

And Ethan's expression... shifts. Confusion? Annoyance? Something else?

Chapter 4

No, that's impossible.
Why would Ethan get jealous?
He's never wanted me like that.
Right?

* * *

Ethan

She looks different today.

Softer. Brighter. Like she's been smiling at something — or someone — all day.

And I hate that I notice.

When her phone buzzes, she looks down and smiles. Not a polite smile. Not a distracted one.

A shy smile.

Something inside me tightens, sharp and surprising.

"New book?" I ask, nodding toward her phone even though I know exactly what a message notification looks like.

"Oh—no." She tucks her hair behind her ear. "Just... someone I've been talking to."

Someone.

My stomach sinks.

"Someone special?" The words slip out before I can stop them.

The question surprises both of us.

I don't usually ask things like that. I don't insert myself where I don't belong. And yet, the idea that someone else is occupying space in her world—space I didn't realize I cared about—sits wrong in my chest.

I tell myself it's instinct. Habit. Protective reflex.

That's all.

But the tightness doesn't fade.

I watch her carefully, noticing things I've never allowed myself to linger on before. The way she hesitates. The way she chooses her words. The way her attention feels... divided.

I don't like it.

And that realization lands heavier than I expect.

"I don't know yet," she says quietly. "Maybe."

And I swear for a second, everything inside me goes still.

But I force a smile, because she deserves support — not whatever complicated mess is happening inside my chest.

"That's great," I say softly. "You deserve that."

The lie sits heavy in my chest.

Why do I care?

Why does it feel like I'm losing something I never had?

I shove the feeling down.

It's nothing.

It has to be nothing.

❄❄❄

Lizzie

As Sasha and I walk away, she whispers, "Ethan was acting WEIRD."

"No he wasn't."

"Lizzie. He looked at your phone like it personally offended him. That man was jealous."

"Ethan doesn't get jealous." But that didn't look like nothing.

"Uh-huh." She sips her drink. "And I don't get Starbucks every morning."

But all the way home, I can't stop replaying the look on his face.

Chapter 4

I shouldn't care.
Not when I'm talking to someone real.
Someone I'm starting to fall for.
Yet my heart doesn't listen to logic.
It never has.

❆❆❆

Ethan

Back in my truck, I open Heartstring, trying to shake off whatever weird moment just happened.

A new message appears.

Paperheart:

Sorry for the late reply earlier. Ran into someone unexpectedly.

I blink.

Someone.

Probably just a friend. Maybe even the guy she's been smiling about.

But I'm tired. The game schedule has been heavy. My brain is fried. Of course the timing feels strange — everything feels strange lately.

I type back:

Frozenfire:

Hope the unexpected person wasn't annoying.

A moment later:

Paperheart:

No. It was... complicated.

I let out a quiet breath.

Complicated.

A lot of life feels complicated right now.

But the idea that paperheart could possibly be someone I know?

Someone like Lizzie?
No.
Ridiculous.
Those two parts of my life don't touch.
Lizzie is someone I've known forever.
Paperheart is someone I'm getting to know in a completely different world.
I'm just tired.
Overthinking.
Reading into things that aren't connected.
Two separate people.
Two separate feelings.
Two separate problems.
NOT the same girl.
I close my eyes, drop my phone onto the passenger seat, and whisper the only truth I understand:
"I am definitely in trouble."
Because for the first time, I don't want to pull away.

Chapter 5

Lizzie

By the time Tuesday night rolls around, I've stopped pretending this is a coincidence.

It's not just that Frozenfire and I talk every evening now, or that my body seems to recognize the soft buzz of my phone before it even lights up. It's the way my days have started to revolve around him—how I catch myself measuring time in before and after his messages, how the quiet hours stretch when he's busy, how my thoughts keep drifting back to a man I've never met but somehow feel closer to than anyone I see in real life. Whatever this is, it's no longer accidental. It's intentional, and that realization is both thrilling… and dangerous.

I still tell myself it's just casual—because that's the lie that lets me keep breathing—but my body doesn't listen. My body knows the difference between distraction and devotion. Distraction is mindless scrolling on TikTok or Instagram, but devotion. Devotion is checking the clock like it owes me something.

I'm in bed earlier than I need to be, hair wrapped, skin freshly moisturized, candle lit like I'm preparing for a man who can't even see me. My laptop is open on the blanket—half a chapter of romance draft blinking on the screen, untouched. You would think that lately I would be able to write, but no, all my thoughts are clouded either with Ethan or Frozenfire. It's honestly driving me crazy.

Tonight I can't focus on the fictional couple. I can only focus on him as the time grows closer to knowing when he's online.

I stare at the Heartstring icon like it might bite me. Then I tap it anyway, because I'm tired of acting like I don't want what I want.

A new message is already waiting.

Frozenfire:
You alive, Paperheart?

My mouth curves before I can stop it.

Paperheart:
Barely. You?

Frozenfire:
Alive. Annoyed. Surrounded by people. Still thinking about you.

My stomach flips, warm and stupid.

A week ago, if someone told me a text could make my pulse jump like this, I would've rolled my eyes and told them to wake up from their fantasy, quickly. Now?

Now I'm smiling at my phone like a woman with a secret. And that's what it is, isn't it?

A secret.

They felt like things you carried because you weren't brave

Chapter 5

enough to be honest. But this one doesn't feel like shame. It feels like privacy. Like something delicate I'm protecting until I understand what it means.

No one is forcing this. No one is pulling me into it.

I'm choosing it.

That realization steadies me in a way I didn't expect. Because wanting something doesn't make me reckless. It makes me honest. And I've spent too long pretending I don't want what I very clearly do.

I don't know where this is going.

But I know I'm walking into it with my eyes open.

I sit up, propping pillows behind my back like I'm settling in for something that matters, like a good book that will have me sucked in for hours.

Paperheart:

You said you've been thinking about talking to me since noon. What happened at noon?

There's a pause.

A longer one than usual.

Then the tying bubbles appear. **Stop. Start. Stop.**

Finally:

Frozenfire:

I had a moment where I realized I was counting down the time. Like "two more hours until I can text her without interruption" type of thing.

My throat tightens.

Not because it's cheesy.

Because it's honest.

Because I do that too.

I glance at my laptop screen, at the blank page where I'm supposed to be writing, and I think about all the times I've poured my feelings into fictional men because real ones were too complicated.

But this isn't fictional.

This is a real person on the other end, choosing me.

Paperheart:
That's not weird. That's... kind of sweet.

Frozenfire:
Sweet isn't really my brand.

Paperheart:
Maybe it should be.

I wait for him to joke. For him to dodge, for him to flirt and pivot into something safer.

Instead, he replies:

Frozenfire:
I don't know how to be soft in real life.

My stomach drops—not in fear, but in recognition. Because I know that feeling too. I've mastered soft. Everyone expects soft from me. The problem is they think soft means weak, and I'm done letting people confuse the two when it comes to me.

Paperheart:
I don't think softness is the same as weakness. I think it's the bravest thing you can be when you've been hurt.

There's silence long enough that I wonder if I said too much. Then:

Frozenfire:
You always say the exact thing I didn't know I needed to hear.

My chest warms, my fingers hover over the keyboard.

I could keep this safe.

I could keep this sweet.

I could stay in the shallow end where it's warm and

Chapter 5

comfortable, and no one drowns, but I don't want safe anymore. Not when I've spent half my life quietly wanting someone to choose me out loud. I want the kind of love that chooses me over everyone else, that sees me as the only person he should want to make his everything. For someone to spoil me and make me feel feminine, to make me feel soft.

Paperheart:
What do you want from this?

The question sits there between us, calm but unflinching. Sasha would be so proud of me.

The typing bubbles appear and instantly, then pause.

Again.

When he finally answers, it's slower than usual.

Heavy.

Frozenfire:
I want... something that feels like peace, and for some reason, you feel like that to me.

My throat tightens so sharply I swallow on instinct.

Paperheart:
Maybe because we don't have to perform here.

Frozenfire:
Yeah. No expectations. No image to live up to and most of all no pressure.

Pressure.

That word rings like a bell in my chest.

I don't know what he does. He's never said, and I've never asked. Heartstring rules are unwritten but understood: you don't go digging too soon. But something about him feels... familiar. Not his words.

His silences. The way he answers is like he's used to making sure every sentence lands perfectly. Like he lives in a world

where one mistake is expensive.
Paperheart:
What are you doing right now?
Frozenfire:
Sitting in my truck like an idiot. Trying to calm down.
I blink
Paperheart:
Why are you in your truck?
Frozenfire:
Because if I go inside, I'm surrounded by people again, and for some reason, you're the only person I actually want to talk to.

My skin prickles.

That's not flirting.

That's attachment.

And attachment is dangerous.

Because attachment is real.

The speed of it should scare me more than it does.

A week ago, this man didn't exist in my life. Now his words sit in my chest like they belong there. That kind of shift usually comes with consequences, with lessons learned the hard way.

I'm aware of that.

But awareness doesn't stop the pull.

What scares me isn't how quickly this is happening. It's how right it feels to stop pretending I'm unaffected. Like I've been holding my breath for years and only just noticed.

I don't want to rush.

But I don't want to deny myself either.

I sit there for a few seconds, staring at the screen, letting that truth settle. Then I type the thing I've been too careful to say.

Chapter 5

Paperheart:
I think about you during the day, too.
A beat.
Frozenfire:
Tell me when.
My lips part. Heat crawls up my neck.
Not because it's sexy.
Because it feels intimate in a way I didn't expect.
Paperheart:
When something good happens and I want to tell someone. When something annoying happens and I want to complain. When I see a couple and I wonder what it would feel like to have that. When I'm at work and a customer is rude and I want someone to make me laugh.

I pause, then add—because I'm not going to play small anymore.
Paperheart:
And sometimes when I'm thinking about someone I shouldn't be thinking about.
My heart thuds.
There.
The truth with its teeth.
The typing bubbles appear, frantic.
Frozenfire:
Someone you shouldn't?
Paperheart:
Mm-hmm.
Frozenfire:
Do I know them?
I laugh softly to myself.
No.

Yes.
Maybe.
Paperheart:
No.
Frozenfire:
Good.
My breath catches on that single word.
Good.
Possessive, but not crude.
Claiming, but not controlling.
The kind of responses that makes my stomach flip and my mind go quiet.
I should be careful.
I know that.
But I'm tired of shrinking.
Paperheart:
You sound jealous.
Frozenfire:
I'm not jealous.
Paperheart:
You are.
Frozenfire:
I'm protective.
My pulse jumps.
Paperheart:
You can't be protective of me. You don't even know me.
Frozenfire:
I know enough.
And there it is again—that strange, steady presence. Like he's the kind of man who doesn't say things he can't back up.
My phone buzzes again.

Chapter 5

Frozenfire:
Tell me something real. Something you've never told anyone.
I stare at the message.
My fingers go cold.
I could give him something small. A safe confession. A cute little secret, but the truth is... I've been lonely in a way I never let anyone see.
I swallow.
Paperheart:
I'm tired of being the girl people assume will be fine. I'm fine until I'm not, and when I'm not, I disappear because I don't want to be a burden.
There's no answer for a few seconds.
Then:
Frozenfire:
Don't disappear on me.
My chest tightens.
Paperheart:
I don't even know you.
Frozenfire:
You do. You know me in the place that counts.
I bring my knees to my chest, hugging them, suddenly too aware of how quiet my room is.
How personal this feels. How fast this is going.
Paperheart:
This is a lot.
Frozenfire:
I know. Tell me to slow down.
I stare at the screen, heart pounding, because this is the moment. The moment, where I decide whether I want this enough to risk it. I inhale slowly, then type:

Paperheart:
Don't slow down. Just... don't make promises you can't keep.
A beat.
Then:
Frozenfire:
I don't make promises lightly.
My chest aches and deep down, a thought rises like a dangerous spark: If he asked to meet me... I might just say yes.

* * *

Ethan

I've played through pain that would make most people tap out. Cracked ribs, split knuckles, a shoulder that still clicks when the weather changes. None of it feels like this. This—this ache behind my sternum when Paperheart says something honest and it lands like a hand on my throat—this is a different kind of weakness.

The kind you can't tape up.

I'm sitting in my truck outside my place, phone in my hand, engine off, the world quiet except for the distant hum of the streetlights.

I could go inside.

The guys are probably still texting in the group chat, talking about practice, talking about tomorrow, talking about bullshit.

But I don't want noise.

I want her.

Chapter 5

When she asks what I want from this, my first instinct is to joke.

Deflect.

Make it easy.

That's what I do in real life. Keep it moving. Keep it light. Keep it controlled.

But she doesn't feel like someone you can lie to.

Not convincingly.

So I tell her the truth.

And the second I hit send, my chest goes tight like I just stepped onto thin ice.

Because I mean it.

I want peace.

I want something that doesn't require me to be perfect.

I want to be seen without being judged.

And apparently, I want it so badly that I'm jealous of a person I don't even know.

When she says she thinks about someone she shouldn't be thinking about, something hot and ugly sparks in my gut.

I shouldn't care.

I have no right to care.

I'm just... a stranger on an app.

But the feeling doesn't ask permission.

So when I say "good," it's not a choice.

It's instinct.

And then she calls it out.

Jealous.

I tell myself it's not jealousy.

It's not.

It's... protective.

Because she's soft in the places the world can bruise. I can tell. And I hate the thought of someone taking advantage of that.

Even if that someone is me.

She tells me she disappears when she feels like a burden.

And my chest turns to stone.

Don't disappear on me.

I don't type it like a plea, but that's what it is.

And then she says this is a lot.

I almost back off. I almost do the responsible thing.

But then she tells me not to slow down—just not to make promises I can't keep.

And something inside me steadies.

I don't make promises lightly.

That's true.

That's always been true.

A week ago, I would've laughed if someone told me I'd be sitting in my truck, talking to a stranger like she owns the best parts of me.

Now?

Now the only thing I can think is: I want more.

And that's the problem.

Because wanting more means wanting her in real life.

Wanting a voice to have a face.

Wanting a stranger to have a name.

I know it instinctively — the same way I know when to pull back on the ice before a hit turns reckless. There's a line here. One I've been skirting all night.

Wanting her is one thing.

Asking for more is another.

Because once faces replace words, once voices replace text, this stops being safe. It stops being contained. It becomes

Chapter 5

something that could collide with the life I already have.
With Lizzie.
The thought lands hard, unwelcome.
I should shut this down. I should protect everyone involved.
Instead, my thumb hovers over the screen.
And I cross the line anyway.
I stare at her last message, then type before I can overthink it.

Frozenfire:
If I asked to meet you someday... would you?
My heart pounds.
I hold my breath like I'm waiting for a referee to call my penalty.
A moment passes.
Then another.
Finally, her reply appears.

Paperheart:
Someday.
If you're serious.
And if you don't ask me to be small.
My hands go still.
I read it again, slower this time.
Don't ask me to be small.
Something in my chest twists, sharp and reverent.
Because that's exactly the kind of woman you don't deserve unless you show up right.
Unless you're willing to risk things.
Unless you're willing to stop hiding behind "it's complicated."
I swallow hard and type the only answer that feels true.

Frozenfire:

I wouldn't ask you to be small.
I'd ask you to be mine.
The second I send it, adrenaline floods my system.
What the hell am I doing?
I should delete the app. I should cut this off. I should stop before it turns into a disaster.

But instead, I sit there in the dark, waiting.
And when she replies, it's one line.
Paperheart:
Then earn it.
My breath punches out of me.
Earn it.
Not flirtation.
A challenge.
A boundary.
A woman who knows her worth.
My mouth curves before I can stop it.
Because whatever this is… it's not harmless anymore.
It's not a joke.
It's not a distraction.
It's the beginning of something that's going to cost me.
And for the first time in my life, the idea doesn't scare me enough to stop.

I look down at my phone, thumb hovering over the screen.
Then I whisper into the empty truck, the only truth I've got:
"I'm definitely in trouble."
And this time, I don't hate it.

Chapter 6

Lizzie

By now, the routine is set.

Nine o'clock comes, my room goes quiet, and Frozenfire is there—steady, familiar, impossible to ignore. Whatever this started as, it's no longer casual. We don't skim the surface anymore. We circle the same questions, the same what-ifs, like we're both aware that something is about to change. I tell myself it's just routine. A harmless one.

But it's not the same as brushing my teeth or turning off the lights. This is something I feel in my body—the subtle tightening in my chest when the clock gets close to nine, the way I'm more careful with my evenings now, like I'm saving the best part for last.

I've started leaving my phone on the bed beside me instead of the nightstand. I've started replying faster than I mean to. I've started rereading his messages at odd times of day, letting them settle into places they shouldn't be able to reach.

It's ridiculous, how quickly a person can become a comfort

when you let them.

And that's the part that scares me.

Because comfort becomes expectation, and expectation becomes need, and I've spent too long pretending I don't need anyone in ways that could hurt me.

But then his name lights up my screen, and my fear doesn't stand a chance.

Frozenfire:

Are you awake? Because I've had the longest day known to mankind, and you're the only thing keeping me sane.

I smile before I can stop myself.

Paperheart:

What happened?

A pause. Longer than usual.

Frozenfire:

Life. Expectations. People wanting more than I have to give. But talking to you... it feels easy. Real.

My breath catches.

He always says things like that—unfiltered, unguarded. He doesn't flirt for the sake of it. He connects. And somehow, without seeing my face or knowing my name, he makes me feel understood.

Paperheart:

It feels real to me too.

Another pause. My heart thuds.

Frozenfire:

I wish I could meet you in real life.

My stomach drops so sharply I sit up like the bed tilted beneath me.

Because we've been circling this for days without saying it outright, both of us careful in that way people get when

Chapter 6

they're afraid a good thing will shatter the second it has edges.

Meeting makes it real. Meeting means faces and voices and the possibility of disappointment. It means I can't hide behind a username when my heart starts doing something reckless.

I press my palm to my chest, grounding myself in the steady beat there.

I want this. I do.

But I also know myself well enough to understand what's at risk: if this goes badly, I won't just lose a conversation. I'll lose the feeling of being seen. And I don't know if I'm ready to grieve that yet.

Still… the idea of never knowing feels worse.

I stare at the screen, pulse roaring in my ears. This was always where this would go. I knew it the moment we stopped skimming the surface and started asking questions that mattered.

I type. Delete. Type again.

Paperheart:
I've been thinking the same thing.
I hit send before fear can talk me out of it.
Frozenfire:
Then why haven't we?
Because I'm scared.
Because I don't want to ruin this.
Because what if reality can't live up to what we've built?
Paperheart:
Because I'm scared.
Three dots appear.
Frozenfire:
Me too.

Two words. Heavy. Honest.

* * *

We don't rush it after that. We circle the idea for days—testing it, respecting it. The conversations change after that—subtly at first, then all at once.

He asks questions like he's trying to learn the shape of me without breaking the rules. I find myself answering with more care than usual, choosing words that feel like they belong to the version of me I want him to meet.
One night he says:
Frozenfire:
What would you notice first about me?
I laugh into my pillow, cheeks warm.
Paperheart:
Your energy. Whether you feel safe.
The typing bubble appears and stays, like he's thinking hard.
Frozenfire:
I want to feel safe with you too.
Another night, I admit:
Paperheart:
I'm scared you'll be different.
His reply comes fast.
Frozenfire:
I'm scared you won't like me when I'm not just words.
That one sits heavy. Because it's the same fear, mirrored. Two people bracing for impact while still walking toward it anyway.

Chapter 6

Frozenfire:
If we met, what would you want it to feel like?
Paperheart:
Soft. Unrushed. Like we already know each other.
Frozenfire:
I'd want to see your face when you laugh.
My chest tightens.
Another night:
Frozenfire:
What's your favorite place in the world?
Paperheart:
Barnes & Noble. The café section. Books and coffee make everything quieter.
The pause is longer this time.
Frozenfire:
Then that's where I'd want to meet you.
I sit up in bed.
Paperheart:
You'd really want to meet me there?
Frozenfire:
Yeah. It feels like you.
And only if you want to.
I don't overthink this one.
Paperheart:
I want to.
The reply is immediate.
Frozenfire:
Saturday. 4 p.m.
If it's awkward, we pretend it never happened.
If it's not... we see where it goes.
My heart feels too big for my ribs.

Paperheart:
Deal.

* * *

The next morning I'm at Sasha's house and she literally screams. Like seriously.
Sasha screams.
Not figuratively. Literally.
"YOU'RE MEETING HIM?! IN PERSON?!"
"Yes!"
"No!" She grabs my shoulders. "Yes, but no, because we need a PLAN."
She's already pulling clothes from her closet.
"Something that says," she declares, "'I'm soft enough to fall for, but hot enough to ruin your life.'"
"Sasha!"
"What? Romance is strategy."
We settle on something simple. Intentional. Me.
When I look in the mirror, I don't see fear.
I see possibility.
Sasha softens, looping her arm through mine.
"Whoever he is... he's already halfway gone."
I swallow.
Saturday at four, everything changes.
And for once?
I'm ready.

* * *

Chapter 6

Ethan

I stare at the message longer than I should.
Saturday. 4 p.m. Barnes & Noble.
I should cancel.

This was supposed to stay contained. Safe. Anonymous. Something I could feel without consequences.

But the idea of her—Paperheart—standing there, waiting? My chest tightens.

Barnes & Noble smells like books and coffee. Like quiet. Like her.

I can picture it too easily.

Not the store itself—just the feeling. Quiet. Intentional. The kind of place where conversation matters more than noise.

Paperheart feels like that. Thoughtful. Careful. Like she chooses her words the way someone chooses where to step when the ice is thin.

I tell myself I'm romanticizing a stranger. That I'm projecting meaning onto a voice because it feels good to be understood.

But the ease of it unsettles me.

I've started noticing things during the day and thinking, I should tell her that.

That's when I know I'm already past the point of pretending this is harmless.

And for reasons I refuse to examine too closely, my mind drifts—unbidden—to Lizzie Harper. To the way she hides behind pages. To the way she smiles like she's keeping a secret.

I shake my head.

Different worlds. Different people.

I lock my phone, lean back in my seat, and exhale.

Secrets On Ice

"This is fine," I mutter.
But deep down, I already know.
Nothing about this is fine.
And I'm walking straight into it anyway.

Chapter 7

Ethan

I know something's wrong the moment I find Ryan waiting for me in the empty film room after practice.

He's sitting in one of the chairs, elbows on his knees, jaw locked tight.

This isn't casual Ryan.

This is captain Ryan.

Big brother Ryan.

There's something else under it too.

Fear.

Not the kind that comes from distrust, but the kind that comes from knowing exactly how much damage one person can do to another if things go wrong. Ryan isn't just protecting Lizzie from me. He's protecting her from hope.

From expectations.

From the fallout that comes when someone like me realizes too late that they should've chosen differently.

The realization settles heavy in my chest. Because I

know Ryan isn't wrong about who I am when things get complicated.

That's the part that scares me.

Not his anger.

His accuracy.

"You wanted to talk?" I ask carefully.

"Yeah."

He motions for me to shut the door.

My stomach knots.

I close it.

He takes a long breath. "This is about Lizzie."

Ice floods my veins.

"What about her?" My voice is too quick. Defensive.

"You tell me," he fires back.

"I don't—"

"Drop it." He stands, crossing his arms. "I've seen the way you look at her lately."

My heart slams against my ribs.

"I don't know what you think you're seeing—"

"I know exactly what I'm seeing," he cuts in. "And we're ending it right now."

The words hit before I understand them.

Ending what?

There's nothing to end. No confession. No crossed line. No moment I can point to and say, that's where it started.

And yet, the certainty in Ryan's voice tells me he's already made the call. That whatever he sees on my face has been loud enough to give me away.

That's the problem with feelings you pretend don't exist.

They still show up.

Just not in ways you can control.

Chapter 7

Nothing's even happened.
But the way he says it feels like an iron gate slamming shut.
Ryan steps closer, voice low, controlled, deadly serious.
"Lizzie is off-limits."
My breath catches.
"Ryan—"
"No." His voice sharpens like a blade. "This isn't up for debate. She has always been off-limits. She will always be off-limits. You do not get to cross that line."
Anger prickles under my skin — unwanted, confusing.
"I'm not doing anything to her," I argue.
"You're staring at her like you are," he fires back. "You're acting weird around her. She's getting attention from other guys, and you're suddenly interested. I know you, Ethan. I know what that means."
I open my mouth, close it.
He keeps going.
"Lizzie may be grown, but she's still my little sister. She's sensitive. She loves hard. She trusts deeply."
He points at me. "You? You're a mess emotionally. You shut down when things get real. You run from anything that looks like commitment."
"That's not fair."
"It's reality," he snaps. "And I'm not letting you drag her into that."
My jaw tightens. A storm builds in my chest — frustration, shame, denial, fear.
It's all tangled.
"I don't like her like that," I say quickly.
Ryan stares at me with that cold, assessing look.
"Good," he says. "Because if you ever did, you need to shut

it down. ASAP."

The words hit like a punch.

My throat tightens. I don't know why it hurts. I don't know why I care this much.

"There are a thousand girls in Wintercrest," he continues. "Pick any of them. Not her."

He lets that sink in.

Lizzie.

Off-limits.

Forbidden.

I've never been good with forbidden things.

Not because I chase them—but because once something is labeled untouchable, it stops being abstract. It becomes something I have to actively avoid.

And avoidance takes effort.

It takes awareness.

It takes admitting that there's something there in the first place.

I tell myself this isn't about wanting Lizzie. It's about respecting Ryan. About doing the right thing. About keeping the peace.

But the truth presses in anyway: if there were nothing there, this wouldn't hurt.

Boundaries don't sting unless they're cutting through something real.

Something in my chest twists painfully.

Ryan grabs his jacket and heads to the door.

"This isn't about friendship," he says quietly. "This is about family. Don't cross the line, Ethan."

He leaves.

The room feels like it collapses inward, heavy and suffocat-

Chapter 7

ing. I sink into a chair, head pounding.

Lizzie is off-limits.

She has always been off-limits.

He's right.

He's always is.

So why does the thought of staying away feel like swallowing glass?

I scrub a hand over my face, trying to shake the conversation off.

I don't like Lizzie like that.

I don't.

I can't.

Ryan would never forgive me.

And yet—

Every time her phone buzzes...

Every time she smiles at someone else...

Every time she walks into a room and my chest tightens...

and I know I'm lying to myself.

My phone buzzes.

Paperheart.

Instant relief.

Instant comfort.

An escape that doesn't ask me to explain myself.

Paperheart:

Tell me something good about your day.

I swallow hard.

Frozenfire:

Someone reminded me what my boundaries are. Guess that's... good?

Three dots appear... then vanish... then appear again.

She finally responds:

Paperheart:
Sometimes boundaries help... but sometimes they just scare us.
I stare at the screen.
Why does she always say the exact thing I can't admit?

Chapter 8

Ethan

By the time I leave the film room, the arena feels too quiet. Not the calm, post-practice kind—this is the kind of silence that presses in, heavy and suffocating, like the building itself is holding its breath. Ryan's words still echo in my head with every step I take down the hallway, each one landing sharper than the last. *Off-limits. Family. Don't cross the line.* I tell myself I'm fine. That I've heard worse. That this shouldn't matter. But my chest feels tight, my thoughts scattered, and for the first time all season, I don't know where to put the weight of what I'm feeling—only that I can't carry it alone.

I'm so wrapped up in my thoughts that I don't notice Madison until she steps into my path, soft smile already in place.

"There you are," she says gently, like she's been waiting to catch me. "You okay?"

Her voice is syrupy sweet — too sweet.

But not sharp this time.

Not cutting.
Just… soft.
Almost kind.
I sigh. "Not in the mood, Madison."
She tilts her head, studying me. "You look upset."
"Just tired."
"That's not tired," she whispers. "That's… hurt."
I freeze.
Because damn it — she's right.
And she steps closer, not smirking, not teasing — but grounding.
"I've known you a long time, Ethan," she says softly. "Longer than most women around here. You don't show when things get under your skin. So when you do…"
She reaches up and touches my arm lightly.
"…someone must have really hurt you."
I swallow hard.
"I'm fine," I lie.
"Sure," she murmurs. "But if you ever need to not think for a while…"
Her eyes lift to mine.
"…I'm good at being a distraction."
My chest tightens.
I should walk away.
I should say no.
I should think about Lizzie — sweet, soft, off-limits Lizzie.
But all I can hear is Ryan's voice saying she's forbidden.
That I'll never be allowed to be with her.
That I shouldn't even be thinking about her.
A pressure builds in my chest — anger, heartbreak, confusion, need.

Chapter 8

All twisted together.

Madison steps closer, slow and patient.

"You don't have to talk," she whispers. "You don't have to explain. Just... let someone take care of you tonight."

My defenses crack.

Not because I want Madison.

Not because she makes my blood rush the way Lizzie does.

Not because she makes me feel seen.

But because her words land at the exact moment I'm unraveling.

And she knows it.

"Come on," she says softly, threading her fingers through mine. "Let me make you forget whatever he said."

This is the moment I should stop.

I know it with the same clarity I know when a hit is coming a second too late to dodge. I could still step back. Still choose the harder thing. Still walk away and sit with the mess Ryan left behind.

But the thought of sitting alone with it—of replaying Lizzie's face, her smile, the way her presence makes everything feel exposed—feels unbearable.

Madison doesn't ask questions. She doesn't expect explanations or growth or honesty.

She's offering numbness.

And right now, numb feels easier than integrity.

That's the part I hate most.

Knowing I'm choosing the wrong thing because it hurts less in the moment.

My breath slips out.

"Okay," I hear myself say.

***

I don't remember deciding to stay.

I just remember not leaving.

One drink turns into another. Conversation blurs into background noise. The part of me that knows better goes quiet, like it's tired of trying to intervene.

I drink more than I should.

She pours the shots.

She laughs at my jokes.

She tells me I'm amazing, talented, misunderstood, special.

She tells me everything I want to believe.

She gives me exactly what I let her.

Everything Lizzie never said — and never would — because Lizzie doesn't think of me that way.

At least… that's what I tell myself.

So when Madison leans in and kisses me, sweet and slow and practiced, I don't pull away.

I let it happen.

I follow her into her bedroom.

And I don't think.

Not once.

I let the alcohol burn in my veins.

I let her hands distract my mind.

I let the noise drown out the ache in my chest.

Because tonight, I don't want to feel.

I don't want to think about Lizzie smiling at her phone.

I don't want to think about Ryan saying she's forbidden.

I don't want to think about how wrong everything feels.

I just want to forget.

And for a few hours…

Chapter 8

I do.

*** * ***

I wake up tangled in sheets that aren't mine.
Madison is asleep beside me, makeup smudged, hair spread over the pillow like she planned the aesthetic.
My head pounds.
My stomach turns.
Because I know...
This didn't solve anything.
It didn't change anything.
It didn't take away the ache.
If anything?
It made everything worse.
As I stare at the ceiling, a single thought hits harder than the hangover:
I didn't want her.
I just didn't want to feel.
I drop back onto Madison's bed with a hard exhale, dragging my hands down my face.
What the hell am I doing?
My pulse is still racing, my skin still hot, but none of it feels good.
Not really.
Not the way it used to.
Hell — *used to* is generous.
The truth is worse.
Madison and I...
Yeah.

We were a regular thing once.
Nothing serious.
Nothing emotional.
Just… convenient.
She liked me for the attention.
I liked her because she didn't ask for anything more.
Especially during away games—
god, those empty hotel rooms, the adrenaline after wins, the frustration after losses—it was too easy to slip into somebody's bed.
Too easy to let my body distract my mind.
Too easy to pretend feelings didn't exist.
And it wasn't always Madison.
Sometimes it was someone else from the opposing city, someone who didn't care about my life or my last name or what team I played for.
Someone who wanted the moment, not the truth.
It was stupid.
Shallow.
Lonely as hell.
And Ryan knew all of it.
He never judged me, not out loud.
But he never forgot it either.
That's why he said Lizzie was off-limits.
Why he looked me dead in the eye and said she wasn't built for the kind of mistakes I used to make.
And the worst part?
He wasn't wrong.
I breathe out, slow and miserable.
Because tonight…
I proved him right.

Chapter 8

I proved every fear he had about me.
And for what?
To feel nothing?
To forget the one person I can't forget?
To pretend the way I feel about Lizzie isn't eating me alive?
My stomach twists.
I didn't sleep with Madison because I wanted her.
Not even close.
I slept with her because for half a second, I wanted to feel like the old me—the guy who didn't ache every time Lizzie walked into a room.
The guy who didn't think about her voice or her laugh or the way she looks at me like she sees something worth holding onto.
The guy who didn't want something real.
Because wanting her is the most dangerous thing I've ever felt.
It's the one thing I can't screw up.
The one thing I should stay away from.
The one thing that makes me feel like I'll ruin her if I get too close.
But lying here, staring at the ceiling, everything burns.
What happened with Madison?
It didn't fix anything.
It didn't numb anything.
It just made everything worse.
Because all I can think about is Lizzie.
Her laugh.
Her smile.
Her stupid little book she pretends to read at games.
The way she blushes when I talk to her.

The way she said my name on the porch like she'd been waiting her whole life to say it like that.

I cover my face with one arm and exhale shakily.

I'm such a coward.

I run to all the wrong places when the right thing is staring me in the face.

And the truth settles in my chest like a punch:

I don't want anyone else anymore.

Not Madison.

Not some random girl in a hotel room.

Not the easy, empty stuff I used to grab when I didn't want to feel anything real.

I want her.

Lizzie.

Always have.

Always will.

And now I've made everything ten times more complicated.

Perfect.

Chapter 9

Ethan

I don't know why I'm tearing apart my closet.

It's not a date.

It's not romantic.

It shouldn't matter.

And yet my palms are sweating like it does.

I hold up a shirt, study it, toss it onto the bed. Try another. Too stiff. Too casual. Too much like I'm trying too hard. I scrub a hand over my face and exhale.

"What the hell am I doing?"

I already know the answer.

I want to look good for her.

Paperheart.

The woman whose voice exists only in text bubbles and late-night confessions. The one who listens without expectations, who sees the parts of me no one else asks about. The one who makes the pressure fade—just a little—every time my phone lights up.

I want her to like me.

That's new.

Wanting to be liked instead of wanted. Wanting approval instead of distraction. Wanting someone to see me and still choose to stay.

With Madison—or anyone else—it was always about the moment. Chemistry. Escape. A way to not feel so damn heavy.

This feels different.

This feels like something that could matter tomorrow. And the next day. And the day after that.

That realization tightens something in my chest, sharp and unsteady. Because things that matter don't come with exits you can slip through unnoticed.

They come with consequences.

And I don't know if I'm ready for those.

That thought lands heavy in my chest, because the second it does, another face flashes through my mind.

Lizzie.

Her laugh.

Her quiet presence.

The way she looks at her phone like someone just handed her something precious.

It shouldn't bother me.

It shouldn't mean anything.

But it does. Because every time I picture her looking at her phone like it holds something fragile, I feel like I'm standing too close to a line I already crossed once.

Lizzie has always felt like something I wasn't supposed to touch. Not because she's delicate — she's not — but because she matters in a way that demands care.

Chapter 9

And the worst part?

I don't think I've ever wanted anything more carefully in my life.

I force myself to breathe and pull on a dark Henley that fits the way I want it to. Jeans. Clean boots. I run my hand through my hair once—just once—until it falls the way it always does.

Controlled. Normal.

I reach for my jacket.

A knock hits the door.

Soft. Familiar.

I already regret opening it.

Madison stands there, glossy lips curved into a smile she knows how to use. She leans against the frame like she belongs here.

"Well," she purrs. "Don't you look nice."

"Not today, Madison."

She steps inside anyway. "Relax. I'm not here to fight."

I shut the door slower than I should. "Then why are you here?"

Her eyes sweep over me—taking inventory. "You're dressed up. That usually means something."

"It doesn't."

She hums, unconvinced, circling closer. "We had a good time once. We could again."

I step back. "No."

The word is firm. Final.

Her smile falters—just for a second. "Why not?"

"Because it was a mistake." The truth lands rough but clean. "I shouldn't have let it happen."

She studies me, recalculating. "If you need comfort—"

"I don't." My voice hardens. "That's over."

Something sharp flashes behind her eyes before she smooths it away.

"That girl must be special," she says lightly. "If you're turning down this."

I don't answer.

Because she's right.

But the person I want to impress isn't standing in front of me.

Madison watches me a moment longer, then steps toward the door. "Good luck," she says sweetly. "Wherever you're going."

The door clicks shut behind her.

I lean my forehead against it, breath leaving me in a slow, controlled exhale.

Guilt presses in—quiet but heavy.

For Lizzie.

For my past.

For wanting something that feels real when it shouldn't.

I grab my jacket, my keys, and force my feet to move.

This is simple.

Just a meeting.

No complications.

I've said the words enough times that they should feel solid.

They don't.

The closer I get to my keys, the more it feels like I'm stepping into something already in motion. Like the choice was made days ago, and I'm just now catching up to it.

I don't feel excited.

I feel braced.

Like a man walking into a moment that's going to change

Chapter 9

something whether he's ready or not.

I repeat it until it almost sounds true.

Then I head toward my truck—toward Barnes & Noble—toward the woman I've fallen for through words alone—completely unaware that the disaster waiting for me already has a name — and I already love the sound of it.

Lizzie.

Chapter 10

Lizzie

I change my outfit twice before settling on the first one.

Not because it's perfect — but because it feels like me.

Soft jeans. A sweater I've worn enough times that it hangs the way I like. Lip gloss instead of lipstick. I'm not trying to impress anyone. I'm not trying to look like a version of myself that only exists for special occasions. I want to show up as I am — the girl who loves quiet corners and warm coffee and conversations that feel like exhaling.

The girl who didn't expect this to happen.

My phone rests on my bed, screen dark, but it feels louder than anything else in the room. I keep glancing at it like it might speak on its own. Like it might reassure me that this is real. That I didn't imagine the way Frozenfire talks to me. The way he listens. The way he makes space for my thoughts without rushing me through them.

I sit on the edge of the mattress and take a breath.

This is just a meeting.

Chapter 10

That's what I tell myself — not because I don't care, but because I do. Because if I let myself spiral into *what ifs* and *maybes*, I'll never make it out the door. I've learned that about myself. Hope has a way of growing teeth if I don't hold it gently.

Still, my hands shake a little as I zip my bag.

I catch my reflection in the mirror and pause.

I look... good. Not in a dramatic, *everyone look at me* kind of way. Just steady. Comfortable. Like I belong in my own skin. That feels important. I smooth my curls once, then stop myself before I can overdo it.

"Enough," I murmur.

The door opens without a knock.

Sasha leans against the frame, arms crossed, eyes already scanning me from head to toe like she's assessing a final draft.

"Well," she says. "Look at you."

I roll my eyes. "You've already seen me today."

"Yeah, but this is different." She steps into the room, grin widening. "This is *meeting-the-mysterious-man-from-the-internet* you."

I groan. "Please don't say it like that."

She laughs, unapologetic. "I'm just saying. You look good. Soft. Intentional."

I glance back at the mirror, suddenly self-conscious. "Too soft?"

Sasha's expression shifts — not teasing now, but thoughtful. She shakes her head. "No. You look like yourself. That's the point."

Something in my chest loosens at that.

She moves closer, lowering her voice like we're sharing a secret. "How do you feel?"

I consider the question carefully.

"Nervous," I admit. "But… good. Like I'm standing on the edge of something instead of waiting for it to happen to someone else."

Sasha smiles slowly. "That's because you are."

I pick up my phone, thumb hovering over the screen. The quiet stretches longer than I expect it to.

Long enough for my brain to start filling in gaps it has no business touching. What if he's late? What if he changed his mind? What if the idea of meeting felt easier than the reality of it?

I hate how quickly doubt sneaks in when something matters.

I remind myself that silence isn't absence. That anticipation doesn't mean rejection. That people are allowed to take their time when they're stepping into something vulnerable.

Still, my chest tightens.

I don't want to be the girl who reads meaning into every pause — but I also don't want to pretend this doesn't mean something to me.

I breathe through it.

Let myself want. No new messages yet. I don't need them. The last one is enough — the one where he said he couldn't wait to finally hear my voice. The one where he told me Barnes & Noble felt right.

"Do you think it's weird?" I ask quietly. "Meeting like this?"

She snorts. "Lizzie, people meet in worse ways every day. At least this one started with conversation."

"That's what I keep telling myself."

"And," she adds, nudging my shoulder, "anyone who talks to you the way he does? He's already halfway gone."

Chapter 10

Heat creeps up my neck. "Sasha."

"I'm serious," she says. "Men don't ask questions like that unless they care about the answers."

I swallow, suddenly aware of how much I want that to be true.

Sasha squeezes my hand. "Whatever happens, you showed up. That matters."

I nod. It does.

My phone buzzes then, like it waited for permission.

Frozenfire:

I'm on my way.

My heart stutters — just once — before settling into a steady, excited rhythm.

"I should go," I say.

Sasha grins. "Text me the second you leave."

"Of course."

"And Liz?" She stops me at the door. "You don't owe anyone anything. Not charm. Not forgiveness. Not a second chance."

Her words settle deeper than she probably realizes.

Because part of me is already preparing — already rehearsing how to be accommodating, how to be understanding, how to make space for someone else's nerves instead of my own.

I've done that my whole life.

Today, I don't want to.

I want to show up open, yes — but not apologetic. Hopeful, but not smaller.

I meet her gaze. "I know."

She studies me for a beat, then nods. "Okay. Go."

* * *

Secrets On Ice

The drive to Barnes & Noble feels shorter than usual, like the road knows where I'm going and wants to help. At every red light, I check my phone even though I know he's driving. At every turn, I feel the weight of what I'm walking into settle more firmly in my chest.

This isn't just curiosity anymore. It's investment.

I'm not meeting a stranger. I'm meeting someone who already knows the parts of me I usually keep tucked away.

That thought is equal parts thrilling and terrifying.

The town looks the same as it always does — familiar storefronts, the quiet stretch of Main Street — but everything feels sharper, more alive. Like the air itself is paying attention.

I park and sit for a moment with my hands on the steering wheel.

This is it.

I think about the way Frozenfire laughs in text — the pauses, the ellipses, the way he never rushes to fill silence. I think about the night he told me he wanted peace, and how something in me recognized that word like an old friend.

I step out of the car.

Inside, Barnes & Noble smells like coffee and paper and comfort. The café hums softly, voices blending together in a way that feels safe. I scan the room without really knowing what I'm looking for. My gaze catches on small details instead — a man standing by the counter checking his watch, someone shifting in their seat like they're waiting too, a half-finished coffee growing cold on a nearby table.

I wonder if any of them are him.

I wonder if I'll recognize him instantly or if I'll hesitate, second-guess myself, wait for a feeling that might not announce itself loudly.

Chapter 10

The idea that he could already be here — watching me without my knowing — sends a nervous flutter through my chest.

I straighten slightly, resisting the urge to fidget.

I don't want to hide.

I want to be found.

I check the time.

Four o'clock.

I take a breath and choose a table near the shelves, close enough to feel surrounded by stories. My bag rests at my feet. My hands fold neatly in my lap.

I'm not pretending this doesn't matter.

I'm just choosing not to be afraid of it.

Whatever happens next, I showed up honestly. I didn't hide. I didn't shrink. I didn't let doubt talk me out of wanting something real.

And for now?

That's enough.

Chapter 11

Lizzie

Barnes & Noble feels too bright.

Too quiet.

Too full of people who are not the man I'm supposed to meet.

I'm twenty minutes early and already sweating through my sweater, fingers worrying the edge of my sleeve as I pretend to browse a display I've memorized by heart. Every time the café door opens, my pulse jumps.

Every time it isn't him, my stomach sinks.

My phone buzzes.

Frozenfire:

Here.

The word feels heavier than it should.

Here means inside. Here means now.

I glance toward the door, my pulse thudding so loud I'm sure people can hear it. For a split second, I consider not turning around at all — just sitting here, suspended in the

Chapter 11

moment before everything changes.

Because whatever happens next will rewrite something.

I don't know what yet.

I just know I won't be able to undo it.

I sit straighter.

Smooth my sweater.

Fix my curls in the reflection of my dark screen.

Then the door opens.

And my world tilts sideways.

Ethan Walker steps into the café.

Tall. Broad. Familiar in a way that steals the air from my lungs. He's dressed casually — dark Henley, jeans — but he looks devastating anyway.

That alone would've been enough to knock me flat.

But he's holding a book.

My brain scrambles, grasping for logic that doesn't exist.

People read books. Ethan reads books. This doesn't mean anything.

Except my chest knows better.

Because he isn't just holding a book. He's holding it carefully, like it matters. Like it was chosen. Like it belongs to something unfinished.

The book.

The one I told Frozenfire changed everything for me.

My heart drops into my stomach.

No.

No, no, no.

This cannot be real.

He scans the room.

His eyes land on me.

He freezes.

My chest tightens so hard it hurts.

"Please," I whisper to no one, "please tell me this isn't happening."

* * *

Ethan

Where is she?

What does she look like?

Does she smile the way she writes?

I step into the café gripping the book she told me to read — the one she said felt like home and heartbreak all at once.

And then—

Lizzie.

Sitting in the exact seat we agreed on.

Looking like she's about to shatter.

The world crashes into place all at once.

The way she texts.

The softness.

The humor.

The honesty.

The girl I've been falling for is—

Lizzie Harper.

Of course it's her.

Of course the one person I let myself open up to — the one person who feels like peace — is the one person I was never supposed to touch.

This isn't fate.

It's my fault.

I should've asked more questions. I should've slowed this down. I should've protected her from me instead of letting

Chapter 11

myself pretend this existed in a vacuum.

Every warning Ryan gave me echoes back, brutal and precise.

I did this.

My best friend's little sister.

The girl who has always been off-limits.

The girl I never let myself want.

My chest caves in.

I can't move.

She can't move.

Everything fractures.

And suddenly, I don't know which version of him hurts more.

Chapter 12

Lizzie

I stand so fast my chair scrapes loudly against the floor.
"No." My voice cracks. "No—this isn't funny."
"Lizzie—"
"Don't." Tears blur my vision. "You don't get to play with me like this."

My chest aches like something has been ripped out of it.
This isn't just embarrassment. It's grief.

Because I didn't just give him my words — I gave him the parts of myself I don't hand over lightly. The lonely parts. The hopeful parts. The parts that believed someone could choose me without already knowing my face or my history.

I trusted that version of him.
I trusted the man who listened.

And now I'm standing here realizing that the safest place I've felt in years was built on something I didn't understand.

"I swear, I didn't—"
"You never even liked me," I choke. "So why pretend to be

Chapter 12

someone else? Why ask me to meet you like this?"

Pain flashes across his face — real, raw, unguarded.

"I didn't pretend," he says, stepping closer. "I didn't know it was you."

I shake my head, hands trembling.

"You expect me to believe that?" My voice drops to a whisper.

"That the man I've loved for so long just *happens* to be the stranger who made me feel seen for the first time in years?"

He looks wrecked.

"Lizzie… if I'd known—"

"That's the point," I whisper.

"You never knew."

His eyes close like I struck something vital.

"You never noticed me," I say softly. "Not in the way that mattered."

* * *

Ethan

Her words hit harder than any punch I've ever taken.

"I noticed you," I say immediately. "More than I ever should have."

Her breath stutters.

"Every laugh in the stands. Every book you carried. Every time you pretended not to watch me."

I should stop.

I should say less. Choose safer words.

Because every truth I'm about to give her comes with a price — and I don't know if she'll ever forgive me for it.

But she deserves honesty, not protection.
So I let it spill.
My voice drops. "I saw you."
Her eyes shine with unshed tears.
"And when I talked to Paperheart…" I swallow.
"I didn't know it was you, but I felt something I've never felt before."
Her lips part.
I lift my hand — hesitating — then brush my fingers against her cheek.
She closes her eyes.
Just once.
If I kiss her, I lose Ryan.
If I don't, I lose her.
I lean in anyway.
Our foreheads almost touch.
Her breath mixes with mine.
Her lips part — unsure, hopeful, waiting.
One second.
One fragile, suspended second.

***

Lizzie

A barista calls out an order.
The sound shatters the moment.
I stumble back, breath shaking.
"I can't," I whisper. "I need time."
My hands curl into fists at my sides, nails biting into my palms like pain might keep me grounded.
If I stay, I will fall apart.

Chapter 12

I will ask questions I'm not ready to hear the answers to. I will lean into something fragile and unfinished and hope it can hold me.

And I don't trust myself not to do that.

Not with him.

Not when everything in me still wants to believe him.

"Lizzie—"

"I'm sorry."

And before I completely fall apart, I turn and walk out of the café, tears burning down my cheeks.

Leaving Ethan standing there—ruined, breathless, and fully awake—

watching me go.

Chapter 13

Lizzie

I wake up the next morning before my alarm.

For a few seconds, I don't remember why my chest feels tight. The room is still, pale light slipping through the blinds, the kind of calm that usually means nothing is wrong.

Then memory settles in.

Barnes & Noble.

The book.

Ethan.

I sit up slowly, letting my feet touch the floor, grounding myself in the present. I don't rush. I don't panic. I breathe in through my nose and out through my mouth like I've been taught a hundred times before—like I know how to do this.

I've always known how to do this.

The part no one sees is how much energy it takes.

How every steady breath feels deliberate. How calm isn't something that happens naturally — it's something I build, piece by piece, because letting myself unravel would take

Chapter 13

longer to recover from.

I sit there for a moment longer than necessary, hands resting in my lap, letting the feeling crest and pass.

I don't cry.

But I don't pretend I couldn't.

The mirror over my dresser reflects a version of me that looks... fine. Puffy eyes, maybe. A little tired. But not shattered. Not ruined. Just real.

I pull my hair into a loose bun and change into leggings and a sweatshirt, movements deliberate, careful. There's comfort in routine. Control in the familiar.

The world didn't stop yesterday. That realization sits heavier than I expect.

The town still woke up. People still went to work. Coffee was brewed. Books were shelved. And somewhere in all of that normalcy, I walked out of a café and left a part of myself behind.

I make it through the morning on autopilot—emails, errands, small talk that requires nothing from me. No one asks the right questions. No one looks at me like they know something cracked.

I'm grateful for that.

What surprises me is the clarity.

I thought I'd wake up confused. Torn between anger and hope. But the truth is quieter than that. Sharper.

I wasn't hurt because Ethan was Frozenfire.

I was hurt because I was finally brave enough to want something—and it fell apart in public.

There's a particular kind of humiliation that comes with being vulnerable where people can see you. With letting your guard down and realizing too late that you weren't protected.

I've spent most of my life learning how to be composed. How to be the girl who doesn't ask for too much. The one who understands timing, optics, patience. I learned early how to be resilient because the world expects it of women like me.

Strong. Graceful. Unbothered.

Soft, but never fragile.

And yesterday, I was fragile.

I open my phone once, then set it back down.

There are a dozen things I could do instead.

I could reread the messages. I could look for meaning in timestamps, in phrasing, in silences. I could imagine what he's thinking right now and whether it hurts as much as this does.

That version of me wants answers immediately.

This version knows better.

Closure that comes too fast is rarely honest. And I won't trade my self-respect for relief that won't last.

Heartstring sits there like it always has. The app didn't disappear. The messages didn't vanish. That almost makes it worse.

Anonymity felt safe because I wasn't asking to be chosen. Not really. I was letting myself be known without demanding space in someone's real life.

That's the truth I can't ignore now.

Being wanted quietly is not the same as being chosen out loud.

And I don't want quiet anymore.

Ethan's face flashes in my mind—not the confident athlete everyone sees, but the man standing frozen in the café, eyes wide like he'd just realized his life had shifted without his permission. I remember the way his voice softened when he

Chapter 13

said my name. Not the confident version he uses with the team or the town — but the quieter one, like he was afraid of getting it wrong.

That memory hurts more than the shock.

Because it tells me this wasn't nothing.

It just wasn't handled with care.

I don't think he lied to me.

That truth lands gently, but firmly.

Believing him doesn't mean forgiving him. It doesn't mean I'm ready to hear explanations or unravel intentions. It just means I'm not going to rewrite myself into a fool to make this easier to bear.

I can hold two truths at once.

He didn't know.

And I still got hurt.

By the time the sun dips lower in the sky, something inside me settles.

I can't change what happened. I can't unsee his face or undo the way my heart leapt when I thought I was finally walking toward something meant for me.

But I can decide what happens next.

I won't chase answers that cost me my dignity.

I won't shrink myself to make someone else more comfortable.

And I won't disappear just because being seen hurt.

If Ethan wants to explain, he can wait until I'm ready to listen.

If he wants me—really wants me—it won't be in secret. It won't be halfway. And it won't be on terms that ask me to carry the weight alone.

I set my phone face down on the counter and pour myself

Secrets On Ice

a glass of water, steady hands, steady breath.
   For now, this is enough.
   I survived the impact.
   The rest can wait.

Chapter 14

Lizzie

I don't remember driving home — only deciding that I wouldn't fall apart in public again.

The door closes behind me, and I stand there for a moment, keys still in my hand, breathing through the ache in my chest. Everything feels bruised, but intact.

Barnes & Noble already feels distant. Unreal.

Then there's a knock at my door.

A knock hits my bedroom door.

"Liz?"

Ethan's voice.

My whole body reacts before my brain can catch up.

Heat floods my chest, sharp and sudden, like I've been burned. My hands shake so badly I have to press them into my thighs to steady them.

This isn't fear.

It's recognition.

The same pull I felt in the café, only now there's nowhere

to hide from it. No table between us. No crowd. Just a door and everything I don't trust myself to say if I open it.

My heart slams so hard it hurts.

"No," I whisper. "No, no, no—"

He knocks again, softer. "Lizzie, please. I just need to talk to you."

I curl in on myself, chest aching.

"I can't," I choke. "I can't do this right now."

"I didn't know," he says through the door, voice strained. "I swear, if I had—"

"Please stop," I whisper.

Silence.

Then, quietly, carefully—

"I didn't lie to you."

"I didn't play with you."

His voice isn't defensive.

It's wrecked.

That's what breaks me.

Because if he were angry, or cold, or trying to control the narrative, I could harden myself against it. I could turn him into a villain and walk away clean.

But he sounds like someone standing in the aftermath of something he never meant to destroy.

And I recognize that tone — the one people use when they're telling the truth even though it won't save them.

"I didn't know it was you. I swear."

Tears spill again.

Because the worst part?

I believe him.

I don't want to — but I do.

And believing him hurts more than thinking he was cruel.

Chapter 14

"I'm sorry, Lizzie," he says softly.

My throat closes. "Please go."

I don't say it to punish him.

I say it because if I hear one more word, I will open the door. I will ask questions I'm not ready to hear answered. I will lean into something that already feels too fragile to survive another hit.

This isn't rejection.

It's triage.

A long pause.

Then a slow, defeated exhale.

"Okay," he says. "But I'm not done explaining. Not until you hear me."

His footsteps fade down the hall.

The moment he's gone, my breath collapses completely.

I break all over again.

Ten minutes later, my bedroom door flies open.

"WHERE IS HE? I'M READY TO COMMIT A FELONY."

Sasha storms in like she's prepared for violence.

"He left," I croak.

She slams the door and climbs onto the bed, wrapping herself around me like a feral guard dog.

"Tell. Me. Everything."

I do.

Barnes & Noble.

The book.

Ethan walking in.

The realization.

The almost-kiss.

Me panicking and running like my soul was on fire.

Sasha stares at me for one long second.

Then she screams into my pillow.

"YOU MATCHED WITH ETHAN WALKER."

"I know," I moan.

"That's not a tragedy, Lizzie. That's destiny wearing skates."

"I accused him of playing me!"

"You were overwhelmed!"

"I RAN."

"YOU WERE EMOTIONALLY AMBUSHED."

"He saw me crying!"

"GOOD."

"SASHA."

She grabs my face. "Listen to me. You didn't imagine that connection. He didn't fake it. That man was falling for you without even knowing who you were."

I sniffle. "Ryan is still going to kill me."

She winces. "Okay, yes. That's… a hurdle."

I bury my face in her lap. "I can't even look Ethan in the eye again."

"Perfect," she says brightly. "Make him suffer."

"That's not advice."

"It absolutely is."

She strokes my hair like she's narrating a documentary. "You shook that man to his core. He knocked on your door like someone realizing his entire life just re-routed."

I laugh weakly through tears.

"Sash… what do I do?"

She smiles, calm and certain.

"You do nothing."

"…Nothing?"

"Nothing," she repeats. "You breathe. You exist. You let him come to you."

Chapter 14

I swallow. "What if he doesn't?"

She snorts. "Lizzie. He left here realizing he's been emotionally falling in love with his best friend's little sister."

I groan and hide my face again.

Hope doesn't arrive loudly.

It slips in carefully, like it knows it isn't fully welcome yet. Like it understands how easily it could be crushed if it asks for too much too soon, but for the first time since Barnes & Noble...

I let myself hope she's right.

Chapter 15

Ethan

I've never felt panic like this.

Not during playoffs.

Not when I shattered my wrist junior year and smiled through the pain because coaches were watching.

Not even when Ryan told me—flat, final—that Lizzie was off-limits, and I nodded like it didn't cut straight through me.

This is worse.

This is realizing I already crossed the line... and didn't even know it at the time.

The arena parking lot is half empty when I finally make it to my truck. The sky is a washed-out gray, the kind that makes everything look colder than it is. My hands shake when I try to start the engine, and when it catches, the rumble doesn't calm me the way it usually does.

It just makes the silence louder.

Barnes & Noble plays in my head like a highlight reel I can't turn off.

Chapter 15

The door opening.

Her sitting there.

Her face going pale.

The way her mouth opened like she was trying to breathe through a punch.

Lizzie.

I press my forehead to the steering wheel and breathe through my nose, slow and controlled, like I'm trying to push the moment back out of my body.

It doesn't move.

I should've known.

Not that it was her—how could I have known that? But I should've known something like this was inevitable. I should've known that the universe doesn't let you cheat consequences. You don't get to build an entire connection with someone—strip yourself down to the parts you hide—without eventually paying for it.

I built that with Paperheart.

And Paperheart was Lizzie Harper.

Ryan's sister.

My best friend's family.

The girl I trained myself not to want.

The girl I still wanted anyway.

The guilt is immediate and physical, like sickness. It crawls up my throat and sits there, bitter and thick.

Because here's the part I can't outrun:

Even if I didn't know…

I still did it.

I still texted her like she was mine to be gentle with. Like I had a right to her honesty. Like I deserved her softness. Like I was safe.

And then I showed up—holding the book she told me about—looking like I was walking into something sweet.

While she looked like she was walking into an ambush.

I slam my fist lightly against the steering wheel. Not hard enough to break anything. Just hard enough to feel it.

"Idiot," I mutter.

I don't mean the reveal.

I mean everything.

I mean thinking I could keep this contained.

I mean pretending I didn't feel it.

I mean using anonymity like a loophole.

As if the truth wouldn't find me.

My phone sits in the cupholder, screen dark. I don't touch it. I can't. The urge to open Heartstring and see her messages is strong—stronger than the urge to breathe—but I don't deserve that right now.

Those words aren't mine to scroll through like comfort.

Not after the way her face fell.

Not after the way she looked at me like she didn't recognize the world anymore.

I pull out of the lot and drive with no real destination. Wintercrest blurs past—the familiar streets, the places that have always been safe because they were *normal*. But nothing feels normal now. Every stoplight feels too bright. Every storefront feels like it's watching.

Like everyone can see what I did.

I make it to the edge of town before I realize I'm heading toward the rink.

Of course I am.

The only place I know how to be when I can't handle my own head is the ice.

Chapter 15

I park and let myself in through the side door, the one that creaks if you don't push it right. The building is empty. No music, no voices, no skates cutting clean lines into frozen water—just the hum of fluorescent lights and my own footsteps echoing down the hallway.

It smells like disinfectant and cold metal.

It smells like control and for the first time, control doesn't help.

I walk until I'm standing at the edge of the rink, staring at the blank sheet of ice like it might offer answers.

It doesn't.

I rest my forearms on the railing and close my eyes.

Ryan's voice from the film room rises up in my memory, calm and lethal:

She's off-limits.

I didn't argue because I didn't have a defense that mattered. I never do.

Because Ryan wasn't wrong. Not about my history. Not about the way I used to run. Not about how easy it was for me to numb out instead of facing anything real.

And I proved him right.

I proved him right even *before* Barnes & Noble, didn't I?

My stomach twists.

Madison's name flashes through my head like a warning light.

I don't even let myself sit in it long enough to spiral into shame, because the truth is simple and brutal:

When Ryan drew the boundary, I didn't rise to meet it.

I broke myself against it.

And now Lizzie is the one bleeding.

I open my eyes and stare at the ice harder, like intensity

could rewrite time. Like I could go back and be a different version of myself—one who deletes the app, who tells Paperheart goodbye the moment it stops being casual, one who walks away before it turns into something that can wreck a girl like Lizzie.

But I can't.

All I can do is accept that intent doesn't erase impact.

I didn't mean to hurt her.

And she still got hurt.

Meaning my intent doesn't matter nearly as much as I wish it did.

My phone vibrates in the cupholder.

Once.

Then again.

My chest goes tight.

I pull it out with stiff fingers, expecting a message from Ryan—because this has Ryan written all over it. Expecting the inevitable *Where are you?* or *We need to talk.*

But it's not Ryan.

It's Heartstring.

A notification.

Paperheart:

...?

Just three little dots and a question mark. Like she's standing on the other side of a wall, hand hovering, unsure if she's allowed to knock.

My throat closes.

I stare at it for too long, like the screen might burst into flames.

I want to answer.

I want to explain.

Chapter 15

I want to fix it so badly it makes my skin hurt.
But I don't.
Because any message I send right now would be for me.
Not for her.
It would be to soothe my own panic, my own guilt, my own need to be forgiven quickly so I can breathe again.
And that isn't love.
That's selfishness wearing a pretty mask.
That question mark holds more restraint than anything I've shown her so far.
She's waiting without demanding.
And if I answer now, I'd be betraying that.
I lock the phone and shove it into my jacket pocket like it's a blade.
Then I inhale slowly and make myself think like someone who isn't allowed to hide behind adrenaline.
What does Lizzie need right now?
Not me.
Not my voice.
Not my explanation.
She needs space.
She needs the dignity of not being chased through her own emotions like her pain is an inconvenience I'm trying to solve.
I press my fingers to the bridge of my nose and exhale.
This is the part where the old me would run straight into damage control.
Text. Call. Show up again. Force the conversation. Force the moment.
Because I've always been good at pushing when I'm scared.
But this isn't a game.
This is Lizzie.

The girl who has always been gentle with everyone else.
The girl who deserves gentleness back.
If I want any chance at being someone safe for her, I have to prove I can do the one thing I'm terrible at:
Wait.
Let the silence exist.
Let the consequences settle.
I pull my hand away from my face and stare at the ice again.
The rink is empty, but I can still hear it—the sound of skates, the thud of a puck, the yell of coaches. All the noise that used to make my world simple.
None of it touches this.
Because this isn't hockey.
This is real.
And the real thing is this:
I fell for her through words.
And now I have to earn the right to speak to her with my voice.
Ryan is going to find out. I don't know when. I don't know how. But he will. Ryan always does.
And when he does, I won't lie.
I won't defend myself like I'm the victim.
I won't pretend this was harmless because I didn't know.
I'll take it.
Because whether I meant to or not, I walked into a place that belonged to Lizzie's heart and left footprints all over it.
I push away from the railing and start walking back toward the exit, footsteps echoing again.
Outside, the air is cold enough to sting, and the sky is starting to darken. I stand there for a moment, letting the cold burn my lungs clean.

Chapter 15

I pull my phone out once more, thumb hovering over the Heartstring app.

Paperheart's message sits there waiting...?

I don't open it.

Not yet.

Instead, I type a note in my phone—something I'll use when the time comes, when she's ready, when she isn't shaking and looking like she might shatter.

A promise to myself more than anything:

No excuses. No pressure. No chasing. Tell the truth. Give her space. Earn it.

I save it.

Then I turn my phone off completely.

The silence that follows is brutal.

But it's honest.

And for the first time since Barnes & Noble, I do the only thing I actually deserve to do.

I let it be hard.

I let it matter.

Chapter 16

Lizzie

Ryan notices something's wrong before I say a word.

He always does.

I'm halfway through pouring coffee when he leans against the counter, arms crossed, eyes narrowed just enough to tell me he's clocking everything I'm not saying. My movements are too careful. My shoulders too tight. Like I'm bracing for something I refuse to name.

"You okay?" he asks.

The question is casual. The tone is not.

I keep my eyes on the mug. "Yeah."

Ryan hums, unconvinced. "That didn't sound like a yeah."

I shrug, taking a sip that's too hot. It burns my tongue, but I don't react. Pain feels easier than explanation right now.

He watches me for a moment longer, then pulls out a chair and sits, turning it backward so he can rest his arms on the back. This is his *I'm not going anywhere* posture. The one he used when we were kids and I'd scraped my knee too badly

Chapter 16

to pretend I was fine.

"Did something happen?" he asks quietly.

I shake my head. Then, because that feels like a lie even to me, I add, "Not... like that."

Ryan's jaw tightens just a little. "Liz."

There it is. Not a warning. Not a command. Just my name, heavy with concern.

I finally look at him.

His expression softens immediately, like he wasn't braced for how tired I look. How worn down.

"Hey," he says, gentler now. "What's going on?"

I exhale slowly and set my mug down before my hands can start shaking again.

"I don't want to talk about it yet."

Ryan studies my face, searching for something—panic, maybe. Fear. The kind of thing that would make him step in and take control.

Whatever he sees must reassure him, because he nods once. "Okay," he says. "Then we won't."

Relief hits me so fast it almost makes me dizzy.

He leans back in the chair. "But I'm still going to ask this once. And you can tell me to shut up if you want."

I wait.

"Are you safe?"

The simplicity of it nearly undoes me.

"Yes," I answer immediately. "I'm safe."

Saying it out loud feels like claiming something I worked hard to protect.

Ryan lets out a breath like he's been holding it in all morning. "Good."

We sit in silence for a few seconds, the familiar quiet of our shared space settling around us. The house smells like coffee and toast and the faint sweetness of whatever Angela baked last night. Home. Solid. Real.

"I don't like seeing you like this," he admits finally. "You're usually better at hiding it."

I huff out a weak laugh. "Wow. Thanks."

He smirks. "You know what I mean."

I do. I've always been the composed one. The calm one. The girl who learned early how to carry herself with grace because the world was always watching a little too closely.

Black girls don't get the luxury of falling apart publicly.

Ryan knows that. He's always known that.

"Whatever it is," he says, voice steady, "you don't have to protect me from it."

"I know."

"And you don't owe me details just because I'm your brother."

I glance at him, surprised.

He shrugs. "I worry. That's my job. But I trust you to tell me when you're ready."

Something warm spreads through my chest at that. Not relief exactly—more like being seen without being cornered.

"Thank you," I say softly.

Ryan nods, then hesitates. "Can I say one thing?"

I brace myself. "Depends."

A corner of his mouth lifts. "Fair."

He sobers. "Whatever line I drew before? Whatever rules I set?"

My stomach tightens, but I don't interrupt.

"They were never about you," he says. "They were about me being scared."

Chapter 16

I blink.

"Scared that someone would hurt you and I wouldn't see it coming," he continues. "Scared that I wouldn't be able to protect you if it mattered."

His gaze holds mine. Honest. Open.

"You're not fragile, Liz," he says. "You never have been. But you are important. And sometimes I forget that protecting someone doesn't mean controlling the situation. Sometimes it means trusting them to stand in the mess and come back on their own terms."

The words settle deep.

"I can take care of myself," I say quietly.

"I know," he replies immediately. "And I'm proud of you for it."

My throat tightens.

He stands, crossing the kitchen to squeeze my shoulder once—a grounding, familiar gesture. "If someone crossed a line with you, I want to know. Eventually."

"I will tell you," I promise. And I mean it.

Ryan nods. "Good. Until then?"

He offers a small smile. "I've got your back. No questions asked."

I let out a breath I didn't realize I was holding.

"Okay," I say.

He grabs his keys, pausing at the door. "And Liz?"

"Yeah?"

"If you ever feel like you have to disappear to keep the peace?" His voice is firm now. "That's when something's wrong. Not with you—with the situation."

I swallow. "I'll remember that."

Ryan gives me one last look, then heads out, leaving the

house quiet again.

I stand there for a moment, hand wrapped around my mug, feeling steadier than I did an hour ago.

Not because anything is fixed.

But because I'm not alone.

And for now?

That's enough to keep going.

Chapter 17

Lizzie

The rink feels colder than I remember.

Or maybe I'm just more aware of everything now—the sharp bite of the air, the echo of skates cutting into ice, the way my shoulders tense the second I step inside. The familiar smells hit me all at once: metal, rubber, cold water, adrenaline.

Home territory.

Which makes it worse that he's here.

I spot Ethan immediately, even though I don't want to. I always do. He's on the ice already, moving through drills with mechanical precision, jaw set, focus razor-sharp. He looks the same as he always has—strong, controlled, untouchable.

Except now I know that's a lie.

I take a seat near the boards, far enough away to feel intentional. Sasha drops down beside me, nudging my knee with hers.

"You good?" she murmurs.

I nod. "I can handle this."

She studies me for a second, then smiles. "I know."

That's the thing. I do know too.

The whistle blows. Players shift. Ethan skates past the bench, close enough that I can see the tension in his shoulders. He doesn't look at me.

I notice immediately.

The old version of me would've taken that personally. Would've wondered what I did wrong, why I wasn't worth acknowledgment.

This version understands restraint and for the first time, it doesn't feel like rejection.

Still, awareness hums between us like live wire. Every time he circles back, every time his skates scrape too close to where I sit, my body reacts before my mind can stop it.

I don't miss the way his movements falter—just barely—when Ryan steps onto the ice.

Big brother. Captain. Boundary.

Ethan stiffens, jaw tightening, but he keeps skating. Keeps his head down. Keeps his distance.

Good.

Practice ends without incident. Players peel off the ice, laughter and chatter filling the space. I stand slowly, giving myself a moment before turning toward the tunnel.

That's when I feel it.

Not a touch. Not a voice.

A presence.

His presence.

I look up.

Ethan stands a few feet away, helmet off, hair damp with sweat. His eyes meet mine for the first time since Barnes &

Chapter 17

Noble.

The air shifts.

He doesn't step closer.

He doesn't speak.

He just looks at me—like he's measuring every word he's not saying.

I hold his gaze.

Not soft. Not angry.

Steady.

"Hey," he says finally. Quiet. Careful.

"Hey," I reply.

His voice doesn't ask for anything and neither does mine.

That's it.

One word each.

It shouldn't feel like this much, but it does. Like something important just passed between us without either of us reaching for it.

Ryan's voice cuts through the moment. "Ethan."

Ethan breaks eye contact immediately. "Yeah."

He turns, shoulders squaring like he's bracing for impact.

I watch him go, something bittersweet settling in my chest.

He didn't chase me.

He didn't explain.

He didn't cross the line.

That matters more than he probably knows.

Sasha exhales beside me. "Wow."

I huff out a breath. "Don't."

"I didn't say anything."

"You were about to."

She grins. "Okay, fine. But... proud of you."

I glance at her. "For what?"

"For not shrinking. And for not letting him pull you back before you're ready."

I think about that as we walk toward the exit. About the way Ethan stopped himself. About the space he left intact.

Maybe this doesn't have to be a disaster.

Maybe it's just… complicated.

And maybe—for the first time—I trust myself enough to let it be that way.

Chapter 18

Ethan

Avoiding Lizzie Harper turns out to require more discipline than a full-contact drill. I don't mean intentionally. I'm not ducking corners or rerouting my life to stay away from her. I'm just… aware now. Of where she might be. Of the spaces she occupies. Of how easily I could cross a line if I'm not careful.

That awareness follows me everywhere.

The locker room is louder than usual, the guys chirping and shoving like nothing in the world has shifted. I go through the motions—untie skates, peel off gear, nod when spoken to—but my mind keeps drifting back to the way Lizzie looked at me in the rink.

Not angry.

Not hopeful.

Just steady.

Like she was watching to see who I'd choose to be.

I fail that test the moment my phone buzzes.

Heartstring.
My chest tightens before I even look.
Paperheart:
Are you okay?
Three words. Simple. Gentle. Still her.

I stare at the screen, thumb hovering, every instinct screaming at me to answer. To tell her I'm not okay. To tell her I'm wrecked and ashamed and trying to do the right thing even though I don't know what that is anymore.

But I don't reply.

Because answering her here—behind a locker room stall, surrounded by noise and sweat and distraction—feels wrong. Like hiding again. Like slipping back into the version of myself that takes the easy connection instead of the honest one.

I lock my phone and shove it into my bag.

Across the room, Ryan catches my eye.

Not suspicious. Not angry.

Just... watching.

That might be worse.

I leave the rink without lingering, the cold air outside hitting my lungs hard enough to ground me. The town is quiet, dusk settling in, streetlights flickering on one by one like they're keeping time.

I don't drive home right away.

Instead, I find myself pulling into the grocery store parking lot, hands tight on the wheel.

Why am I here?

The answer comes immediately.

Because Lizzie shops here. Because this is normal. Because some part of me wants to prove—to myself, maybe—that I

Chapter 18

can exist in the same world as her without reaching for what I'm not allowed to touch.

I grab a basket and head inside.

Bad idea.

I spot her near the end of the aisle, comparing two jars of pasta sauce like it's the most important decision she'll make all day. She's dressed casually, hair pulled back, glasses perched on her nose. She looks… real. Grounded. Like she belongs exactly where she is.

My feet stop moving.

She hasn't seen me yet.

I could turn around. Walk away. Let this be another almost.

But then she looks up.

Our eyes meet.

There it is again—that quiet recognition. The pause where the world seems to hold its breath.

She doesn't smile.

She doesn't frown.

She just nods once, acknowledging me like I'm… human.

I nod back.

We stand there for a beat too long, the space between us heavy with everything we're not saying.

"Hey," I say finally.

"Hey," she replies.

Same word. Different setting.

Progress? Maybe.

She gestures weakly to the jars in her hands. "Do you know if there's actually a difference between these, or is it just marketing?"

The question catches me off guard.

She's talking to me.

About pasta sauce.

Like nothing exploded between us.

"Uh," I clear my throat. "The one on the left," I say. "Less acidic. Fewer regrets."

Her lips twitch despite herself.

A small victory.

"Good to know," she says, dropping it into her basket.

Silence stretches again. Not awkward. Just… loaded.

"I got your message," I say before I can stop myself.

Her eyes flicker—just once. "Okay."

"I didn't answer because—" I hesitate, choosing honesty over comfort. "I didn't want to do it halfway."

Something softens in her expression. Not forgiveness. Not yet.

Understanding.

"I appreciate that," she says quietly.

We stand there, two people orbiting the same truth from different angles.

"I'm not ready to talk," she adds. Not apologetic. Just factual.

"I know," I say immediately. "I'm not asking you to."

She studies me for a moment, like she's testing the weight of that promise.

"Okay," she says.

That's it.

No resolution. No next step.

Just… okay.

She turns her cart toward the checkout.

I watch her go, something tight and aching settling in my chest.

I didn't fix anything.

Chapter 18

But I didn't take anything from her either.
And for now, that has to be enough.
As I leave the store, my phone buzzes again.
Paperheart:
Thank you for not pushing.
I stop walking.
I type back before I can overthink it.
Frozenfire:
I meant what I said. No pressure.
I send it, then slip the phone into my pocket, heart pounding.
This isn't the easy path.
But it's the right one.
And for the first time in a long while, I don't run from that.

Chapter 19

Lizzie

I don't expect to see him at the fundraiser.

That's probably my mistake.

The Wintercrest Youth Hockey fundraiser is exactly the kind of thing neither of us can avoid without it being noticeable. Everyone who matters is here—players, families, donors, coaches. The rink lobby is dressed up with string lights and folding tables covered in raffle baskets and baked goods.

Normal. Community. Safe.

I tell myself that when I walk in.

Sasha brushes my arm. "You okay?"

Chapter 19

"Yeah," I say. And this time, it's mostly true.

I spot Ryan first, already deep in conversation with one of the coaches. He catches my eye and gives me a quick smile—the same one from this morning. Solid. Grounding.

Then I feel it.

That awareness. That quiet pull that has nothing to do with sound or sight.

I turn.

Ethan stands near the silent auction table, dressed in dark jeans and a sweater that looks unfairly good on him. He's laughing at something one of the boosters says, posture relaxed, shoulders loose.

He looks... normal.

The realization hits harder than I expect.

He's still Ethan Walker. The world didn't stop for him the way it did for me.

And somehow, that hurts more than if it had.

Our eyes meet.

There's no jolt this time. No shock.

Just recognition.

He doesn't come over.

Neither do I.

Good.

The night moves in fragments. I help Sasha at the bake sale. I chat with people who've known me since I was a kid. I smile when appropriate, laugh when expected.

But I'm aware of him the entire time.

Of where he stands.
   Of when he shifts.
   Of how his gaze flickers toward me and then away, like he's testing his own restraint.

At one point, I reach for a napkin at the same time he does.

Our fingers don't touch.

They hover, close enough that I feel the heat of him.

"Sorry," he says immediately, pulling back.

"It's fine," I reply.

Our eyes lock for half a second too long.

Chapter 19

Something tightens in my chest.

I step away first.

Later, the crowd thins. Music hums softly from someone's speaker. Ryan disappears into a conversation near the doors.

I'm studying a photo display when Ethan's voice comes quietly from behind me.

"You did a good job with this."

I turn slowly. "With what?"

"The fundraiser," he says. "It matters."

"Yeah," I say. "It does."

Silence settles between us. Not awkward. Just heavy.

"I won't stay long," he adds, like he needs me to know. "I just wanted to say that."

I nod. "Okay."

Another pause.

"You don't have to answer," he says carefully, "but… are you doing alright?"

I consider the question.

"I'm doing better than I was," I say honestly. "That's all I can offer right now."

He accepts that without argument. I see it in the way his shoulders ease just slightly.

"I'm glad," he says. "You deserve that."

The words land softly. No expectation attached.

It would be easier if he pushed. If he demanded clarity or forgiveness or something I could react against.

But he doesn't.

"I should go," he says.

"Okay."

He hesitates, then adds, "For what it's worth… I meant what I said at the store."

"I know," I reply.

And I do.

He gives me a small nod and steps away, disappearing into the thinning crowd.

I let out a breath I didn't realize I'd been holding.

Chapter 19

Sasha appears at my side like she's been summoned. "You alive?"

Barely, I think.

"I'm fine," I say instead.

She eyes me knowingly. "You two look like you're one bad decision away from combusting."

I huff a quiet laugh. "That's dramatic."

"Is it?" she asks gently.

I don't answer.

Because the truth presses in, undeniable and uncomfortable:

Avoiding him isn't getting easier.

It's getting harder.

Every shared space makes the silence louder. Every almost-moment sharpens the edge of what we're not saying.

I don't want to rush this. I don't want to undo the control I fought to regain.

But I'm starting to understand something I didn't before.

Restraint isn't the same as distance.

Secrets On Ice

And pretending we don't feel this?

That's starting to feel like its own kind of lie.

Chapter 20

Ethan

The worst part is that I know better.

I know exactly where this is heading the second I see her name light up my phone.
Lizzie:
Can we talk?
No qualifiers.
No softening.
Just four words that land like a warning.
I don't answer right away.
Not because I don't want to—but because I do. Because every instinct in me says go, and I've learned the hard way that instinct alone isn't enough.
I type. Delete. Type again.
Ethan:
Yeah. Where?
The reply comes almost immediately.

Lizzie:
The old bleachers. If that's okay.
My chest tightens.

The outdoor rink sits on the edge of town, half-forgotten and rarely used anymore. We spent summers there as kids— Ryan teaching me slap shots, Lizzie reading on the sidelines, pretending she wasn't watching.

It's neutral ground.

That makes it dangerous.

The night air is cold enough to sting when I pull into the lot. The lights above the rink flicker weakly, casting long shadows across the empty ice. Lizzie is already there, leaning against the boards, arms folded tight around herself.

She looks calm.

That scares me more than tears ever could.

I stop a few feet away, giving her space.

"Hey," I say.

"Hey."

Silence stretches between us, thick and charged.

She exhales slowly. "I didn't want to do this over text."

"Me neither."

Another pause.

"I'm not here to fight," she says. "And I'm not here to forgive you."

I nod. "Okay."

Her eyes lift to mine. Steady. Searching. "I just need you to be honest with me."

Something in my chest shifts. "I will be."

She steps closer—just one step. Close enough that I can smell her shampoo. Close enough that my body reacts before my brain can stop it.

Chapter 20

"Do you still want me?" she asks quietly.

The question hits like a punch.

There it is. No dancing around it. No safe phrasing.

"Yes," I say immediately. Too fast. Too honest. "But that's not the point."

Her breath catches. "Then what is?"

"The point," I say carefully, "is whether wanting you makes this better or worse."

She studies my face, searching for cracks. "And?"

"And I don't trust myself not to hurt you if we rush this."

The words cost me something to say. I feel it in the way my jaw tightens, the way my hands curl at my sides like they're resisting a pull.

"I don't want to be another man who takes what feels good and leaves you to deal with the fallout," I continue. "I don't want to prove Ryan right."

Her lips press together. "This isn't about Ryan."

"I know," I say. "But it's about me."

She takes another step closer.

Now she's right there.

My pulse roars in my ears.

"You don't get to decide what hurts me," she says softly. "I do."

"I know," I reply. "That's why I'm trying not to."

Her hand lifts—hesitant—and rests against my chest.

Right over my heart.

I freeze.

Every nerve in my body lights up. My breath stutters. I don't move, don't touch her back, don't give in to the instinct screaming to pull her closer.

"You feel this too," she says.

"Yes," I breathe.

"Then why are we standing here pretending we don't want the same thing?"

Because if I touch you, I won't stop.

Because if I kiss you, I'll cross a line I can't uncross.

Because you deserve more than heat and apologies.

I don't say any of that.

Instead, I say the truth that matters most.

"Because I want the first time we cross that line to be something we don't regret."

Her fingers curl slightly in my shirt.

The space between us is gone now. Our foreheads almost touch. Her breath brushes my mouth. My hands lift instinctively—then stop, shaking, midair.

I give her the choice.

She leans in.

Just barely.

Enough that I feel the promise of her. The pull. The ache.

For one suspended second, the world narrows to this—her warmth, my restraint, the line trembling between us.

Her lips part.

My thumb brushes her

Not a kiss.

Not yet.

She closes her eyes, breathing me in like she's memorizing the moment.

Then she pulls back.

Just as slowly as she leaned in.

Her hand drops from my chest.

"Okay," she whispers. "Not yet."

Relief and loss crash into me at the same time.

Chapter 20

"Not yet," I echo.

She steps away, wrapping her arms around herself again, reclaiming the space between us.

"But Ethan?" she adds, meeting my gaze.

"Yes?"

"When it happens…" Her voice steadies. "I don't want it to be careful. I want it to be real."

Something fierce and reverent settles in my chest.

"It will be," I promise.

She nods once, then turns and walks toward her car, boots crunching softly against the gravel.

I don't follow.

I don't call after her.

I stand there in the cold, heart pounding, body buzzing, restraint burning through me like fire.

Because tonight, we didn't cross the line.

But we stopped pretending it isn't there.

And that makes what's coming inevitable-whether we're ready or not.

Chapter 21

Lizzie

I don't see Ethan again that night.

    I drive home alone, just like we agreed, the road stretching quiet and empty in front of me. The cold air seeps through the vents, grounding me, cooling the heat that lingered under my skin after the bleachers. I don't rush. I don't replay every second on a loop.

    I let the silence do its work.

    At home, I shower. Change into soft clothes. Sit on the edge of my bed with my phone resting face-down beside me like it might burn if I touch it.

    I tell myself I don't have to do anything.

    That choosing nothing is still a choice.

    But the truth settles in slowly, unmistakable.

    I don't want nothing anymore.

    I want him — without pretending, without running, with-

Chapter 21

out crossing a line we'll regret in the morning. I want what we almost had at the rink, but with clarity. With intention. With both of us standing in it fully awake.

So this time, I decide.

I pick up my phone before doubt can talk me out of it and type carefully, deliberately.

Lizzie:

If you're still awake… you can come over.

Only if you want to. Only if this is intentional.

The response doesn't come right away.

I pace. Breathe. Remind myself that this invitation is mine to take back if I need to.

Then my phone buzzes.

Ethan:

Yes.

Only if you're sure.

I close my eyes.

Lizzie:

I am.

The knock comes twenty minutes later.

Not loud.

Not urgent.

Measured.

I open the door, and there he is — hands in his jacket pockets, posture careful, eyes searching my face like he's still making sure this is what I want.

He doesn't step inside right away.

"Hey," he says quietly.

"Hey."

The space between us holds.

"This is okay?" he asks. "Still?"

"Yes," I answer without hesitation.

Only then does he step inside.

The door closes softly behind him, the apartment settling into a hush that feels intimate without being overwhelming. He doesn't touch me immediately. He stays a step away, letting the moment breathe.

That matters more than anything.

I move first.

When my hands rest against his chest, I feel his breath hitch — just once — like he's been holding it longer than he realized. His hands come up slowly, resting at my waist, grounding instead of claiming.

"This isn't careful forever," I tell him softly.

"No," he says. "Just right now."

He kisses me then.

Not like the almost-kiss at the bleachers.

This one is unhurried. Warm. Certain.

His mouth moves against mine like he's not trying to prove anything — like he already knows we're here because we chose to be. I lean into him, fingers curling into his sweater, pulling him closer until the distance we kept all night finally disappears.

His kiss deepens slowly, like he's giving me time to change my mind — and when I don't, when I melt into him instead, something in his chest loosens.

His hands slide from my waist to my back, broad palms warm through the fabric, pulling me closer until I can feel the steady thrum of his heart. It's fast. Controlled. Like he's holding himself together by sheer will.

I tilt my head, letting him in, and his breath stutters against my mouth.

Chapter 21

"Lizzie," he murmurs, barely louder than a thought.

The way he says my name sends a spark straight through me. My fingers slip beneath the edge of his sweater, brushing warm skin, and he inhales sharply — the sound low, involuntary.

There it is.

The proof that this affects him just as much.

His grip tightens, not rough, not desperate — just honest. Like he's anchoring himself to me. His kiss turns hungry then, still unhurried but full of intent, like he's been thinking about this moment longer than he'll ever admit.

My pulse races. My body leans into his without permission from my brain. Every place where we touch feels too small and not enough all at once.

He rests his forehead against mine, breathing hard.

"Tell me to stop," he whispers.

I don't.

I kiss him again instead, slower this time, softer — and that seems to undo him more than anything else. His hands roam, learning, lingering, leaving heat everywhere they pass.

The world narrows to sensation.

The sound of his breath.

The steady pressure of his hands at my back.

The quiet noise I make when his lips trail along my jaw, down my neck — unguarded, real.

He pauses, forehead resting against mine.

"Still okay?" he murmurs.

"Yes," I breathe. "More than okay."

That's when the restraint breaks — not recklessly, not all at once — but fully.

He sets me down at the edge of the bed like he's afraid of

startling me, hands lingering at my hips, thumbs brushing slow, grounding circles.

"Still okay?" he asks quietly.

I nod, breath unsteady. "Yeah. I want this."

Something soft breaks across his face — relief, want, something dangerously close to reverence.

"Tell me if that changes," he murmurs.

He leans in again, kissing me with a patience that makes my chest ache. His mouth moves against mine like he's memorizing me, like this moment matters just as much as everything that's about to follow. When his hands slide up my sides, it's unhurried, asking instead of taking.

I reach for him without thinking, fingers curling into his shirt, tugging him closer.

A quiet sound leaves him — approval, restraint thinning.

He presses his forehead to mine, breathing me in. "You don't know how long I've wanted this," he admits, voice low. "Not just the touching. This. Being here with you."

My heart stumbles.

"Then stay," I whisper.

He does.

The world softens around us — the bed, the warmth, the steady rhythm of shared breath. His hands learn me slowly, deliberately, like there's no finish line he's racing toward. Every touch feels intentional. Every kiss feels chosen.

When he finally draws me down with him, it's with a tenderness that steals the air from my lungs.

I kiss him again, slower this time, deeper.

This isn't a secret.

This isn't stolen.

This is chosen.

Chapter 21

When the bedroom door closes behind us, the rest of the world fades away — expectations, rules, lines drawn by other people.

There's a quiet that settles between us, thick and charged, like the air before a storm finally breaks.

Ethan's hands frame my waist, steady and sure, thumbs brushing slow arcs into my skin. He looks at me like this moment matters — not like something he's taking, but something we're stepping into together.

"This is still okay?" he asks softly.

I don't answer with words.

I step closer.

His breath catches — just once — and then his forehead rests against mine, our noses brushing, our breaths tangling. The closeness is overwhelming in the best way, like standing at the edge of something inevitable.

"I choose you," I whisper.

That's all it takes.

His mouth finds mine again, deeper now, slower, like he's savoring every second. The kiss isn't rushed or desperate — it's certain. Hands slide, bodies align, and the heat between us builds until it's impossible to tell where I end and he begins.

Time stretches.

There's no hurry.

Only the rhythm we find together — breath, touch, the quiet sounds we don't bother to stop. Every movement feels intentional, every moment anchored by the knowledge that neither of us is leaving.

When the world finally narrows down to sensation — warmth, closeness, the steady beat of his heart beneath my hand — I know this isn't about losing control.

It's about choosing it.
For tonight, there's only this:
The way he holds me like something precious.
The way I trust him enough to let go.
The certainty that we didn't rush — and we didn't run.
And when we finally settle together, wrapped in each other's presence, I know something has shifted for good.
Not because he followed me.
Not because we lost control.
But because this time, I opened the door —
and he stepped through it only after I asked.

Chapter 22

Lizzie

Morning comes quietly.

No alarm. No rush. Just pale light slipping through the blinds and the slow awareness of warmth beside me.

For a second, I let myself stay still with it.

Ethan is asleep on his back, one arm bent above his head, hair mussed in a way that makes him look younger. Softer. Not the composed version everyone else sees — just a man who spent the night holding me like it mattered.

Because it did.

I shift carefully, testing the space between us. He stirs immediately, fingers brushing my hip like his body knows where I am even before his mind catches up.

"Hey," he murmurs, voice rough with sleep.

"Hey."

He opens his eyes and looks at me — really looks — and something quiet passes between us. No panic. No regret. Just awareness.

"You okay?" he asks.

"Yes," I answer without hesitation. Then, because honesty feels important now, I add, "Are you?"

He exhales slowly. "Yeah. I think so."

We lie there for a moment, neither of us reaching for the easy comfort of jokes or distraction. The room smells like clean sheets and my lavender body wash drifting in from my bathroom. Normal things.

That's what makes it feel heavier.

"I should probably get up," I say eventually.

"Yeah," he agrees. "Me too."

Neither of us moves.

When he finally sits up, he does it carefully — like he's conscious of every inch of space between us. He pulls on his shirt, glances around for his boots, gives me privacy without asking for it.

That matters too.

In the kitchen, I start the coffee while he leans against the counter, arms crossed, watching me like he's trying to memorize something.

"This doesn't change what I said," I tell him quietly.

He nods immediately. "I know."

"I meant it," I continue. "I'm not rushing anything. And I'm not pretending this fixes everything."

"I wouldn't ask you to," he says. "Last night wasn't about fixing. It was about choosing."

The words settle warm and steady in my chest.

Still — something presses at the edge of my thoughts.

"What happens now?" I ask.

He doesn't answer right away.

Chapter 22

That hesitation is my answer.

I turn, meeting his gaze. "You don't have to explain," I say gently. "I just need to know you're not disappearing."

"I won't," he says immediately. Too fast to be calculated. "I just... I don't want to mess this up."

"I know."

But knowing doesn't erase the truth.

We're still standing in the same world we were yesterday. Ryan still exists. The team still exists. Madison still exists. And whatever Ethan feels, he hasn't figured out how to hold it out in the open yet.

I don't push.

Not today.

After coffee, I walk him to the door. No kiss. No lingering touches. Just a quiet moment where his hand brushes mine and stays there — grounding, deliberate.

"Thank you," he says.

"For what?"

"For trusting me," he replies. "And for stopping me when we needed to."

I nod. "That goes both ways."

He hesitates, then adds, "I'll see you later?"

"Yes," I say. "You will."

When the door closes behind him, the apartment feels different.

Not empty.

Just... changed.

I lean back against the counter and let myself breathe.

Last night didn't solve anything.

But it clarified something important.

I don't regret choosing him.

Secrets On Ice

What I'm not willing to do anymore is choose silence.

And if Ethan wants to keep standing beside me — not just behind closed doors — he's going to have to figure out what that looks like.

I pour myself another cup of coffee and stare out the window, letting the morning settle around me.

Whatever comes next, it won't be accidental.

Chapter 23

Lizzie

By Monday, the world has reset.

Practices. Schedules. Familiar faces moving through Winter-crest like nothing monumental happened over the weekend.

Nothing monumental did happen — not in a way anyone else can see.

That's the problem.

Ethan and I don't talk about Saturday night.

Not because it didn't matter.

Because it mattered too much.

I see him in the hallway outside the rink, laughing with a couple of teammates. Madison is there too — close enough to touch, close enough to feel intentional. Her hand rests on his arm like it's always belonged there.

It shouldn't bother me.

It does.

When Ethan notices me, his smile falters for half a second.

Not guilt — awareness. He doesn't come over. Doesn't wave.

Doesn't acknowledge me beyond that flicker of recognition. The message is quiet but clear.

Not here. Not now.

Sasha notices immediately.

"Wow," she mutters under her breath. "So we're pretending you didn't rearrange his entire nervous system."

"Stop," I say softly.

But I can't stop watching.

Madison leans in to say something, her mouth close to Ethan's

ear. He laughs — easy, practiced — like this version of him hasn't spent the night in my bed learning where I soften and where I tense.

Something twists in my chest.

Later, I catch Ryan by the vending machines.

"You good?" he asks, tossing me a drink.

"Yeah," I say automatically.

He studies me a beat longer than necessary. "You sure?"

I nod. He lets it go.

That night, my phone stays silent.

No check-in. No did you get home okay. No acknowledgment of what we crossed together.I tell myself I didn't ask for more.

But wanting isn't the same as asking.

By Thursday, the quiet has stretched thin.

I run into Ethan again — this time alone — outside the gym.

Chapter 23

Our eyes meet. The moment sharpens.

He opens his mouth like he might say something.

Madison appears at his side before he can.

"Hey," she says brightly, eyes flicking to me with polite curiosity. "We were just talking about Friday."

Something in her tone makes it sound like a claim.

Ethan nods. "Team thing."

I swallow. "Cool."

He looks like he wants to say more.

He doesn't.

I walk away before I can read into it.

That night, I sit on my bed scrolling through my phone, thumb hovering over an app I hadn't opened in weeks.

The anonymous one.

Not because I want a stranger.

Because I want to be chosen — openly, without hesitation, without feeling like a secret.

Sasha's words echo in my head.

Don't make yourself small for someone who's still afraid to be seen.

I open the app — not to escape, but to remember.

Not to hide.

But to remind myself that I don't have to wait quietly for someone to decide I'm worth claiming.

By the time I close it, my decision is already made.

If Ethan can't choose me in the daylight…

I won't keep choosing him in the dark.

Chapter 24

Lizzie

By the end of the week, I understand something I didn't want to admit before.

Ethan didn't disappear after Saturday night — but he didn't step forward either. And there's a difference between patience and waiting quietly for someone else to decide how much space you're allowed to take up.

I'm done doing the second one.

Quietly.

Politely.

Alone.

* * *

My shift at Barnes & Noble ends at nine.

By the time I clock out, my feet ache and my head feels full

Chapter 24

in that quiet, satisfied way it always does after a long night surrounded by books. I change in the bathroom, smoothing my sweater and fixing my curls in the mirror, taking an extra second before I leave.

Not because I'm nervous.

Because I'm deliberate.

His name is Marcus.

We matched earlier this week — no drama, no mystery, no emotional excavation. He asked me out like it was the most normal thing in the world, and I said yes without overthinking it.

That alone felt like progress.

We meet at a small bar downtown, the kind with warm lighting and no TVs blasting sports highlights. Marcus stands when he sees me, smiling easy and open, like he's not trying to impress anyone.

"Lizzie?" he asks.

"That's me."

He pulls out my chair. Orders my drink without asking what it says about me. Listens when I talk.

It's… nice.

Not electric. Not consuming. But steady.

And for the first time in days, my chest doesn't feel tight.

"So what do you do?" he asks casually.

I hesitate — just for a second.

"I work at Barnes & Noble," I say. True. Not the whole truth, but enough for tonight.

"That explains the calm vibe," he says with a grin. "I could never work around books all day. I'd never leave."

I laugh. "That's the point."

We talk about music. About travel. About how Wintercrest

feels too small and too comforting at the same time. He doesn't know my brother. Doesn't know hockey politics. Doesn't know Ethan Walker.

And that feels like freedom.

When he asks if I want to grab food somewhere louder, I agree.

The place he suggests is already buzzing when we arrive.

Music. Laughter. Bodies packed shoulder to shoulder.

And then I see the jerseys.

My stomach drops.

Of course.

The hockey team party is already in full swing — players scattered across the room, familiar faces everywhere. Ryan stands near the bar, drink in hand, laughing with two teammates.

I freeze.

Marcus notices immediately. "Everything okay?"

"My brother," I say weakly. "He's... a lot."

"Should I be scared?" Marcus jokes.

"Only a little."

Ryan spots me a second later.

His smile vanishes — then reappears sharper.

He strides over like he's about to inspect a suspicious package.

"Lizzie Harper," he says slowly. "Why are you here?"

"Nice to see you too," I reply. "Ryan, this is Marcus."

Marcus offers his hand immediately. "Nice to meet you, man."

Ryan shakes it, grip firm, eyes scanning him head to toe like he's assessing a draft pick.

"So," Ryan says, clapping Marcus on the shoulder, "what's

Chapter 24

your position?"

Marcus blinks. "Uh... marketing?"

Ryan nods seriously. "Good stamina?"

"Ryan," I warn.

He grins. "Kidding. Mostly."

Marcus laughs, unfazed. "She warned me you'd be intense."

"She warned you correctly," Ryan agrees.

Then Ryan leans in closer to me, lowering his voice. "You good?"

"Yes," I say firmly. "I am."

He studies me for a long beat — then nods.

"Alright," he says. "You two have fun."

As he walks away, relief washes through me.

Until I feel it.

That familiar pull.

I turn.

Ethan stands across the room.

He's frozen.

Eyes locked on me.

On Marcus's hand resting casually at my back.

Something sharp flashes across his face — surprise, confusion, and then something darker.

Jealousy.

For the first time, he doesn't look controlled.

He looks undone.

Our eyes meet.

I don't look away.

I don't step back.

I don't explain.

Marcus leans in to say something in my ear, unaware of the storm forming ten feet away.

Ethan watches.
Jaw tight. Hands clenched. Breath shallow.
And for the first time since Saturday night, the imbalance shifts.
I didn't come here to make him jealous.
But I won't pretend it doesn't feel like reclaiming something I gave too freely before.
Across the room, Ethan takes a step toward me.
Then another.
And I know — with sudden, dangerous clarity —
This night is not going to end quietly—for any of us.

Chapter 25

Ethan

I'm already in a bad mood.

Not because of the win — we crushed it.

Not because of the party — these are routine.

I'm in a bad mood because Lizzie hasn't texted me all day.

No good morning.

No quiet check-in.

No sign that Saturday night existed outside my own head.

I tell myself it's fine. That this is what we agreed on. Distance. Space. Control.

Then the doors open.

And she walks in.

With another man.

The hit is immediate and brutal — like my lungs forget how to work.

Lizzie looks unreal.

Not dressed to impress. Not trying too hard. Just confident. Effortless. Like she knows exactly who she is and doesn't need permission to take up space.

The guy beside her has his hand resting lightly at her lower back.

Not possessive.

Familiar.

Comfortable.

My jaw tightens.

Someone laughs nearby, but it sounds distant — like I'm underwater.

Because she's smiling.

Actually smiling.

Not the careful one she's worn lately. The real one. The kind she hasn't given me in days.

My chest burns.

Ace follows my line of sight and whistles low.

"Well damn."

I don't answer.

Nico leans in. "Is that—"

"Yes," I snap.

Too sharp. Too fast.

They exchange a look.

The guy says something to Lizzie and she laughs, tipping her head back, resting her hand briefly on his arm.

Something in me fractures.

I grab a drink I don't need and immediately regret it. Jealousy and alcohol are a bad combination — and I'm already losing control.

I tell myself not to watch her.

I fail.

She moves through the room like she belongs there. Easy. Unafraid. The guy — Marcus, I hear someone say his name

Chapter 25

— stays close, but not hovering. Like he's confident she wants him there.

That's what gets me.

Not that she's with someone else.

That she looks comfortable.

Ace steps into my line of sight, blocking her from view.

"Okay," he says carefully. "You wanna tell me why you look like you're about to set something on fire?"

"Move."

He doesn't.

Instead, he glances over his shoulder — then back at me.

"Oh," he mutters. "That's why."

I say nothing.

Because if I open my mouth, I might say something I can't take back.

Ace lowers his voice. "That Lizzie?"

My silence answers him.

"Shit."

"Don't," I warn.

"Too late." He shifts closer. "So... that's why you iced Madison."

My jaw clenches.

"You didn't just get bored," he says.

"No."

"Didn't think so." He looks back at Lizzie. "She's... not what I expected."

That almost makes me laugh.

"She's not like anyone," I say quietly.

Ace nods. "Yeah. I can see that."

Across the room, Lizzie laughs again. Real. Unfiltered.

My chest tightens.

Ace studies me. "You look like you're losing your damn mind."

"I feel like I already did."

He exhales. "Listen to me."

I finally meet his eyes.

"You do anything stupid tonight," he says seriously, "and you'll regret it. Not because of Ryan — because of her."

That lands.

"She didn't do anything wrong," I mutter.

"No," he agrees. "She didn't."

Silence stretches.

Ace sighs. "If she wanted you to chase her, she would've looked at you by now."

My stomach drops.

"She hasn't," I say.

"No." He pauses. "Which means this isn't about jealousy. It's about whether you're finally going to stop hiding."

I swallow hard.

"Because if you storm over there," he continues, "you don't look brave. You look like a guy who waited too long."

That one hurts.

Across the room, Lizzie finally looks up.

Our eyes meet.

She doesn't smile.

Doesn't look away.

She just holds my gaze — calm, steady, unreadable.

She's not trying to hurt me.

She's watching.

Seeing what I'll do.

And for the first time all night, I don't know the right answer.

Chapter 25

Then she leans closer to Marcus — not intimate, not teasing — just enough to say something in his ear.

And the pressure in my chest spikes all over again.

I don't plan it.

She steps away from Marcus — just for air, just for space. I follow, stopping short of touching her.

My hand closes around her wrist.

"Ethan," she says sharply. "Don't."

Too late.

I pull her into the nearest bathroom and shut the door, locking it with a sharp click that echoes too loud in the quiet.

The music outside dulls to a distant thrum.

Just us.

She spins on me, eyes blazing.

"What the hell do you think you're doing?"

I step closer.

Her back hits the counter.

She doesn't move away.

"You don't get to do this," she says, breath uneven. "You don't get to watch me all night like I belong to you and then—"

"You're right," I interrupt. "I don't."

That stops her.

"But don't pretend you didn't feel it," I add, voice low and wrecked. "Because I felt every second of him touching you."

Her eyes darken.

"Good."

Something feral twists in my chest.

I lift her onto the sink in one smooth motion. She gasps, hands flying to my shoulders as I step between her knees, close enough that there's no space left to argue. I grip her chin forcing her to look up at me.

"You went on a date," I murmur.

"You noticed."

"I noticed everything."

Her legs hook around my waist before either of us thinks better of it.

"You don't get to touch me like this," she whispers, "when you won't choose me."

"Then tell me to stop."

She groans, fists my shirt and drags me in.

"Don't."

I kiss her — hard, reckless, desperate — pouring every second of frustration and want into it. She kisses me back just as fiercely, breath breaking, hands gripping like she's done waiting.

I pull back just long enough to breathe.

"This doesn't fix anything," she says softly.

"I know."

"But you don't get to keep me in the dark," she adds. "Not anymore."

I nod.

Because she's right.

She slides off the counter, smooths her clothes, eyes steady.

"Figure your shit out," she says. "Then come find me."

She unlocks the door and walks out.

Leaving me alone — heart racing, hands still warm from her skin — finally understanding one brutal truth:

If I don't step up now,

I will lose her.

And I won't survive watching that happen.

Chapter 26

Lizzie

I don't look back.

Not when I step out of the bathroom.

Not when the music swells again.

Not when my pulse is still racing and my lips still feel warm.

I walk straight past the bar and find Marcus where I left him.

He looks up immediately. "You okay?"

"Yes," I say. And this time, it's true.

I don't explain. I don't owe him that. He nods, easy and respectful.

"I think I'm going to head out," I add.

"Want company?" he asks, gentle. No pressure.

"I'm good," I say. "But thank you."

He smiles. "Text me when you get home."

I do not look back when I leave.

The night air is sharp, grounding. By the time I get to my car, my hands are steady.

I sit there for a moment, forehead resting against the steering wheel.

Not because I regret it.

Because I don't.

What happened tonight didn't confuse me — it clarified everything.

Ethan didn't take anything from me.

He showed me exactly how far he's willing to go—and where he stops.

At home, I move slowly, deliberately. Shoes off. Face washed. Pajamas on. Control reclaimed.

My phone buzzes once.

Ethan:

Can we talk?

I stare at the screen for a long moment.

Then I set it face-down.

Not out of spite.

Out of self-respect.

The knock comes the next morning.

I already know it's him.

When I open the door, Ethan looks wrecked — jaw tight, eyes shadowed, like he hasn't slept. His hands are shoved into his jacket pockets like he doesn't trust them.

"Hey," he says quietly.

"Hey."

I don't invite him in.

That's intentional.

"I'm not here to argue," he says quickly. "Or make excuses."

"Good," I reply. "Because I'm not interested in either."

That lands.

He swallows. "You meant what you said last night."

Chapter 26

"Yes," I say calmly. "Every word."

"I care about you," he says. "More than I ever meant to."

"I know," I reply. "That's not the issue."

He frowns slightly. "Then what is?"

I meet his eyes, steady and unflinching.

"The issue is that you want me in private," I say, "but you don't have the courage to stand beside me in public."

His chest rises sharply.

"And before you say anything," I continue, "no — this isn't about labels or rushing or forcing something you're not ready for."

"This is about respect."

He opens his mouth. I don't let him.

"I am not one of the girls from your past," I say, voice firm but even. "I'm not here for late-night decisions followed by daylight silence. I'm not here to be pulled into corners and told 'it's complicated.'"

Something flickers in his eyes — guilt, recognition, fear.

"I won't shrink myself to make your life easier," I continue. "And I won't wait around while you figure out whether you're brave enough to choose me."

"Lizzie—"

"No," I say softly, and somehow that's more powerful than shouting. "You don't get to interrupt this."

He goes still.

"I like you," I say. "I care about you. But if you keep playing this halfway game, I will walk away — and I will find someone who doesn't hesitate to show up for me."

The words hang between us. Heavy. Final.

His voice is rough when he speaks. "You'd really do that."

"Yes," I say without hesitation. "Because I respect myself

too much not to."

Silence stretches.

"I'm not asking you to disappear," I add. "I'm asking you to decide who you are when it counts."

He nods slowly, like that truth is settling somewhere deep.

"I hear you," he says.

"I need you to understand me," I reply. "Hearing isn't enough anymore."

Another pause.

"I'm not going to reach out for a while," I tell him. "Not to punish you. To give you space to decide what you're actually willing to stand behind."

He swallows. "That's fair."

I step back, hand on the door.

"Take care, Ethan."

He hesitates — then nods and steps away.

When the door closes, I don't collapse.

I don't cry.

I lean against it for a moment, breathing through the ache — because choosing yourself doesn't feel good right away.

But it feels right.

I'm done being someone's almost.

Whatever Ethan does next?

It won't be because I waited quietly.

It'll be because he finally decided to stop fucking around with my heart.

And if he doesn't?

I'll be just fine without him.

Chapter 27

Ethan

I don't sleep.

I lie in bed staring at the ceiling, replaying her voice until it loses its edges and still cuts anyway.

I'm not one of the girls from your past.

I will walk away.

I won't shrink myself to make your life easier.

By the time morning comes, my body feels heavy and hollow all at once.

I skate like shit.

I know it.

The whole team does.

Hell — even Coach knows it.

I miss a pass in warm-ups. Over correct on a turn. Nearly eat ice chasing a puck I should've had.

My head isn't here.

It's standing in Lizzie's doorway.

It's watching her walk away without looking back.

After the third mistake, practice screeches to a halt.

Ryan slams his stick against the ice and skates straight toward me, eyes blazing.

"Dude, what the **hell** is wrong with you?"

I grit my teeth. "Back off."

"No."

He gets in my face. "Get your shit together, man!"

The rink goes quiet. Matty curses under his breath. Ace lets out a low whistle like he's watching a fight about to break out.

Ryan shoves my shoulder.

"You're playing like you don't even want to be here!"

"I said back off," I snap.

He shoves me again — harder.

"You think you get to tank practice for no reason?" he explodes. "You think Coach won't bench your ass? What's your problem?!"

Lizzie.

Lizzie.

Lizzie.

But I can't say that.

Ryan scoffs when my jaw tightens. "Seriously, Ethan — you're skating like a damn rookie."

My temper spikes. "I'm **fine**."

"Bullshit!" he barks. "You look like you haven't slept in a week! You're sloppy, distracted, and one bad mistake away from getting your head taken off!"

His chest rises and falls hard.

And beneath the anger, I see it — worry.

Classic Ryan. He masks concern with aggression.

The whole team is watching now.

Chapter 27

"Whatever is going on," Ryan says tightly, "**fix it**. Before you drag us down with you."

He skates off, muttering, "Get your shit together, Walker," as he joins a passing drill with Ace.

I stand there, breathing hard, hands shaking inside my gloves.

Matty skates past and murmurs, "Damn, dude... what the hell is going on with you?"

I don't answer.

Because I know the truth.

And it's killing me.

Practice ends in a blur.

In the locker room, Ryan avoids my eyes. Ace doesn't.

"You wanna talk?" he asks quietly.

"Not here."

He nods. "Figured."

Madison hovers near my stall — too close, too aware — watching me with that knowing smirk like she can sense the cracks forming.

I don't look at her.

Lizzie isn't here.

Not at the arena.

Not in the hallway.

Not answering my texts.

Not even opening them.

That hurts more than Ryan's shove ever could.

Later, I sit alone in my truck outside the arena, engine off, hands resting uselessly on the steering wheel.

The building looms in front of me — familiar, safe, full of rules I've followed without question for years.

Inside those walls, I know who I am.

Outside of them?

I've been hiding behind silence.

I pull my phone out, thumb hovering over Lizzie's name.

I don't text her.

She asked for space. I respect that.

Instead, I sit there and finally let the truth settle — not the convenient one, not the excuse-wrapped one.

The real one.

I wasn't protecting anyone by keeping her in the shadows.

I was protecting myself.

From Ryan.

From fallout.

From having to stand behind what I want when it counts.

She doesn't want apologies.

She wants honesty — in daylight.

Ace's words echo in my head.

If she wanted you to chase her, she would've looked at you.

She didn't.

Because this isn't about chasing.

It's about choosing.

And for the first time, the fear shifts.

It's not fear of Ryan.

Not fear of the team.

Not fear of the consequences.

It's fear of losing her — not because I couldn't have her…

…but because I didn't step up when it mattered.

I start the truck.

Not to chase her.

Not to corner her.

But to figure out what it actually looks like to stop hiding — and mean it.

Chapter 27

Because when I see Lizzie again, I won't be asking for more time.

I'll be showing her who I decided to be.

Chapter 28

Ethan

The arena is quieter on non-game days, but it never really sleeps.

Even with the stands empty, you can feel it — the low hum of compressors, the echo of skates from a youth practice on the secondary rink, the distant clang of metal gates rolling up. Staff move around like they own the rhythm of the place, not the players.

Maybe they do.

I'm walking through the back corridor in sweats and a Wolves hoodie, headed for a film session I'm already late to, when I see her.

Lizzie.

She's coming out of a door marked OPERATIONS with a lanyard around her neck and a clipboard in her hand like she belongs there.

Chapter 28

No — not like.

She does.

She's talking to one of the arena staff, pointing down the hallway with calm, precise direction. There's no nerves on her face. No uncertainty. Just... competence.

It knocks the air out of me.

She turns slightly, and her curls catch the fluorescent light. Her expression is focused, serious, the kind of beautiful that has nothing to do with makeup and everything to do with being in control of yourself.

And I realize two things at once:

One — she wasn't exaggerating when she said she has a life outside of me.

Two — I have been a damn fool for acting like my fear gets to be the loudest thing in the room.

I slow before I reach her.

Not to hide.

To make sure I'm not about to do something selfish.

She lifts her gaze.

Her eyes meet mine.

For a second, her face gives nothing away. She's calm — that same calm she wore at the door when she told me she'd walk away.

Then, slowly, she looks past me.

Down the hall.

Like she's checking who's watching.

I follow her glance.

A couple interns in Wolves polos are wheeling a cart of bottled water. A staff member from PR is chatting with someone near the press-room doorway. A few guys from the team are further down, laughing about something on a phone.

Normal arena life.

Normal audience.

My chest tightens.

This is where I always choose the easy route.

The quiet route.

The route that keeps Ryan from noticing, keeps Madison from spinning, keeps the world quiet.

Lizzie's chin lifts slightly, like she's bracing herself.

Not for me to say something sweet.

For me to prove something real.

So I do the one thing I've been avoiding for weeks.

I walk to her anyway.

No corner. No shadows. No private doorway.

Right there in the open hallway.

Her expression flickers — surprise, then guarded.

"Ethan," she says, voice even.

"Liz," I reply.

She tucks the clipboard tighter to her chest, posture straight. "You shouldn't be back here."

It's said like a fact, not a flirtation.

I glance at the lanyard on her neck. "You're back here."

A muscle in her jaw jumps.

"Does your dad know you're doing this?" I ask quietly, nodding at the clipboard.

Her eyes sharpen, like she's deciding how much she can trust me with.

Then she says, "Yes."

But the way she says it is… measured.

Like there's more to it.

I clock it. I don't pry.

Chapter 28

Not right now.

"I'm not here to question your life," I tell her. "I'm here because I owe you something."

Her brows lift a fraction. "An apology?"

"No," I say immediately.

Her mouth twitches, almost amused. "Oh?"

"I already apologized," I say. "You didn't need words. You needed change."

That wipes the hint of humor right off her face.

Good.

This is not the moment for charm.

She looks down the hall again, toward where the interns are now closer.

I don't move. I don't step back. I don't lower my voice like I'm ashamed.

I take a breath.

Then I do it — the smallest public step that still feels like jumping off a cliff.

"I'm choosing not hide you anymore," I say.

Her eyes snap back to mine.

I keep going before fear can bite down.

"I'm not saying it has to be a headline," I add. "I'm not saying you have to be comfortable with cameras or comments or any of it."

Her fingers tighten around the clipboard.

"But I am saying this," I continue, voice steady. "You will not be my secret. Not because I want you in private and panic in public. Not because I'm scared of my own choices."

She studies me like she's trying to find the lie.

"Ryan doesn't know," she says, blunt.

"I know."

"And Madison—"

"I know," I repeat. "And I'm still standing here."

For a beat, her face stays hard.

Then she exhales through her nose, almost like she's fighting an emotion she refuses to give me for free.

"This is a hallway," she says. "Not a revolution."

"I'm aware," I say. "It still matters."

Her eyes dip to my mouth for half a second.

Then she catches herself and looks away again, offended at her own body.

I swallow.

"I'm not asking you to take me back," I say, softer. "I'm not asking you to trust me because I showed up once."

She looks at me again.

"I'm asking you to watch me," I continue. "I'm asking you to let me prove I can be the man you deserve — out loud. In places like this."

A door opens down the hall. Laughter spills out. Two players walk by, nodding at Lizzie like she's staff.

They don't even look twice.

She is part of the arena.

I'm the outsider here.

And still, I don't move away from her.

Lizzie's throat works as she swallows. Her expression is guarded, but I see the crack — the part of her that wants to believe me.

"Okay," she says finally.

One word.

Not forgiveness.

Not acceptance.

A door left unlocked.

Chapter 28

"Okay?" I repeat, careful.

She lifts her chin. "Okay. I'm watching."

My pulse hits hard.

"Good," I say, because I don't trust myself to say anything else.

She shifts the clipboard under one arm, eyes narrowing. "And Ethan?"

"Yeah?"

"If you make me look stupid," she says quietly, "I won't cry about it."

I almost smile, but her stare is deadly serious.

"I'll replace you."

The words hit like an adrenaline shot.

I nod once. "Fair."

She turns like she's done.

Then pauses.

Just long enough to add, "And for the record…"

She glances at the lanyard at her neck, then back at me.

"I'm not a secret at Barnes & Noble either."

And then she walks away down the corridor, boots clicking softly, posture straight, leaving me standing there like my whole life just recalibrated.

I watch her go, chest tight with something that feels like hope and fear in equal measure.

She's watching.

Which means the work actually starts now.

And this time, I'm not going to waste it.

Chapter 29

Lizzie

Barnes & Noble at night feels like a secret you're trusted to keep.

The overhead lights are dimmer. The café smells like espresso and vanilla syrup instead of desperation. The world outside the windows has slowed to a crawl, and inside, everything is quiet enough to think.

Which is dangerous.

I'm re-shelving romance when Sasha appears at the end of the aisle like a gremlin summoned by emotional instability.

She doesn't say anything.

She just stares.

I slide a book into place without looking at her. "If you're about to ask me if I've cried today, the answer is no."

"Liar," she says. "Your eyeliner is doing that thing where it's brave but tired."

I sigh and lean the cart against the shelf. "What do you

Chapter 29

want?"

She grins. "To know why you look like someone just handed you a loaded weapon and said, 'Don't blink.'"

I freeze.

Damn it.

She notices immediately.

"Oh," she says softly. "Oh. He did something."

I glance toward the front of the store, making sure the manager is still distracted, then lower my voice. "He came up to me today. At the arena."

Sasha's eyes widen. "Public?"

"Yes."

"Like—people present public?"

"Yes."

She grips my arm. "DETAILS."

I shake her off, but I'm smiling now, and that's the problem. "He didn't touch me. He didn't corner me. He didn't whisper. He just... stood there. And said he wasn't hiding me anymore."

Sasha goes very still.

"He said that?" she asks.

"Yes."

"And he didn't immediately follow it up with 'but—'?"

"No."

She exhales like someone just released a held breath. "Wow."

I tuck a strand of hair behind my ear, heart doing that stupid flutter thing again. "I told him I was watching."

Sasha's mouth curls into a feral smile. "As you should."

I grab another stack of books, needing something to do with my hands. "I meant it, Sash. I'm not doing this halfway. I'm not going to be his secret comfort while he figures out whether he's brave enough to stand next to me."

"Good," she says. "Because I already picked out his replacement in my head."

I snort. "You absolutely did not."

"I absolutely did," she insists. "Tall. Accountant. Emotional availability of a golden retriever."

I glance at her. "You don't even like accountants."

"I like security," she says. "Anyway — does this mean you're… back together?"

I pause.

That word — together — feels heavier now. More intentional.

"I don't know," I say honestly. "I'm not pretending the noise isn't there. Ryan still doesn't know. Madison still exists. The media is still circling."

Sasha nods. "But?"

"But," I say, "for the first time, it feels like he's not asking me to carry it alone."

She softens. "That matters."

"It does," I whisper.

The bell over the café counter dings. Someone orders a drink. Life keeps moving.

I slide another book into place and straighten the spine.

I don't miss the way my phone buzzes in my apron pocket.

I do miss the way my heart jumps anyway.

Ethan:

Did you make it through your shift?

I stare at the screen.

Then I type.

Me:

Still alive. Haven't replaced you yet.

Three dots appear immediately.

Chapter 29

Ethan:
That feels... promising.
I smile before I can stop myself.
Me:
Don't get cocky.
Ethan:
Noted. Just... wanted you to know I meant what I said today.
I hesitate.
Then:
Me:
I know.
And I do.
The problem isn't that I don't believe him anymore.
The problem is that believing him means I have to be brave too.
Sasha watches my face change and bumps my shoulder. "He texted, didn't he?"
"Yes."
She smirks. "You're glowing."
"I am not."
"You are," she says. "And I'm proud of you."
"For what?"
"For not folding," she says simply. "For letting him step up without chasing him or punishing him. That's grown-woman behavior."
I swallow.
Because she's right.
And because grown-woman behavior means the next steps are going to hurt if they go wrong.
But I finish my shift anyway.
I clock out.

Secrets On Ice

I walk to my car alone.

And for the first time in days, the future doesn't feel like something that's already decided without me.

Chapter 30

Ethan

The thing no one tells you about choosing something or someone out loud?

The world listens.

I feel it the second I walk into the arena the next morning. It's subtle. Not dramatic. No confrontations. No headlines plastered across screens. Just... awareness. A few extra glances that linger too long. Conversations that stop when I pass. A couple of guys from another line going quiet mid-sentence.

Nothing I can call out.

Everything I can feel.

I drop my bag at my stall and start taping my stick like it's the only thing grounding me. I'm halfway through when Ace slides into the stall beside mine, elbow resting on his knee. "You good?" he asks.

"Fine," I say automatically.

He snorts. "You always say that when you're about to punch a wall or make a life-altering decision."

I don't look at him. "Already made it."

That gets my attention.

He studies my face for a beat. "So it's real, then."

I pause.

Not long.

"Yeah," I say. "It is."

Ace nods slowly. "Okay."

That's it.

No lecture. No warning. No jokes.

Just okay.

Relief hits me harder than I expect.

Practice is clean. Focused. My body does what it knows how to do. Muscle memory takes over where my brain tries to spiral. I skate hard, finish checks, bury two shots in drills like I've got something to prove.

Maybe I do.

When Coach blows the final whistle, I'm drenched in sweat and steady again. Like hockey scraped the static off my skin.

That's when I see her.

Madison.

She's leaning against the glass near the tunnel, arms folded, lips curved into that familiar, calculated smile. The one that says I know something you don't.

I freeze for half a second.

Chapter 30

Then I keep walking.

I don't owe her a conversation.

She falls into step beside me anyway.

"Wow," she says lightly. "You're avoiding me now? That's new."

I don't slow. "I'm busy."

She laughs softly. "You always were terrible at pretending I don't exist."

I stop.

Turn.

Meet her eyes.

"That's because I never needed to pretend," I say evenly. "I'm

doing it now."

Something sharp flashes across her face before she smooths it away.

"This is about her," she says.

I don't respond.

Which is answer enough.

She steps closer, lowering her voice. "You know how this looks, right? You making a show of things all of a sudden. Walking up to her in the open. Standing there like you're proud."

"I am," I say.

Her smile tightens. "You didn't used to be."

"I didn't used to be a lot of things," I reply. "Turns out people change."

She scoffs. "Do they? Or do they just get bored and need a new audience?"

That does it.

"Watch it," I say quietly.

She tilts her head. "Or what?"

I lean in just enough that she understands this isn't a game anymore.

"Or you stop being part of my life entirely," I say. "No friendly check-ins. No 'accidental' run-ins. No commentary. You don't get to orbit me anymore."

Her breath stutters.

Good.

"You don't get to talk about her," I continue. "You don't get to speculate. You don't get to spin. Whatever you're thinking of doing — don't."

Madison laughs, brittle. "You think you can control the narrative now — after all this?"

"No," I say honestly. "I think I can control myself."

Her eyes search my face like she's looking for the crack. She doesn't find one.

"This won't end the way you think it will," she says finally. "She's not built for this world."

I straighten.

"You don't know her," I say flatly. "And you never will."

She watches me for a long moment, then steps back, lips curling.

"Good luck, Ethan," she says sweetly. "You're going to need it."

She walks away.

I don't watch her go.

Because at the end of the hall, Lizzie is standing near the operations office again — clipboard tucked under her arm, talking to someone from facilities like she belongs exactly where she is.

Chapter 30

She glances up.
Sees me.
Doesn't look away.
Doesn't hesitate.
She gives me a small nod.
Acknowledgment.
Not possession.
Not performance.
Just I see you.
And for the first time since this all started, I understand something crystal clear:
Choosing her isn't the risk.
Losing her because I was too afraid to choose her?
That would've been the real mistake.

Chapter 31

Ethan

Ryan almost figures it out on a Tuesday.

Which feels unfair, honestly. Of all days.

We're halfway through video review when it happens — the kind of meeting where Coach pauses footage every ten seconds and asks questions he already knows the answers to. The room smells like burnt coffee and sweat that never quite leaves hockey gear.

Ryan's sitting two seats down from me, arms crossed, jaw tight in that captain way that means he's clocking everything even when he looks relaxed.

Chapter 31

I'm answering a question about zone entries when I feel it.

His stare.

Not angry.

Not explosive.

Focused.

I finish my sentence and lean back, stretching my shoulders like nothing's wrong.

Ryan doesn't say anything.

That's worse.

After the meeting breaks, guys file out in clumps, arguing about lunch plans and chirping each other over missed passes. I'm stuffing my notebook into my bag when Ryan stops in front of me.

"Walk with me," he says.

Not a question.

My pulse ticks up, but I nod. "Yeah."

We head down the quieter hallway that loops past the auxiliary rink. The echo of skates on ice bleeds through the walls — a youth team practicing drills, laughter bouncing in sharp bursts.

Ryan shoves his hands into the pockets of his hoodie.

"You've been… different," he says.

Here it is.

I keep my eyes forward. "Different how?"

"Don't do that," he mutters. "You know what I mean."

I do.

I just don't know how much he knows.

"You're focused," he continues. "Locked in. But not in that 'playoff tunnel vision' way. More like…" He exhales. "Like you figured something out."

I stop walking.

He stops too, turning to face me.

"You sleeping?" he asks abruptly.

That almost makes me laugh.

"Yeah," I say. "Why?"

"Because you look like someone who finally is," he says.

Chapter 31

"Which is new."

I swallow.

Ryan studies me, eyes sharp. He's not accusing. He's assessing.

"You're not doing the Madison thing anymore," he adds.

I stiffen before I can help it.

There it is.

He catches it instantly.

"Thought so," he says quietly.

I force myself to breathe. "That ended a while ago."

He nods. "Good."

Relief flashes through me — brief, dangerous.

Then he ruins it.

"And Lizzie's been… busy," he says.

My heart stutters.

"She has?" I ask, too casually.

Ryan gives me a look. "Careful."

I shrug. "She's got two jobs. She's always busy."

"That's not what I mean." He hesitates, then says, "She's at the arena more. Talking to ops. Asking questions. Taking notes like she's studying for something."

I nod slowly. "She likes learning."

"Yeah," he says. "She does."

He looks down the hall, jaw flexing.

"You know," he says, "I always figured if Liz ever brought someone around, I'd know right away."

My chest tightens.

"Why's that?" I ask.

"Because she's terrible at hiding how she feels," he says. "She wears it all over her face."

I think of her nod to me in the hallway. The way she didn't flinch.

"She's grown," I say carefully.

Ryan scoffs. "That doesn't mean I stop noticing."

Silence stretches.

Chapter 31

I can feel the truth pressing against my teeth.

This is the moment where one wrong word cracks everything open.

Ryan turns back to me. "You're not doing anything stupid, are you?"

There it is.

I meet his eyes.

"No," I say.

And for once?

It's not a lie.

He watches me, searching for something — guilt, defiance, arrogance.

Whatever he's looking for, he doesn't find it.

"Good," he says finally. "Because I don't have the bandwidth to deal with your bullshit right now."

I let out a breath I didn't realize I was holding.

He claps my shoulder once. Hard. Familiar.

"We need you," he adds. "All of you. Whatever's going on in

your life, don't let it mess with the room."

"It won't," I say immediately.

He nods, satisfied — for now.

As he turns to leave, he pauses.

"And Ethan?"

"Yeah?"

"If Lizzie ever looks like she's hurting because of someone?" His voice drops. "I won't ask questions first."

My stomach flips.

I don't look away. "She won't."

Ryan studies me for one long second.

Then he walks off down the hall, already pulling his phone out, already thinking about something else.

I stand there alone, heart pounding.

That was too close.

But as my pulse steadies, something else settles in.

He didn't see fear.

Chapter 31

He didn't see a secret.

He saw a man who wasn't screwing around anymore.

And when the time comes — because it will — I won't be blindsiding him.

I'll be standing there.

Just like I was in the hallway.

Out in the open.

Chapter 32

Lizzie

Madison finds me where she thinks I'll be polite.
Barnes & Noble.
Tuesday night.
Low traffic. Soft lighting. Public enough that I won't "cause a scene."
She's wrong.
I'm at the café counter waiting on a latte for a customer when I feel it — that subtle shift in the air that has nothing to do with temperature and everything to do with intention.
Someone watching.
I don't look up right away. I finish tapping the screen, slide the cup down the counter, and say, "Next."
That's when she steps forward.
Madison looks exactly like Madison always does. Perfect hair. Perfect coat. That calm, curated confidence of someone who's used to being the loudest presence in any room without ever raising her voice.

Chapter 32

She smiles at me like we're acquaintances.

"Lizzie," she says warmly. "Hi."

I meet her eyes.

No surprise. No nerves.

"Madison," I reply. "Can I help you find something?"

Her smile flickers — just a fraction.

"I was hoping we could talk," she says. "Privately."

I glance around the café. Two students studying. A couple tucked into the corner with paperbacks and pastries. My coworker restocking mugs behind the counter.

"This is a bookstore," I say calmly. "Not a confessional."

She laughs lightly. "Fair enough."

Then she leans in, lowering her voice anyway.

"I just wanted to check in," she says. "There's been… a lot of attention lately. For someone who didn't ask for it."

I don't respond.

She keeps going.

"People talk," she adds. "And sometimes they don't realize how fragile things can get when they mix business, family, and athletes with reputations."

There it is.

I sip the water beside the register, buying myself half a second.

Then I say, "Are you here as a customer or a warning label?"

Her eyes sharpen.

"I'm here as someone who knows Ethan," she says. "Better than most."

I smile.

Not sweetly.

Precisely.

"That's interesting," I say. "Because the version of Ethan I know doesn't invite unsolicited commentary from exes."

Her jaw tightens. "You think this is about jealousy?"

"I think this is about relevance," I say. "And I'm not interested in giving you any."

She straightens, clearly not expecting push back.

"I'm trying to protect you," she insists. "This world eats girls like you alive."

I tilt my head. "Girls like me?"

She hesitates. "Soft. Private. Not built for scrutiny."

I step out from behind the counter.

Now we're eye level.

"Let's be clear," I say evenly. "I didn't ask to be analyzed. I didn't ask to be discussed. And I definitely didn't ask you to decide what I'm built for."

Her smile is gone now.

"You don't know what he's like when the cameras turn," she says. "When the season gets ugly. When he gets restless."

I nod once. "And you don't know what it's like to be chosen after someone finally grows up."

That one lands.

Hard.

She exhales sharply. "He's going to hurt you."

"Maybe," I say. "But that would be between him and me."

She studies my face, searching for doubt.

She doesn't find it.

"You think this ends well?" she asks.

"I think," I say carefully, "that whether it ends or not isn't your concern."

Her lips press together.

"I'm not one of the girls from his past," I continue. "I'm not waiting around hoping he'll change. I already told him what

Chapter 32

I expect. And if he doesn't meet me there?"

I shrug.

"I'll walk. With my dignity intact."

Her eyes flicker — not triumph.

Something closer to uncertainty.

"And you're okay with that?" she asks.

"Yes," I say. "Because I don't lose myself for men who can't show up."

A beat.

Then she scoffs softly. "You're very confident for someone standing in the middle of a media storm."

I smile again.

This one is sharp.

"I work three night shifts a week at a bookstore," I say. "I grew up in an arena where men yell at glass for a living. And I'm training for a job where every decision gets second-guessed."

I lean in just enough that she hears me clearly.

"I am not afraid of noise."

Silence stretches between us.

Finally, she steps back.

"Well," she says coolly. "Good luck, Lizzie."

I nod. "You too."

She turns and walks out.

The bell over the door chimes softly behind her.

My coworker peeks over from the café. "Everything okay?"

I exhale slowly.

"Yeah," I say. "Everything's fine."

And for the first time, I mean it.

Because whatever Madison thought she was doing tonight? She didn't shake me.

Secrets On Ice

She confirmed something.
I'm not here to be chosen quietly.
And I'm definitely not here to be scared off.
If Ethan wants me, he'll keep proving it.
And if he doesn't?
I already know how to walk away.
With my head high.

Chapter 33

Ethan

Ace tells me without meaning to.

We're in the weight room post-practice, the low hum of machines and shitty music filling the space while I rack a bar I probably shouldn't be lifting with the amount of sleep I didn't get last night.

Ace wipes sweat from his neck.

"By the way—"

He says, casual as hell.

"Madison stopped by Barnes & Noble last night."

The world narrows.

I set the bar down harder than necessary.

"What?" I say.

Ace blinks. "Uh. Yeah. I thought you knew?"

My hands curl around the knurling. "Why would she be there?"

He hesitates. That's my answer.

"She said something about 'clearing the air,'" he adds

carefully. "Didn't seem… friendly."

Something cold and precise settles in my chest.

I don't ask anything else.

I grab my phone and walk out.

I don't text Madison. I don't call. I don't give her the satisfaction of a reaction she can twist.

I text Lizzie.

Ethan:

Did Madison come to see you last night?

Three dots appear.

Disappear.

Appear again.

Lizzie:

Yes.

That's it.

No panic.

No drama.

Which somehow makes it worse.

Ethan:

Did she say anything that crossed a line?

This time the pause is longer.

Long enough for my jaw to tighten.

Lizzie:

I handled it.

I exhale sharply through my nose.

Because that's Lizzie — steady, composed, capable.

And because it should never have been her job.

Ethan:

I'm sorry.

The reply comes almost immediately.

Lizzie:

Chapter 33

I'm not hurt.

I'm just… done being polite with people who don't matter.

That's when something in me snaps.

Not explosively.

Decisively.

I don't go looking for Madison.

She comes to me.

She's leaning against the glass near the players' exit like she owns the place when I walk out, phone in hand, lips already curved like she's been waiting for the moment.

"Wow," she says. "You look intense."

I stop in front of her.

Low voice. No audience.

"You went to her work," I say.

She shrugs. "Public place."

"You don't get to do that."

Her smile sharpens. "You don't get to control me."

"I'm not trying to," I say. "I'm setting a boundary."

She laughs softly. "That's new."

"So is being done," I reply.

Her eyes flicker.

"I told you to stay away from her," I continue. "You ignored that."

"She needed a reality check," Madison says. "Someone had to tell her—"

"You don't ever get to speak about her like that again," I cut in.

The air goes tight.

"I didn't insult her," she says coolly.

"You tried to scare her," I say. "You tried to make her doubt herself. That ends now."

She studies my face like she's looking for the crack.
She doesn't find one.
"This isn't going to end quietly," she says.
"No," I agree. "But it *will* end."
I step closer, just enough that she hears every word.
"If you mention her name on air again," I say, "if you speculate, hint, imply, or smile through some 'concerned commentary' — I will shut it down. Publicly. Completely. And I will not soften it for your career."
Her breath stutters.
"That would hurt you too," she says.
"I'm aware," I reply. "Worth it."
She stares at me for a long moment.
Then she scoffs. "You're serious."
"Yes."
She straightens, mask sliding back into place.
"Good luck, Ethan," she says lightly. "You're choosing the hard way."
I nod once.
"Always have."
She walks away.
I don't watch her go.
I text Lizzie instead.
Ethan:
She won't bother you again.
That's not a promise — it's a fact.
A minute passes.
Then:
Lizzie:
Thank you.
Two words.

Chapter 33

But they land like relief.
Because protecting her isn't about fighting her battles.
It's about making sure she doesn't have to.

Chapter 34

Lizzie

Ryan notices the moment I stop avoiding him.

Which is unfortunate, because I was hoping to delay this until at least next week.

He corners me in the kitchen early Saturday morning, coffee in hand, still wearing the hoodie from last night's game like he slept in it.

"You've been weird," he says.

I grab a mug. "Good morning to you too."

"Don't," he replies. "You're not bad at lying, but you are terrible at pretending I don't exist."

I pour coffee. Slowly.

"I'm fine," I say.

He leans against the counter. "You've been at the arena more."

"I work there."

"You've been smiling at your phone."

I freeze.

Chapter 34

Damn it.

He clocks it immediately.

"Oh," he says. "So that's a yes."

I meet his eyes. "Ryan—"

"How long," he interrupts. Not angry. Just bracing.

Here we go.

I choose my words carefully. "Long enough that it matters. And I'm not going to give you details," I add calmly. "Not because I'm hiding — but because this isn't about permission."

His jaw tightens. "Is it serious."

"Yes."

He exhales through his nose, sharp. "Is there someone?"

I don't answer.

I don't have to.

He drags a hand down his face. "Jesus, Liz."

"I didn't plan it," I say quietly. "And I didn't do anything wrong."

He looks at me — really looks.

Not angry.

Worried.

"You know what this world is like," he says.

"I do," I reply. "That's why I'm not disappearing into it."

"That's not the same thing."

"Maybe not," I say. "But you don't get to decide that for me."

He flinches.

That hurts him.

I see it.

But I keep going.

"I'm not asking for permission," I say steadily. "I'm telling you because I respect you. And because I won't sneak around like I'm ashamed."

He looks away, jaw working.

"And if this hurts you?" he asks.

"I'll walk," I say. "That boundary is already set."

Ryan studies me, searching for cracks.

He doesn't find them.

"You're serious," he mutters.

"Yes."

He nods slowly. "This is going to be messy."

"I know."

"And public."

"I know."

"And it might blow back on the team."

I swallow. "I know."

Silence stretches.

Then he says quietly,

"I don't like it."

I nod. "You don't have to."

He sighs, rubbing the bridge of his nose. "But I see you."

That almost breaks me.

"I see you choosing yourself," he continues. "And I can't pretend you're still a kid anymore."

I let out a breath I didn't realize I was holding.

"This doesn't mean I approve," he adds.

"I didn't ask you to," I say gently.

He huffs a short laugh. "Yeah. I noticed."

He straightens.

"Just… don't let this turn into something you disappear inside of," he says. "You're more than whoever you're dating."

"I know," I say. "And so does he."

Ryan studies me one last time.

Then he nods. "Okay."

Chapter 34

Not approval.

But not rejection either.

As he walks out, my phone buzzes.

Ethan:

Everything okay?

I stare at the screen.

Then type:

Me:

It's getting closer.

But I'm still standing.

Three dots.

Ethan:

So am I.

And for the first time since this started, I believe him without bracing for impact.

Chapter 35

Ethan

The arena on game night is a living thing.

The bass from the sound system thumps through the concrete under my skates as we walk down the tunnel. The roar of the crowd is a constant hum, even back here.

We pass kids in Wolves jerseys pressed against the glass of the walkway, waving signs and homemade posters.

"RYAN MARRY ME"

"WE BELIEVE IN ETHAN"

"BRING US THE CUP"

I tap my stick against the glass where a little girl holds up a sign with my number on it. Her face lights up.

I should be nervous.

We're one series away from the Stanley Cup Final. This is the kind of game people work their whole lives for.

But all I can think about is Lizzie's hand on my chest this morning, her whisper: I'll be there. I'll watch every second.

"Walker," Ryan says, falling into step beside me.

Chapter 35

He's already in game mode—jaw set, eyes forward, helmet dangling from his hand. There's a coiled energy in him that I recognize. He lives for this.

"You good?" he asks.

I nod. "You?"

"Yeah." He bumps my shoulder with his. "Tonight? No distractions. No stupid penalties, no extra drama. We got one job: get to the Final."

I don't know if he saw the headlines earlier and chose to ignore them, or if he really hasn't been paying attention. There hasn't been a big reveal yet. Just whispers, blurry photos, nothing concrete.

So I take the out he's offering.

"Got it," I say. "I'm locked in."

He gives me a quick, sharp grin. "Good. Let's hunt."

The lights dim as we crowd near the end of the tunnel. The announcer's voice booms through the arena.

"WINTERCREST... MAKE SOME NOISE FOR YOUR WOLVES!"

The place explodes.

We burst onto the ice to a wall of sound.

Spotlights, smoke, the opening riff of some rock song that's been playing in this arena since before I could grow facial hair. Fans are on their feet, clapping, waving towels, stomping.

It never gets old.

I skate a warm-up lap, shaking out my arms, feeling the cold bite up through my blades. I glance toward our bench, then up, scanning the lower bowl.

It doesn't take long to find her.

She's in one of the family sections, Wolves hoodie, my number on the back, standing up with Sasha, yelling something I can't hear but can definitely feel.

The second our eyes meet, she freezes.

Then she smiles.

My chest tightens.

I tap my stick against the boards twice in their direction, a tiny, stupid little acknowledgment no one else will think twice about.

Ryan skates by and slaps his glove against my helmet. "Stay sharp, lover boy."

"Shut up," I mutter, but my grin is helpless.

The anthem plays. We line up. I put my blade on the ice and bow my head, letting the noise blur.

When the puck finally drops, it's like a switch flipping.

Everything narrows.

We come out flying in the first period.

Our line's clicking. First shift, we hem their top guys in for almost a full minute. Ryan wins the draw back to Ace at the point, I swing low for the return. We cycle, move our feet, work it around.

Crowd roaring on every shot.

Ten minutes in, it pays off.

I cut behind the net, draw the defenseman with me, and flip a quick pass through his skates.

Ryan's there on the doorstep.

He one-times it top shelf.

The red light flashes. The horn blares. The entire arena erupts.

"WOOOO!" Matty screams from the bench. "Let's go, baby!"

Ryan skates past the glass, slapping the logo on his chest, and the fans scream his name.

Chapter 35

1–0.

We're buzzing.

A few shifts later, I get my chance.

Neutral zone turnover, Ace sends it up the boards, I pick it up with speed. One defenseman between me and the goalie. I fake outside, cut inside, feel his stick jab at my hip.

For a second, everything slows.

I see a gap glove-side and rip it.

The puck hits the top corner, dents the back bar with a satisfying ring, and drops.

Goal.

2–0.

Sound hits me like a wave.

I do my usual low-key celebration—nothing wild—and as I circle back past the boards, I glance up.

Lizzie's on her feet, hands around her mouth, screaming like I just achieved world peace.

I don't drink on game days, but I still feel drunk.

We end the first up 2–0.

Second period is tighter.

They come out desperate, throwing their bodies around, finishing every hit. I get flattened into the boards once and shake it off, feeling the bruise bloom already.

They get one back on a weird deflection. 2–1.

The crowd groans but stays loud.

We push back.

Power play. I'm on the half wall, puck on my stick. I fake the shot, slide it down to Matty, he taps it across the crease—

Ryan again.

He slams it home like he's angry at the puck.

3–1.

Secrets On Ice

He and I bump helmets in the corner, yelling over the noise.

"Keep going," he shouts.

"Always," I yell back.

Later in the period, I swipe a loose puck at the hashmarks, banking in a greasy rebound after a scramble in front of their net.

4–1.

We go into the second intermission with a three-goal cushion, the building rocking like the roof might come off.

We're one solid period away from the Final.

I should be elated.

In the locker room, guys are fired up. Music's playing low, water bottles cracking open, tape being adjusted. The huge flat-screen in the corner is showing the in-arena feed: crowd shots, replays of our goals, intermission desk analysis.

I strip off my gloves, flex my fingers, shake out my wrists.

Madison's segment intro flashes across the screen.

A few guys hoot.

"Oh boy," Matty says. "Local gossip hour."

I ignore it at first.

But then I hear her voice.

"Wolves fans, we've got something a little extra interesting for you tonight," she chirps. "Because it looks like star winger Ethan Walker might have more than hockey on his mind as we head toward the Stanley Cup Final…"

My stomach goes cold.

My head snaps up.

The feed cuts to a graphic beside her: my headshot and a blurred-out second picture, the blur sliding away in a cheesy animation.

It's us.

Chapter 35

Me and Lizzie outside Barnes & Noble.

Her laughing up at me, my arm braced on the door, the kind of easy, soft moment that was never meant for millions of eyes.

Bold text underneath:

ETHAN WALKER'S SECRET ROMANCE—

OWNER'S DAUGHTER & HARPER'S LITTLE SISTER.

The room goes dead silent.

Madison keeps talking, voice syrupy.

"Sources tell us Walker's been spending a lot of time with Lizzie Harper, daughter of arena co-owner David Harper and younger sister of Wolves captain Ryan Harper. Looks like someone's mixing business, pleasure, and playoffs…"

The air feels sucked out of my lungs.

Someone mutters, "Oh, shit."

Ace lets out a low whistle.

I don't look at the screen.

I look at Ryan.

He's staring up at the TV like he just got hit with a puck to the chest.

His eyes flick from the image.

To me.

Back to the image.

Something ugly flashes across his face.

"Turn that off," I say, voice low.

No one moves.

"Turn it OFF!" I bark.

Someone fumbles for the remote, but before the screen cuts to black, Madison's last sentence rings out:

"…and with the Cup on the line, you have to wonder—will love be Walker's ultimate distraction?"

Click.

Silence.

Ryan stands.

The bench creaks under the sudden shift of his weight.

He crosses the room in three strides and slams me back into the lockers so hard my head rattles.

The whole wall shakes.

"MY SISTER?" he roars.

Hands grab at him—Matty, Ace, a couple guys from the second line—but he shrugs them all off, eyes burning holes into me.

"How long?" he demands. "How long have you been sneaking around with her?"

Adrenaline spikes hot under my skin. I shove him back just enough to get space.

"This isn't how—"

"How LONG?" he shouts again, spit flying.

"A while," I snap.

It's the truth. It's also the wrong answer.

He laughs once, harsh. "A while. Great. That's real specific, Walker."

"Harper!" Coach's voice cracks across the room. "Back off!"

Ryan ignores him.

"You knew she was off-limits," he snarls at me. "I told you. I told you not to go near her. And you did it anyway. Behind my back. Like a coward."

"I'm not gonna apologize for caring about her," I shoot back. "I—"

"Caring?" His voice goes brutal. "You cared about Madison, too, right? About every girl you left behind in whatever city we played in? That's what this is to you. A new toy."

Chapter 35

White-hot anger flashes through me.

"Don't talk about her like that."

"Like what? Like she's not just another name on your list?"

"She's not on a fucking list," I growl. "She's—"

"ENOUGH!" Coach bellows, stepping between us, one hand on Ryan's chest, the other on my shoulder. "You two want to tear each other to shreds, you do it after we win this damn game. You hear me?"

No one breathes.

"You are leaders," Coach spits. "You are my top line. I don't care who's dating whose sister. I care about that scoreboard. You lock it in, or I sit you both. Got it?"

I drag my eyes off Ryan and force out, "Got it."

Ryan's jaw flexes. "Yeah," he mutters. "Got it."

Coach glares at both of us for another second, then storms off, barking at the assistants about the power play.

The room slowly exhales.

Guys go back to taping and stretching and pretending they didn't just watch a grenade go off.

Ryan sits on the far end of the bench now, shoulders heaving.

I stare down at my skates, knuckles white where I'm gripping my stick.

I knew this would be bad when he found out.

I didn't think it would feel like losing my brother and my future in the same breath.

In the third period the ice feels different.

Heavier.

We hit the surface to the usual roar, but it sounds muffled in my helmet. Every sense is tuned too high. Every shadow feels like a threat.

We're up 4–1. If we were any other team, we could probably coast.

We're not any other team.

And the other guys are desperate.

Two minutes in, a bad bounce off the boards turns into an odd-man rush. Our defenseman slips, their winger walks in, flicks it high glove.

Goal.

4–2.

The crowd groans.

"Forget it!" Coach yells from the bench. "Next shift! Next shift!"

We reset.

Ryan and I jump over the boards with Matty, our usual line. I swing wide on the right, ready for the breakout pass.

Ryan retrieves the puck behind our net, wheels up, surveys the ice like he always does.

For a split second, our eyes meet.

I'm wide open.

He looks right past me and sends it to the opposite wing.

My chest pinches.

The play dies at the blue line. They turn it over again. Another scary rush. Our goalie bails us out with a sprawling save.

"Harper! Walker!" Coach roars. "Figure it out!"

We limp through the rest of the shift.

On the bench, my lungs burn. Sweat drips down my temples. The noise in the arena is anxious now—edgy, nervous.

Ten minutes left.

11:58 on the clock.

Chapter 35

The other team smells blood.

They press hard, hemming us in. We ice the puck twice in a row. Guys are gassed. The building buzzes with that particular playoff panic—no one sitting, everyone chanting, trying to will the puck out of our zone.

Then it happens.

Loose puck in the slot. Our defenseman fans on a clear. Their center pounces, snaps it five-hole.

Goal.

4–3.

The roof almost blows off—but not in a good way.

The away fans are screaming. Our fans are yelling, too, but it's pure desperation now.

Timeout.

We huddle around the bench, bent over, sucking air.

Coach leans in, face bright red. "I don't know what the hell is going on with the two of you," he snarls, eyes flicking between me and Ryan, "but you fix it. Right now. Or I bench you both and throw the rookies out there to sink or swim."

He jabs a finger in our chests. "Do. Your. Job."

He skates away, still muttering.

For a second, no one says anything.

The noise swirls around us. Stomping, chanting, the pounding of a thousand stressed-out hearts.

I grab a fistful of Ryan's jersey and yank him closer.

"You want to beat the shit out of me?" I growl, low enough that only he can hear. "Do it after the game. But if you blow this because you're pissed at me, you're not just punishing me. You're punishing the whole team. The whole damn city. Your parents. Lizzie."

His eyes flash at her name.

"Leave her out of this."

"She's already in it," I snap. "Because of us. Because I care about her. You can hate me later. Right now we win."

His chest heaves.

"You hurt her, Walker," he says finally, "and I swear to God—"

"I won't," I say, and it's not a promise, it's a vow.

He stares for a beat longer.

Then he nods once, jerky.

"Fine," he mutters. "Let's finish this."

The ref blows the whistle.

We jump back over the boards.

Next faceoff, Ryan wins it clean, kicking the puck back with his skate. Our D flips it to me along the boards, and I take off, adrenaline surging.

I fly down the wing, feel the defenseman shadowing me, waiting for me to cut inside like I always do.

So I don't.

I hold, hold, hold, then at the last possible second, I thread a pass through his skates.

Ryan is exactly where he's supposed to be.

He catches it in stride.

One move.

One shot.

Back of the net.

5–3.

The arena detonates.

Towels whirl. People scream. I swear I feel the whole building shake.

Ryan doesn't celebrate with me.

He does his usual celly near the corner, points his stick up

Chapter 35

to the rafters, bangs the glass where our families sit. I don't follow his gaze. I know Lizzie's up there.

I just skate back to the bench, lungs burning, trying not to puke from adrenaline and emotion.

The last four minutes are pure survival.

They throw everything at us. Our goalie stands on his head. We block shots with anything we can—hips, shoulders, ribs. Every clear is a small miracle.

When the final horn finally, finally blares and the red light flashes, it takes me a second to process.

We did it.

We won.

We're going to the Stanley Cup Final.

The boys mob the ice—helmets tossed, gloves in the air, everyone yelling. I get pulled into hugs, headlocks, fists bumping my helmet.

Ryan hugs Ace. Then Matty.

He doesn't come near me.

The cameras love it.

Two heroes, two goals each. The dynamic duo that just refuses to break.

Anyone watching on TV probably thinks we're tighter than ever.

On the ice, the space between us feels like a mile wide.

* * *

Lizzie

I have never been more stressed in my life.

The energy in the arena is unreal. Every seat filled, every fan on their feet those last few minutes. My voice is shredded from screaming.

When Ethan's line hits the ice for that final push, I swear I stop breathing.

Then he threads that pass to Ryan like they share one brain and one heartbeat.

When Ryan scores and the red light flashes, the sound that rips out of my throat doesn't feel human.

Sasha grabs me, shaking me. "YOUR MAN, BABE. YOUR MAN DID THAT."

"He's not—" I start to protest, then just give up and scream some more.

We win.

We actually win.

People are crying. Strangers hug each other. Some guy in front of us throws his beer in the air and gets tackled by his girlfriend. The announcer is yelling something about "for the first time in franchise history" but I can't hear it past the roaring in my ears.

For a few minutes, it's perfect.

For a few minutes, it's just my boy on the ice, looking huge and bright, hair damp, smile tight but real, raising his stick to the crowd.

Then I see the Jumbotron highlights flash again in my peripheral vision.

Not of the goals.

Of Madison's segment.

Chapter 35

Of my face next to his.

Of my name underneath his.

The people around us start to notice.

A girl two rows back whispers, "Is that her?"

Someone else points. "That's gotta be her, right?"

I feel my skin crawl.

Sasha sees my expression and grabs my hand. "Don't run."

"Everyone's staring," I whisper.

"They're not." She glances around. "Okay, some are. But if you bolt, it looks like you have something to be ashamed of. You don't."

I try to stand tall. I clap. I smile. I cheer when Ethan skates off.

Inside, my stomach is twisting.

After the game, Mom insists we all go back to the house.

"Family celebration," she says, almost vibrating with excitement. "We're going to the Final! Do you know what this means?"

"It means my stress levels will never recover," I mutter.

Dad laughs, slinging an arm around my shoulders. "You did great screaming, kiddo."

"Thanks," I say weakly.

By the time Ryan arrives, the house smells like pizza and champagne and whatever candle Mom lit to be festive.

He walks in to applause.

Mom kisses his cheek. Dad claps him on the back. I hover near the edge of the room, feeling weirdly like an intruder in my own house.

"Hell of a game, son," Dad says.

"Thanks," Ryan mutters.

His eyes scan the room.

Find me.

Stop.

I've known my brother my whole life.

I've seen him furious at refs, gutted by losses, wrecked over injuries.

I have never seen this look on his face.

"Hey," I say softly.

"Can we talk?" he says, voice flat.

Mom, oblivious, is already in the kitchen, humming to herself. Dad heads that way, too, talking about ice buckets.

Ryan nods toward the hallway.

My pulse skitters as I follow him toward the den—empty, quiet, door half-closed behind us.

He turns on me the second it clicks shut.

"You couldn't pick literally anyone else?" he says.

The words are sharp enough to cut.

"That's how we're starting?" I ask, trying for a small smile. It doesn't land.

"How long?" he demands.

I hug my arms around myself. "A while."

He laughs once, harsh, and scrubs a hand over his face. "Jesus, what is it with you Walker idiots and that answer?"

Tears prick my eyes. "Ryan, I—"

"You know what he's like," he snaps. "You've watched him. You've watched girls show up, disappear, repeat. You've seen Madison all over him. You've seen the way he lived."

"He's not like that with me," I say quietly.

He stares.

"And how would you know?" he asks. "Because he took you to a bookstore? Because he says pretty words? Because he scored a few goals and looks good on the Jumbotron?"

Chapter 35

"It's more than that," I whisper.

"He's my best friend," Ryan says. "You think I don't know him? He's a good guy in a lot of ways, but he's a player. He always has been. I told him—" He breaks off, jaw clenching.

"You told him what?" I ask.

He looks away. "I told him you were off-limits."

The words land like a slap.

My vision blurs. "You... did what?"

"I knew you had a thing for him," he says. "You've been making heart eyes since you were, like, twelve. I told him not to mess with you. To keep you out of whatever... cycle he had going."

Anger flashes through the hurt.

"You don't get to make that decision for me," I say, voice shaking. "You don't own me."

"I'm trying to protect you," he snaps.

"From what?" I demand. "From being happy? From loving someone? From making my own choices?"

"From getting your heart ripped out!"

We're both breathing hard now.

He steps closer, expression pained.

"You don't see it," he says. "You're blinded. You see this version of him he gives you. The anonymous texts, the sweet moments, the guy who reads books for you or listens when you talk. You don't see him in other cities. On off-nights. The way he used to be with Madison."

My stomach curdles at her name.

"That was before," I say. "He's different now."

"People don't change that much."

"He has," I insist, even as doubt twists in my chest. "He—he's careful with me. He listens. He shows up. You didn't see him this morning, you—"

Ryan holds up a hand. "I really don't need details about that, thanks."

Heat floods my face.

"I'm not stupid, Lizzie," he adds quietly. "I know you're not that little girl following us around the rink anymore. But that doesn't mean I want you tangled up with him when everything is this loud, this messy. You're not just dating a guy. You're dating the guy the entire league is suddenly obsessed with."

His words hit too close to everything I've already been thinking.

The headlines.

The photos.

The whispers in the stands.

"I can handle it," I say, but my voice wobbles.

"Can you?" he asks. "Because it looked like you wanted to disappear during that intermission."

My mouth snaps shut.

He sighs, running a hand through his hair. "Look. I'm mad, yeah. At him. At you. At Madison. At the whole circus. We're on the edge of the biggest series of our careers and now this is the story?"

"I didn't ask for that," I whisper.

"I know," he says. "But it's here. And when he screws up—and he will—I'm the one who has to keep playing beside him. I'm the one who has to choose between punching him and passing him the puck."

Tears spill over. "He won tonight," I say weakly.

"We won," Ryan says. "In spite of the two of you, not because of it."

Chapter 35

That hurts more than I want it to.

He exhales sharply, stepping back.

"I don't hate you," he says. "I hate that you picked him."

Then he walks out, leaving me in the quiet.

My legs give out.

I sink onto the nearest chair, pressing my trembling hands over my face.

I can hear Mom laughing in the kitchen. Dad's voice booming about how they're "going all the way this year." The clink of glasses. The TV replaying highlights of the game.

All of it feels far away.

My phone buzzes in my pocket.

I fumble it out, swipe at my eyes.

Ethan: Where are you?

Ethan: I want to see you.

Ethan: We did it. I want to celebrate with you.

I stare at the screen, chest tight.

I picture the morning. His hands. His mouth. His smile when I promised I'd be there.

I picture the Jumbotron with my name next to his.

Madison's smug face.

The locker room, him getting shoved into the wall, my brother's betrayal written all over his face.

I picture a thousand strangers watching, deciding who I am based on who I'm kissing.

My fingers hover over the keyboard.

I type. Erase. Type again. My hands shake so hard I have to backspace twice.

Finally, I send:

Me:
I'm happy you won.

Me:
I'm so proud of you.
Me:
But I'm... overwhelmed. Everyone knows now. Ryan is furious. The media is already tearing into it.
Me:
I care about you. I just need time to breathe before I drown.

The moment it leaves, I want to grab it back.

Three dots appear.

Disappear.

Appear again.

I hold my breath.

Ethan:
So you're pulling away.

The words scratch down my ribs like claws.

Another bubble.

Ethan:
Got it.

Another.

Ethan:
I'll give you space.

It feels like the floor drops out from under me.

I sink back, curling around my phone like it's a lifeline instead of the thing that just cut me.

I wanted to protect him.

To protect Ryan.

To protect our family, our team, our season.

Instead I feel like I've hit some giant eject button.

On him. On us. On everything we were just starting to build.

Sasha's text pops up a second later.

Chapter 35

Sasha:
I saw the segment replay. You okay, baby?
I type back, fingers numb.
Me:
No.
But I hit send anyway.
I bury my face in my pillow and cry until my chest hurts.
I don't know how to make this right.
I just know that for the first time since we started this, I'm not sure love is going to be enough to survive the noise.

And somewhere across town, I know Ethan is staring at his own phone, reading my words and hearing something else entirely:
She left.
Just like everyone else did.
Just like his mom.
Just like the people he never talks about.

And I hate that I'm the one who made that wound bleed again.
But I don't know how to be with him and not drown in all of this.
So for now, I do the only thing I think will keep us both from breaking completely.
I pull away.
And it still feels like shattering.

Chapter 36

Lizzie

I don't leave my room for a day and a half.

It's pathetic, I know.

But every time I think about opening the door, I picture stepping into the kitchen and seeing my own face on the news behind my parents. Or scrolling my phone and seeing another headline with his name and mine. Or bumping into Ryan in the hallway and watching that disappointed look cross his face again.

So I stay in bed.

I let my phone buzz itself half to death on my nightstand. I swipe away notifications without reading them. I only answer texts from my parents with the bare minimum:

Mom:
Honey, do you want grilled cheese?
Me:
No thanks.
Dad:

Chapter 36

Proud of you for being there for the team. Even when things got... loud.
Me:
Love you too.

They knock sometimes, checking in. They don't push. Mom pokes her head in once with clean laundry and this soft, searching look like she's trying to gauge my emotional temperature without spooking me.

"You know your father and I aren't mad, right?" she says eventually, folding a hoodie and setting it on my dresser.

I blink. "You're... not?"

Her mouth tugs up at the corner. "Lizzie, sweetheart. We watched you make heart eyes at that boy since he broke his front tooth on our driveway when you were twelve. We're not shocked. Maybe... concerned about the timing, the media, Ryan's temper. But mad?" She shakes her head. "We like Ethan. We just don't like seeing our kids in pain."

Tears burn instantly behind my eyes.

I nod because my throat won't work.

Mom comes over, smooths my hair back like she used to when I was little. "You don't have to talk until you're ready," she murmurs. "But you don't have to be alone, either."

As soon as she leaves, I cry anyway.

At some point, I drift off. At some point after that, there's another knock.

"Go away," I say into my pillow.

The door opens anyway.

"Rude," Sasha says. "What if I was Harry Styles?"

I roll over and squint at her. She's standing there with a tote bag, a messy bun, and her "I'm about to emotionally waterboard you with love" face.

"No offense," I croak, "but I'd rather kiss Harry Styles than you right now."

She kicks the door shut with her heel. "Noted. I'd rather kiss your brother, so we're even."

My eyes narrow. "What?"

"Nothing," she says quickly. "Don't worry about it. You're in crisis. This isn't about me."

She drops the tote bag on my bed and starts pulling things out like a chaotic Mary Poppins:

– A pint of my favorite ice cream
– A giant bag of Hot Cheetos
– Two face masks
– A bottle of sparkling water
– A fuzzy pair of socks

"And," she says grandly, "an emotional intervention."

I groan and flop back. "Hard pass."

"Too bad." She climbs onto the bed and sits cross-legged, staring me down. "You've been ghosting me since the game. You text me 'no' when I ask how you are. That's not a mood, that's a cry for help."

"I'm just tired," I mumble.

"You're heartbroken and terrified," she corrects gently. "Big difference."

The words sit between us like a weight.

I don't talk.

She doesn't rush me.

After a minute, she reaches over and squeezes my ankle through the blanket.

"So," she says softly. "You and Ethan. You told him you needed space?"

My chest aches. "Yeah."

Chapter 36

"And he said...?"

I stare at the ceiling.

"So you're pulling away. Got it. I'll give you space."

Saying it out loud makes my stomach twist all over again.

Sasha winces. "Oof. That sounds like a man about to write sad playlists."

"It sounds like someone who's used to being abandoned," I whisper. "And I just... pushed the exact button he's terrified of."

She watches me for a second. "Do you regret it?"

I suck in a shaky breath.

"I regret hurting him," I say. "But I couldn't breathe, Sash. Everyone in that arena saw my face on the Jumbotron. They know my name. They know where we live. Some of them recognized me in the stands. Ryan looked at me like I'd betrayed him. Madison's out there throwing lighter fluid on everything as a hobby. I felt like if I didn't hit pause, I was going to shatter into a thousand tiny pieces."

"That's fair," she says immediately. "You're allowed to freak out. You're allowed to need a second. You're allowed to have boundaries, even with a man who apparently has magic hands and a playoff beard."

My cheeks heat. "Sasha."

"What?" she says innocently. "I'm just assuming. Your face when you talk about him is not PG."

I bury my face in my hands.

After a beat, she says quietly, "Do you love him?"

My heart stumbles.

I know my answer before I even think it.

"Yes," I whisper. "I think I do. I don't know. It feels like it. He... feels like home and adrenaline at the same time."

She smiles, soft and satisfied. "There it is."

"It doesn't matter," I say quickly. "Love doesn't magically make the media disappear or make Ryan not hate this or make Madison stop being a snake. It doesn't change the fact that he has a reputation and I don't know how to live in a world where my boyfriend's hookups are archived on Twitter."

Her eyes sharpen. "Is that what this is about? His past?"

"It's about everything," I say, voice getting tight. "His past, his job, my family, the pressure. I'm not some cool, unbothered socialite. I literally had to Google what icing was last year. I work at Barnes and Nobles and read romance novels on my breaks. I wasn't built for front-row seats to sports gossip chaos."

Sasha is quiet for a moment.

Then she says, "Okay. Can I be honest?"

"I'm terrified," I warn.

"Good." She leans closer. "Because you're doing that thing again."

"What thing?"

"The thing where you decide fear equals intuition," she says. "Where instead of asking for what you want, you pre-break your own heart so no one else can."

I stare at her.

"That's not what I'm doing," I say, even though it feels uncomfortably true.

"Really? Because from where I'm sitting, it looks like you finally got the thing you've quietly wanted for, oh, a decade—and the second it went from dreamy and secret to real and messy, you decided you don't deserve it."

I swallow.

"He's... Ethan," I say helplessly. "He's this huge thing. He

Chapter 36

fills rooms. People chant his name. They write articles about him. They post pictures of his arms. I'm just—"

"Do not finish that sentence," she snaps.

I shut my mouth.

"You are not 'just' anything," she says, eyes fierce. "You are Lizzie Harper, the girl who reads three books a week and roasts elite athletes in group chats and makes the best hot chocolate in Wintercrest. You are smart and kind and stubborn as hell. He's lucky you even answered his first message on that app."

My throat burns.

"It doesn't feel like that," I whisper.

"I know," she says, softer now. "Because fear is loud. And messy. And it loves to tell you stories about how everything good is secretly a trap."

She shifts closer, tucking one leg under herself.

"Let me ask you something," she says. "If the media wasn't involved—if there were no headlines, no Madison, no Jumbotron reveal—would you still have texted him that you needed space?"

The answer slices through me.

"No," I breathe.

"Okay." She nods like she expected that. "So you didn't pull away from him. You pulled away from the noise. But he can't see that. Not from where he's standing."

Guilt twists my stomach.

"He thinks I don't want him," I say.

"Right now? Yeah," she says gently. "Because you told him you needed space and then vanished."

"I'm scared," I repeat, because it's the only thing that feels solid.

"I know," she says. "And I'm not telling you to slap on a jersey and show up at his door with a boombox and a speech about destiny. I'm just saying... don't let fear be the only voice in the room when you make this choice."

I stare at my hands.

"I don't know how to do this," I whisper. "I don't know how to be someone whose relationship is content for other people. I don't know how to date a man who has a history and not get swallowed by comparisons. I don't know how to look Ryan in the eye and keep choosing Ethan anyway."

Sasha exhales slowly.

"You do it like this," she says. "One conversation at a time. One boundary at a time. One day at a time. You tell Ethan, 'This is what I can handle and this is what I can't.' And then you see if he meets you there. If he doesn't? Then we hate him and write thinly veiled revenge novellas. If he does? Then you keep walking."

A broken laugh slips out of me. "You make it sound easy."

"Nothing about this is easy," she says. "But love's not supposed to be completely safe. Comfortable, yes. Safe with each other, yes. But risk-free?" She shakes her head. "That's not love. That's hiding."

She hesitates.

"And you deserve real love, Liz," she says quietly. "The kind that's worth fighting for. Not the kind you pre-quit because it might hurt."

Tears spill over, hot and fast.

"I don't want to lose him," I admit in a rush. "But I also don't want to lose myself."

"Then don't," she says. "You get to have boundaries and a boyfriend. You get to tell him, 'I need you to shut Madison

Chapter 36

down publicly,' and 'I need time away from cameras,' and 'I need you to understand that this is my first everything, so you can't treat me like everyone else.' If he's the guy you think he is, he'll say, 'Okay. I'll figure it out.'"

"And if he's not?" I whisper.

"Then we find out now," she says. "Before you build your whole life on something that can't hold your weight."

We sit there in silence for a moment, my tears dripping down onto the blanket.

Finally, she nudges my shoulder.

"Do you want him?" she asks. "Forget the team. Forget the headlines. Forget Ryan. In your chest, in your bones—do you want him?"

The answer is so bone-deep it scares me.

"Yes," I say. My voice trembles, but it doesn't break. "I want him. I want... us. I want stupid domestic stuff like him stealing my socks and me stealing his hoodies. I want to kiss him after games and not pretend I'm just the owner's daughter. I want to argue with him and make up with him and—" I break off, wiping my nose. "I want it."

Sasha smiles through suddenly glossy eyes.

"Then that's your truth," she says. "Everything else we can work around. Fear can sit in the backseat. It doesn't get to drive."

I let that sink in.

Fear can sit in the backseat.

"How?" I ask hoarsely. "What do I do?"

"First?" she says. "You shower. You eat something that's not your own tears. You put on real clothes. You stare in the mirror and remind yourself you're hot."

"That seems shallow."

"That seems essential," she argues. "Then… if you're not ready to see him yet, fine. But you at least text him something that isn't 'I'm disappearing now, bye.'"

My lip wobbles. "What do I say?"

She grins. "Lucky for you, you're friends with a communication genius."

"That's not a real thing," I sniff.

"It is if I say it is," she says. "Now scoot. You smell like anxiety."

I snort despite myself.

She hops off the bed and tosses me the fuzzy socks.

"Start with these," she says. "Then we write something honest. Not perfect. Not easy. Just… honest."

I look down at the socks in my hands.

They're stupid and soft and covered in tiny cartoon wolves.

I pull them on.

It feels like the smallest possible step.

But it's still a step.

As Sasha raids my closet and mutters about "main character energy," a quiet thought curls up in the back of my mind:

I don't know how this ends.

I don't know if we make it to the other side of this storm.

I just know I'm tired of letting fear speak louder than the part of me that reached for him first.

When I'm dressed and my hair doesn't look like a cautionary tale, Sasha pats the space beside her on the bed and hands me my phone.

"Ready?" she asks.

"No," I say.

She smiles. "Good. That means it matters."

I stare at my phone until the screen dims.

Chapter 36

Sasha doesn't rush me. She just sits there, solid and stubborn, like if I bolt she'll tackle me back into my own bed.

My thumb hovers over Ethan's thread.

I scroll up to the last thing he said.

I'll give you space.

It shouldn't hurt the way it does—how easy it was for him to make himself smaller. How fast he offered me an exit like he's used to watching people take it.

My throat tightens.

"Not perfect," Sasha reminds me softly. "Just honest."

I inhale and type before I can overthink it.

Me: I'm not pulling away from you.

Me: I'm pulling away from the noise.

Me: I'm overwhelmed and I panicked... but I don't want to lose you.

Me: Can we talk soon? Just us. No cameras.

I read it twice, heart pounding.

Sasha leans in. "Send."

I do.

The message whooshes away and my stomach drops like I stepped off a ledge.

For a second there's nothing.

Then three dots appear.

I stop breathing.

Sasha grins like she just won something. "There. See? You didn't die."

I laugh—wet and shaky—and press my palm to my chest like it might calm the frantic beat under my ribs.

Whatever happens next, at least he won't have to guess where I stand.

And maybe—just maybe—I won't either.

Chapter 37

Ethan

Giving her space feels a lot like losing her.

I told her I'd back off. I meant it. She said she was overwhelmed, and she has every right to be. But every hour that goes by without her name lighting up my phone feels like someone's slowly tightening a band around my chest.

We're three days out from Game 1 of the Final.

Practice is sharp, heavy, focused. Coach has us running drills until our legs burn. Guys are dialed in, talking systems and matchups and which one of their forwards we need to shut down early.

Me?

I'm skating like a machine.

No emotion. Just reps.

Hit the blue line. Cut in. Release. Again.

I'm scoring in practice the way I always do. But it doesn't feel like anything. It doesn't feel like those nights when I'd look up after a perfect shot and see her in the stands, hands cupped around her mouth, screaming like she believed in me more than anyone else.

Now I don't even know if she'll be there.

After practice, Coach does the usual "media's waiting, don't say anything stupid" speech, then nods at me and Ryan.

"League wants you both for the big availability," he says. "Top line, top pressure. Keep it to hockey as much as you can. We don't need any more sideshow bullshit."

His eyes flick to me on that last part.

I nod, jaw tight. "Got it."

Ryan says nothing, just yanks his hoodie on, eyes unreadable.

We walk down the hallway together without speaking, the buzz of the arena muted but still there. Even empty, the place hums. Techs move lights into place. Camera guys adjust angles. There's a low murmur of voices from the press room ahead.

PR catches us at the door.

"Okay," she says, efficient, tablet in hand. "They're going to ask about the Final. They're going to ask about the last series. They're going to ask about how you're preparing mentally and physically. Say all the usual clichés. Do not take Madison's bait. We are not feeding the machine today."

At the sound of Madison's name, something ugly twists in my gut.

"What if they ask about Lizzie?" I ask.

PR's eyes flick up, quick. "They will. Deflect. 'My personal life is my personal life,' that whole thing. The more you say, the more they spin."

I nod, but something in me is already pushing against that.

Because the last few days, I've seen the spin.

Chapter 37

Clips of Madison's segment replayed over and over. Threads picking apart every blurry photo. Comment sections speculating on Lizzie's life like she's a character in a show instead of a real person who reads in the upper rows and brings her parents coffee on game days.

People calling her a distraction. A problem. A liability.

They don't even know her favorite coffee order or how she cries at the same book twice.

"Got it," I lie.

We step into the media room.

The stage lights are too bright. There's a long table with mics, nameplates, little bottles of water. The league backdrop behind us is covered in logos: team, sponsors, Stanley Cup Final branding plastered everywhere.

Cameras aim like weapons. Reporters fill the seats, some familiar faces, some national.

Ryan takes the seat in the middle. I sit to his right. Our coach anchors the end.

Flashbulbs pop.

"Alright, let's get started," someone from PR says. "Questions?"

They ease into it.

"How does it feel to make it this far?"

"What are you expecting from your opponents?"

"Ryan, what does it mean to you as captain to lead this team to the Final?"

We give the usual answers.

"It's an honor."

"One shift at a time."

"Stay focused, stick to our game."

I can do this part on autopilot. Smile a little. Nod when

Ryan talks about our leadership group. Drink water when Coach says something about depth scoring and goal tending.

Then a reporter from one of the national outlets lifts her hand.

"Ethan," she says, "there's been a lot of talk about 'off-ice distractions' this past round. How do you balance a high-profile relationship and the pressure of chasing a Cup?"

PR shifts at the back of the room.

I lean toward the mic.

"My focus is on hockey," I say evenly. "On my team, on this series. That's what matters right now."

It's safely vague.

She presses. "So you won't deny that you're in a relationship with the owner's daughter?"

Ryan's shoulders tense beside me.

Coach starts to lean toward his mic, ready to step in.

I hold up a hand slightly, stopping him.

"I'm not here to talk about my personal life," I say. "I'm here to talk about the Final."

There's a rustle in the room.

Another guy jumps on it—local tabloid, the kind that lives for clicks.

"Ethan, there's concern that your relationship might be a distraction for the team," he says. "Some have called it inappropriate, given that she's the captain's younger sister and the owner's daughter. Do you think it reflects poor judgment on your part?"

The phrasing makes something snap low in my spine.

Ryan shifts in his seat, jaw grinding.

I stare out at the sea of raised phones and lenses.

They're waiting for me to tuck my head down. To apologize.

Chapter 37

To make this easier for them to turn into a chewable narrative.

My mind flicks to Lizzie, curled in her hoodie, probably reading every cruel comment and wondering if she made my life harder just by loving me.

I think about the text she sent, about needing space.

I think about how many times in my life people have walked away and I've just let the story be whatever looked best from the outside.

I lean forward.

"No," I say.

The room stills.

"No, I don't think it reflects poor judgment," I continue, voice steady. "And no, I don't think she's a distraction."

A few reporters exchange glances. Someone's camera light shifts a bit brighter.

I hear PR inhale sharply in the back.

"You're confirming the relationship, then?" the first reporter asks quickly. "You and—"

"Her name is Lizzie," I cut in. "Lizzie Harper. She's not a rumor. She's not a segment. She's a person."

You could hear a pin drop.

I could stop there.

I don't.

"You've all seen the clips," I say, looking out over them. "You've seen the way some of this coverage has gone. Talking about her like she's a storyline, or a liability, or some kind of joke because of who her dad is and who her brother is."

I shake my head, anger prickling hot and controlled.

"She didn't ask for that," I say. "She's known this team her entire life. She grew up in this arena. She cheers for us, worries for us, shows up for us. She works her own job.

Secrets On Ice

She lives her own life. She didn't sign up to be dissected by strangers because I happen to wear this jersey."

A murmur ripples through the room.

The tabloid guy clears his throat. "So you admit the relationship is real?"

I look straight at him.

"Yeah," I say. "I'm dating her. I care about her a lot. And if anyone wants to question judgment, question mine. Not hers. Drag me, not her. Put my face on your graphics before a game, not hers on the Jumbotron. Leave her and her family out of the circus."

Ryan is staring at me from the side now. I can feel it without looking.

Another hand shoots up. "Ethan, do you think it creates any conflict in the room, given that you're involved with your captain's sister?"

I glance at Ryan.

His jaw is tight. His eyes are dark. But he doesn't look away.

I turn back to the mic.

"Look," I say. "Ryan and I… we're working through stuff. That's not a secret. We care about the same people and we care about this team. We'll handle that like grown men in our room."

I pause.

"As for the relationship? I'm not apologizing for loving someone who makes me better. On and off the ice."

Someone in the back actually whispers, "Holy shit," a little too loudly.

"Do you think it's worth the attention and the pressure it brings?" another reporter asks. "Going public like this—"

"It's not about publicity for me," I say. "It's about respon-

Chapter 37

sibility. You all are going to keep talking either way. That's your job. But I'm not going to sit here and let you paint her like some puck bunny or a mistake I made on the way to the Final. She's not a mistake."

My throat tightens, just a fraction.

"She's the person who's had my back when nobody else knew what I was going through," I say quietly. "She's the one who texts me after a loss before anyone else has the guts to. She's the reason I've gotten up on the mornings when everything felt heavy as hell. You can call that a distraction if you want, but to me? That sounds a lot like support."

The words hang there.

I can feel the weight of them. The risk of them.

You're not supposed to say things like that at a podium with league logos behind you. You're supposed to say things like "one game at a time" and "I'm just here so I won't get fined" and keep your heart someplace no camera can find.

But I'm tired of hiding.

I'm tired of watching her get treated like collateral damage in a story she didn't ask to be in.

"Last question," PR says quickly, sensing the tension.

A quieter reporter near the front raises a hand.

"Ethan," she says, "given everything that's been said online and in certain segments…"—a pointed glance at Madison's network—"what would you want fans to know about Lizzie?"

It's the easiest question I've gotten all day.

"That she's real," I say without hesitation. "She's not some stereotype. She's the girl in the stands who actually reads the program, not just looks at selfies. She knows everyone's stats, not just mine. She remembers the staff's birthdays, not just the players'. She shows up, even when it's hard."

Secrets On Ice

I exhale slowly.

"And I'm asking you all—" I look around the room, making eye contact where I can "—to show her the same respect you'd want for your own families. Talk about my game, my mistakes, my goals, whatever. That's fair. That's part of this. But you don't get to tear her up for clicks. Not without hearing from me that she deserves better than that."

There's a long beat of silence.

Then PR jumps in, voice tight. "That's all for today. Thank you."

Microphones are cut. Reporters start talking in low, excited voices. Cameras stay trained on us as we stand.

Coach leans over, whispering under his breath, "You just gave our PR team a heart attack."

"Sorry," I mutter.

He sighs. "But… not your worst answer."

He pats my shoulder once and walks off.

I turn to leave, but Ryan's still sitting there, watching me.

We look at each other.

For the first time since the blowup, there's something in his gaze that's not just anger.

It's… wondering.

He doesn't say anything.

He doesn't have to.

For the first time in days, I feel like I did something right.

Maybe I just torched my media image.

Maybe I just made Lizzie's life harder before it gets better.

But if she sees this—if she hears me call her by name and choose her out loud—maybe, just maybe, she'll know:

I'm not going to pretend she's an accident.

Chapter 37

***

Lizzie

Sasha is halfway through lecturing me on proper hydration when my phone buzzes with a notification from the Wolves app.

LIVE NOW: STANLEY CUP FINAL MEDIA AVAILABILITY — WALKER, HARPER, COACH LEIGHTON.

She's rummaging in my mini-fridge. "You can't just live on coffee and vibes, babe, you need actual—why is your face doing that?"

"Nothing," I say too fast.

She pads over and peeks at my screen.

"Oh," she says. "Do you want to watch it?"

"No," I say immediately.

"Yes," she says at the same time.

We stare at each other.

"Fine," I mutter.

We pull the stream up on my laptop, curl up on my bed, and lean in.

At first, it's the usual stuff.

How does it feel to make it this far?

What are you expecting from the other team?

Ryan does Captain Mode perfectly. Calm, focused, cliché in the best way.

Then someone asks about "off-ice distractions."

Sasha makes a face. "Here we go."

I brace myself for the usual brush-off. The brushed-back hair, the tight half-smile, the deflection.

Instead I watch Ethan lean toward the mic, eyes darker than

I've seen them in any highlight reel.

"My focus is on hockey," he says. "On my team, on this series. That's what matters right now."

It's safe.

Then they say my name.

Or close enough.

"Owner's daughter."

"High-profile relationship."

"Poor judgment."

I feel my spine lock up.

Sasha squeezes my wrist. "Want me to turn it off?"

I should say yes.

I don't.

Then I hear him say it.

"No," he says. "No, I don't think it reflects poor judgment. And no, I don't think she's a distraction."

My breath catches.

He looks angrier than I've ever seen him in front of a camera. Not uncontrolled—just done.

"Her name is Lizzie," he says. "Lizzie Harper. She's not a rumor. She's not a segment. She's a person."

My throat closes.

He keeps going. He talks about the coverage. About the way they've used my face. About dragging family into stories for clicks.

He says, Drag me, not her.

He says, Put my face on your graphics, not hers.

He says, She's not a mistake.

Then he says the thing that absolutely wrecks me.

"As for the relationship?" He looks straight into the cameras. "I'm not apologizing for loving someone who makes me better.

Chapter 37

On and off the ice."

My heart stops.

Sasha lets out a very quiet "Oh my God."

I can't breathe.

He talks about my texts after losses. About showing up. About support. About asking the media to treat me like I'm human.

By the time PR cuts it off, my eyes are full.

Sasha pauses the stream on his face.

He's not smiling.

He looks scared and stubborn and raw.

"Lizzie..." she whispers. "He just soft-launched 'I love you' on national TV."

I laugh, wet and shaky. "Shut up."

She nudges my shoulder. "I'm serious. That wasn't damage control. That was a man planting a flag."

I swipe at my cheeks.

On the screen, his image is frozen mid-sentence, eyes fierce, mouth set like he's bracing for impact.

"He chose you," Sasha says quietly. "Loudly. When he didn't have to."

I think about all the ways this could blow back on him—on the team, on the run, on his reputation.

He did it anyway.

For me.

Fear is still there, coiled in my stomach. These words won't make Madison disappear or fix Ryan overnight or erase the headlines.

But something inside me shifts.

Because he didn't do that for optics.

He did it because he doesn't want me standing in front of a

story by myself.

"Do you still want him?" Sasha asks softly, even though she already knows the answer.

I look at the screen.

At the boy who just told the world I'm not a mistake.

"Yeah," I whisper. "I really do."

"Then fight for it," she says. "Maybe not today. Maybe not with a grand gesture and fireworks. But eventually, you're going to have to stop letting fear and everyone else's opinions be louder than your own heart."

I close the laptop gently.

My hands are still trembling when I pick up my phone.

I don't text him yet.

Not quite.

I just open our thread. Read his last three messages over and over.

So you're pulling away.

Got it.

I'll give you space.

For the first time since I sent that awful text, space feels like something I might be able to cross.

Not today.

But soon.

Because whatever happens next—whether we survive this or not—I want to at least know I didn't just walk away without trying.

And now I know one thing for sure:

I'm not the only one willing to stand in the light anymore.

Chapter 38

Lizzie

I don't know how people deal with big feelings in normal, functional ways.

Some cry.

Some eat entire pints of ice cream.

Some cut bangs.

Me?

I write.

Not because I want to share it.

Not because I want anyone to read it.

But because when something hurts too much to hold, putting it into a story lets me breathe without breaking.

So I open my laptop, take a deep breath, and tell myself the truth in a language I'm not brave enough to speak out loud yet.

A blank document fills the screen.

My fingers hover.

Then the words spill.

Secrets On Ice

* * *

The Man Made of Winterfire

There was once a man who lived on the ice, though everyone swore he was made of fire.

They said he was born for cold arenas and bright lights, for roaring crowds and impossible goals.

They said he was fearless.

Untouchable.

Unbreakable.

But the girl who watched him from the quiet corners knew better.

She knew the fire wasn't armor — it was a warning.

A flare sent into the dark so no one would come close enough to see the cracks beneath the blaze.

When the world looked at him, they saw a star.

When she looked at him, she saw a constellation trying desperately to hold itself together.

He never knew she watched the way his shoulders carried victory like it cost him something,

or how he smiled like joy was a habit he was trying to relearn.

He never knew she memorized the shape of him —

the way he pulled his gloves tight before a face-off,

the way he touched the ice like it was an old friend,

the way his eyes softened, only for a heartbeat, when he spotted someone he cared about in the stands.

And the girl — she tried not to love him.

She tried to pretend her heart wasn't already stitched to the outline of his shadow.

She tried to pretend the universe didn't tug her toward him

Chapter 38

every time he walked into a room.

She tried to pretend her pulse didn't recognize him long before her mind admitted anything at all.

But love is stubborn.

And hers grew like frost on glass — slow, quiet, impossible to ignore once the sun touched it.

She loved him when he didn't know.

She loved him when she thought he never would.

She loved him the way winter loves the first warm day — fiercely, helplessly, with relief so sharp it almost hurt.

And when he finally looked back at her — truly looked — it felt like the world opened a window she'd been pressing her forehead against for years.

But the world can be cruel to hearts that love in the open.

Storms came.

Lies came.

Fear came in a hundred small whispers, telling her she wasn't strong enough, brave enough, worthy enough to walk beside a man who burns for a living.

So she stepped back.

Not because she wanted to.

Because she was afraid her soft heart would melt into nothing next to all his heat.

But here is the truth she could not say aloud:

She has never loved anything the way she loves the man made of winterfire.

Not gently.

Not carefully.

But wholly.

And if he ever reads these words…

She hopes he knows he changed her.

That he made her braver than she knew how to be.

That every story she writes now has a boy with fire in his veins and a girl who finally learns how to reach for him without burning.

And she hopes he knows:

She never pulled away because he wasn't enough.

She pulled away because, for the first time in her life, something mattered enough to lose.

And she hopes — quietly, impossibly — that he'll still be there when she learns how to be brave.

* * *

When I finish, my hands are shaking.

It's not a perfect story.

It's not polished.

It won't win awards.

But it's true.

And the truth feels like a confession I didn't know how to speak.

My cursor blinks at the end of the page. A quiet, patient heartbeat.

There's no way I can give this to him.

Not yet.

Not when fear still has its hand around my throat.

So I do the next best — or maybe worst — thing.

I call Sasha.

She answers on the first ring. "If you're crying again, I brought more Cheetos."

"I'm not crying," I say. "I wrote something."

Chapter 38

Her inhale is sharp. "Is it...?"

"It's... honest," I whisper.

"Lizzie." Her voice softens. "Are you going to send it to him?"

"No."

A beat.

"Not myself, but he'll know it's from me." She's silent for exactly three seconds.

"You want me to deliver it."

I swallow. "I don't want to see him. Not yet. But he deserves... something. After everything he said today. After how he defended me."

Sasha doesn't tease. She doesn't sigh dramatically. She just says:

"Send it to me. I'll take care of it."

I email her the file.

My stomach twists when I hit send.

"Want me to bring you coffee after?" she asks.

"No," I say quietly. "I just want to hide for a little longer."

"You're allowed," she says. "I'll handle the delivery today. You already did the brave part."

When the call ends, I curl up on my bed and press my face into my pillow.

I don't know if this is stupid.

I don't know if this is brave.

I don't know if this will fix anything.

I just know that I finally told the truth — even if it's in a story.

And now it's out of my hands.

Sasha

I'm not nervous.

I'm not.

I'm just… sweating aggressively for no reason while standing in the parking lot of the Wolves' practice facility like I'm about to drop off the nuclear codes.

Ethan is exiting the building when I spot him — duffel over his shoulder, hair damp from a shower, looking like a man who hasn't slept since the Reagan administration.

Perfect. Great. Excellent timing.

"Ethan!" I wave before I can change my mind.

He stops immediately, shoulders tensing before he recognizes me.

"Sasha?" He blinks. "Is she okay? Did something happen?"

Oh boy.

He's in Full Concern Mode.

"She's fine," I say quickly. "Mostly. Emotionally wobbly, but fine."

He exhales shakily.

I take a breath.

Then I hold out the folded paper.

"What's this?" he asks.

"A story," I say. "She wrote it. For you. But she's… still scared. So she asked me to give it to you."

His throat works as he swallows.

"You read it?" he asks softly.

"I skimmed enough to know it's real. Then I stopped, because it's yours." I admit.

Chapter 38

He nods. His hand closes around the paper like it's made of glass.

"Is she... mad at me?" he asks.

"No," I say. "Terrified? Yes. Conflicted? Yes. Deeply emotionally compromised because you went full Romeo in front of national media? Also yes."

He laughs once, short and rough.

I soften.

"She's trying," I say. "Even if it doesn't look like it."

He nods, looking at the story like it contains answers he's starving for.

"Tell her..." He stops, rubs his jaw, shakes his head. "Never mind. She won't want to hear it from me right now."

I reach out and squeeze his forearm.

"Read it," I say. "Then... maybe give her a little time before you text her."

He nods again, tighter this time.

"Thank you," he says.

I smile. "I'm rooting for you two. Even if her brother kills you eventually."

His smile cracks through for real at that.

Then he walks away, story clutched in his hand like a lifeline.

* * *

Ethan

I read it in my truck.

Engine off.

Gear in park.
Phone face down.
The world stops existing somewhere between the third line and the fourth.
By the time I reach the end, my hands are shaking.
Not because it's pretty.
Not because she wrote well — though she did. God, she did.
No.
I'm shaking because she opened her rib cage and handed me her heart, disguised in metaphors and heat and honesty she could never say out loud.
She loves me.
Not puppy love.
Not crush love.
Not infatuation born from proximity.
Real love.
The kind that sees my sharp edges.
The kind that sees the fears I hide.
The kind that sees the boy I've always been under the man everyone else thinks they know.
And she still chooses me in the story.
Even when she couldn't choose me in real life.
I press the pages to my forehead.
Breathe once.
Twice.
Three times.
I don't text her.
Not yet.
She asked for space.
But for the first time since everything blew up, it doesn't

Chapter 38

feel like a goodbye.

It feels like a beginning trying very hard to be brave.

So I open my notes app and type the only thing I can allow myself for now:

When she's ready…

I'll be here.

Fire and all.

And for the first time in days… the world doesn't feel like it's ending.

It feels like it's waiting.

Chapter 39

Ethan

I don't move for a long time after reading her story.

I just sit there in my truck with the echo of her words in my chest, feeling every wall I built peeling back one line at a time. She didn't write a pretty metaphor. She wrote a confession. A map. A wound. A truth.

And for the first time in my life, I don't want to run from that kind of honesty.

I want to meet it.

So I stay late at the arena.

Playoff schedules mean no one questions me staying late.

I ask for the lights.

I ask for the music.

I ask for the space.

And then I build the moment I should've given her months ago.

At center ice, I mark the spot where I've always looked for her—that exact place she always sat as a kid, leaning forward

Chapter 39

with a book in her lap, pretending not to watch me.

A small glowing heart sits there now, cast by a spotlight.

Her place.

Her presence.

Her importance.

And on a white carpet path leading to that heart, I set down a blank journal, tied with a thin red ribbon.

Inside the cover, in my handwriting:

Write the rest with me.

No pressure.

No demands.

Just an invitation to build something we're both finally brave enough to reach for.

Sasha texts me.

We're here.

I take my place at center ice.

And I wait.

* * *

Lizzie

The arena is dark when Sasha opens the door, and cold air spills around my ankles.

"Why here?" I whisper.

"Because this is where everything began," she says softly.

Her answer makes my stomach twist.

We walk through the tunnel, my black ankle boots tapping on the rubber flooring. The air gets colder as we approach the ice. My heart beats faster with every step.

And then—

I freeze.

The rink is glowing.

Snowflake projections drift lazily across the ice.

Golden spotlights illuminate a long white carpet runner stretching from the tunnel all the way to center rink.

But what tears a breath from my chest is the heart-shaped light glowing at center ice.

My spot.

The place I used to sit as a kid.

The place he always looked for me.

And standing inside that heart, with his hands in his pockets and his chest rising like he's afraid to breathe—

Is Ethan.

He lifts his head the instant I appear.

"Lizzie… come here."

My boots step onto the carpet, sinking softly into it. The cold air brushes my cheeks. The lights shimmer off the ice like stars.

And all I can do is walk toward him, heart pounding, throat tight.

When I reach him, he swallows hard.

"You made it."

"I didn't know what to expect," I whisper.

"You weren't supposed to expect anything," he murmurs. "You were just supposed to show up."

He steps aside slightly—revealing the blank journal sitting on the carpet between us.

My breath catches.

He nods at it.

Chapter 39

"Open it."

Hands shaking, I lift it gently, sliding the ribbon off. The first page is blank.

Then the inside cover.

Four handwritten words:

Write the rest with me.

My vision blurs with tears.

"Ethan…" I whisper.

And then he speaks.

***

Ethan

"Lizzie… I've spent my whole life pretending I didn't need anyone.

Pretending love was something dangerous.

Something that would slow me down.

Something I wasn't built for.

But then there was you.

You, sitting in that exact spot—" he gestures to the glowing heart "—with your book and your shy smile and your whole world in your eyes. I noticed you before I understood what noticing meant.

You were my calm before I even knew I needed calm.

You were my comfort before I had the courage to call it that.

You were my favorite part of every game, even when I didn't know why.

And then this…" He gestures between us. "This became

real. Bigger. Scarier. And I failed you in ways I shouldn't have."

My breath trembles.

"But then you wrote your story. And Lizzie… it was the most beautiful thing anyone has ever given me. You didn't just write about love. You wrote about seeing me. All of me. Even the parts I spent years hiding."

He steps closer, voice softer.

"So I made this. For you. For us. The place where I always looked for you. And a journal for the pages we haven't lived yet."

His eyes shine—raw, honest, terrified.

"I'm not asking you to decide everything tonight.
I'm not asking you to promise a future you're not ready for.
I'm asking for a chance.
To write the next pages together.
Messy. Beautiful. Real."

He reaches up, thumb brushing a tear from my cheek.

"I choose you, Lizzie. I always have. I just didn't know how to say it."

* * *

Lizzie

A sound escapes me—half sob, half breath.

"I'm still scared," I whisper. "I don't know how to be brave the way you think I am."

He leans in, forehead resting on mine.

"Then be scared with me," he murmurs. "As long as you're

Chapter 39

here... I'm not afraid of anything."

My heart cracks open.

So I kiss him.

The moment our mouths meet, everything inside me turns molten.

His hands slide to my waist, gripping tight, pulling me against him with a hunger that steals my breath. I gasp, and he groans softly, head dipping, lips taking mine deeper.

He kisses me like he's relearning how to breathe.

My fingers slide into his hair, tugging him closer. He lifts me slightly, my toes grazing the carpet as my back hits the boards behind us—cold enough to make me gasp again.

"Lizzie..." he murmurs against my mouth, voice wrecked. "If you kiss me like this, I'm never letting you go."

"Then don't," I breathe.

His kiss grows hungrier, deeper—his hand tilting my jaw up, thumb stroking just under my chin, guiding the angle of my mouth against his.

Heat spirals low in my stomach.

My knees weaken.

His grip tightens.

And every fear I had dissolves into the cold air around us.

When we finally break away, we're both shaking—breathing each other in like the world hasn't stopped spinning.

He presses his forehead to mine.

"Tell me this is the start," he whispers.

"It is," I whisper back. "It always was."

And then he kisses me again—slow, reverent, like he's writing the first line of a brand-new story.

Chapter 40

Lizzie

Wintercrest the next morning feels different.

Maybe it's the sunlight making the snow on the sidewalks glow.

Maybe it's the way my phone won't stop buzzing.

Or maybe it's because I'm walking beside Ethan—our hands brushing, not quite holding yet, but so close my whole body buzzes from the heat of him.

His confession.

His kiss.

His journal.

His spot on the ice.

I didn't sleep.

Not because I was stressed.

Because every time I closed my eyes, I replayed the way he touched my face. The way he looked at me. The way he said:

"Write the rest with me."

Now we're heading toward the arena together, because of

Chapter 40

course the universe wants to raise the stakes immediately.

Reporters are waiting outside the Wolves' facility.

Cameras.

Microphones.

Phones held high.

All for him.

And now… a little bit for me.

My stomach flips.

Ethan notices instantly.

His hand finds mine.

Warm. Solid. Certain.

"You okay?" he murmurs.

I nod, even though I'm absolutely lying.

He squeezes my hand.

"You don't have to do anything. I'll handle it."

But I surprise both of us by stepping closer to him.

"I'm not hiding this anymore," I whisper.

"I'm not hiding us anymore."

His breath catches—hot, soft—like he wasn't expecting that.

Then he lifts our joined hands and brushes his thumb along my knuckles.

"Then let's show them."

The second we walk up, the crowd goes louder.

"Ethan! Ethan, is this official?!"

"Lizzie, are you two dating?"

"How long has this been going on?"

"Is this serious?"

I freeze for half a second—but Ethan?

He doesn't hesitate.

He wraps his arm around my waist, pulling me right to his side.

"Yes," he says clearly. "It's official."

There's a gasp.

A ripple of noise.

Flashes burst like fireworks.

"And yes," he continues, voice steady, "it's serious."

I can literally hear someone whisper, "Holy shit."

Ethan's hand stays firm at my waist. Protective. Grounding. Proud.

Not possessive—just present in a way that makes my chest feel warm.

Cameras snap.

Reporters ask questions.

People cheer.

And for the first time, I don't feel overwhelmed.

I feel... seen.

With him.

Beside him.

Then someone steps out of the arena doors.

Ryan.

And everything stops.

His eyes travel from Ethan's arm around me...

to my hand resting on his chest...

to the way Ethan doesn't move or back down.

Ryan's jaw flexes.

"Oh crap," I whisper.

Ethan mutters, "Yeah. That looks about right."

Ryan doesn't blink.

He doesn't speak.

He just jerks his head toward the building.

"Inside. Now."

Oh boy.

Chapter 40

***

The second the door closes behind us, Ryan's anger hits like a shockwave.

He's not confused.

He's not surprised.

He is hurt.

"Unbelievable," he snaps, pacing hard. "You two really went behind my back. Again."

Ethan shifts slightly in front of me, protective.

"Ryan—"

"No." Ryan cuts him off sharply. "You knew. You BOTH knew how I felt about this. And you still did it in secret. And now?"

He points toward the hallway, toward the media chaos outside.

"My baby sister is on every sports site in the damn country. Every camera pointing at her. Every headline dragging her name into your world."

I swallow.

"Ry—"

"And YOU—" he jabs a finger toward Ethan, "—didn't even respect me enough to ask. Not that I would've said yes, but you didn't even try."

His voice cracks—just barely—and that's when it hits:

He isn't just angry.

He feels betrayed.

"I'm your best friend," Ryan says, lower now, almost gutted. "I thought that meant something."

Ethan's jaw flexes with guilt.

"It does," Ethan says quietly. "It means everything. And I

should've come to you first. I should've told you the minute it stopped being… complicated."

Ryan laughs bitterly. "Complicated? You think this is complicated? She's my sister, Ethan. My responsibility. One of the most important woman in my life. And now the whole damn world is watching her because of you."

Ethan steps forward.

"I know. And I'm sorry for how it happened. But I'm not sorry that I love her."

My breath stops.

Ryan goes still.

Ethan continues, steady:

"I'm not using her. I'm not playing with her. And I'm not backing out because the world suddenly noticed."

Ryan looks at him long and hard.

Then he turns to me—eyes soft, heartbreaking.

"You really love him?" he asks, voice hushed.

"I do," I whisper. "And I chose this. Not because he asked me to—because I wanted him."

Ryan squeezes his eyes shut, pained, like he's fighting every protective instinct screaming inside him.

Then he steps closer to Ethan—too close.

His voice drops into a lethal murmur.

"You didn't ask me," he says quietly. "So now hear me loud and clear."

Ethan meets his eyes, unwavering.

"If she cries because of you—real tears, not stress, not nerves—if you break her heart, our friendship is dead. I don't care how long we've known each other. I don't care what we've survived together."

Ryan's jaw tics.

Chapter 40

"If you break her heart, I will end you. You hurt her and I will put your ass six feet under. I don't care what we've survived. I don't care what we've built. Do you understand me?"

Lizzie gasps softly.

Ethan nods—serious, accepting.

"Fair. I'd deserve it."

Ryan stares a moment longer.

The anger doesn't leave his face…

but something in his shoulders loosens.

Just slightly.

He turns to me then and pulls me into a tight, rib-crushing hug.

"I hate this," he mutters into my hair. "I hate how fast it happened. I hate that you're in the spotlight. I hate that he didn't ask. But…"

His voice softens.

"I love you. And I'm trying."

A small laugh breaks out of me. "You're still the best brother."

"I know," he mutters dramatically, sniffing once.

He releases me, then points at Ethan while refusing to make eye contact.

"And YOU. Don't touch her around me. Ever. Especially not before games. I swear to God."

Ethan snorts. "Deal."

Ryan mutters, "Disgusting," under his breath, then storms out of the room.

But… he didn't say no.

And for Ryan?

That's a blessing.

Secrets On Ice

* * *

By noon, Wintercrest has decided we're a story worth rooting for.

Fans post edits. Teen girls scream "we knew it." Adults smile about how we grew up together. Someone coins a hashtag that trends locally before lunch.

For the first time, the attention doesn't feel like a threat.

It feels like momentum.

* * *

Lizzie

By late afternoon, the story of me and Ethan has gone from rumor → to confirmation → to full Wintercrest meltdown.

People are rooting for us.

Comment sections are cheering.

Fans are posting edits.

But the Wolves organization?

They've had enough of Madison's behavior.

So now I'm standing backstage in the arena's media room with: my dad, Ethan's dad, Ryan, and Ethan.

And most horrifyingly…

Madison.

She's in full broadcast makeup, heels clicking, eyes slicing over me with that condescending smile she always saves for women she thinks are beneath her.

"You shouldn't be here," she says lightly. "This is a staff meeting."

Chapter 40

I don't flinch.

My dad steps forward.

"Actually, sweetheart," he says—not to Madison, but to me—"you should be standing front and center."

Madison's smile falters.

Ethan's hand brushes mine, hidden from cameras.

A reminder.

A grounding point.

The doors swing open.

The press waits inside—cameras, lights, reporters, the whole frenzy.

Dad and Mr. Walker walk to the podium first.

Ryan and Ethan flank them.

I stay just behind until Dad gestures me forward.

"Lizzie," he murmurs, "this is yours."

My heart stumbles.

But I step forward.

The room quiets.

Flashbulbs go off.

Madison tilts her head, confused—then annoyed.

And Dad begins.

* * *

"Thank you all for coming," my dad says in his calm, CEO voice. "Today's briefing concerns recent conduct by one of our media partners."

He glances at Madison.

Her jaw tightens, but she lifts her chin like she's untouchable.

"Earlier this week," Mr. Walker continues, "content was released that violated our organization's harassment and ethics policy."

Reporters murmur.

Cameras shift.

Madison steps forward.

"If this is about the Harper girl—" she scoffs.

"Miss Harper," my dad corrects firmly.

Her eyes flash irritation.

"She's not an employee," Madison says sharply. "You can't claim harassment of a civilian."

The room goes dead quiet.

And then Dad smiles.

The kind of smile that says

You just played yourself.

"Actually," he says clearly, "my daughter is the Assistant General Manager of the Wintercrest Wolves organization."

Gasps.

Reporters whip their cameras toward me.

Ryan looks smug.

Ethan looks proud.

Madison looks like someone slapped her.

"She signed her contract two months ago," Mr. Walker adds. "And as her position states, she is a full-time executive employee of the franchise."

Madison's face drains of color.

"And per section 14B of the league's media partnership agreement," Dad continues, "any employee may file harassment claims against contractors, vendors, and broadcasters."

"Which brings us to today," Mr. Walker says.

He turns to me.

Chapter 40

"Lizzie? Go ahead."

My pulse hammers.

I step to the mic.

When I speak, my voice is steady.

Clear.

Strong.

"Madison Tate," I say, "you have repeatedly violated the professional boundaries outlined in your contract. You have targeted me publicly, encouraged rumors, interfered with player performance, and attempted to weaponize personal information for media gain."

She sputters. "You're twenty-five!"

"And your contract says," I continue, lifting a highlighted clause, "'Harassment of any employee or staff member of the Wolves organization results in immediate termination. No appeal. No exceptions.'"

The room ERUPTS.

Flashbulbs explode.

Reporters shout questions.

Madison stares at me like she can't process what just happened.

"You can't fire me," she breathes. "You don't have the authority to do this."

"No," I say softly.

"I'm your superior."

Dead silence.

I lift the termination letter from the podium.

"Effective immediately, your credentials with the Wintercrest Wolves and Wintercrest Sports Broadcasting are revoked pending formal termination."

Her mouth falls open.

Security steps forward.
She looks to Ethan.
"Ethan," she whispers. "You're really letting her—?"
He doesn't hesitate.
"Goodbye, Madison."
And for the first time ever, she has nothing to say.
Security escorts her out.
She doesn't look back.

* * *

Ethan

The moment the door shuts behind Madison, I exhale for the first time in ten minutes.

Lizzie stands there, breathing hard, a little shaken, but solid.
Strong.
Terrifyingly beautiful.
Ryan reacts first.
"Holy shit."
He grins.
"My sister just fired Madison Tate on live television."
Dad laughs.
Mr. Walker beams.
And me?
I walk straight to her.
"You okay?" I ask quietly.
She nods, still processing, eyes wide.
"That was…" Ryan starts.
"Badass," Ethan finishes for him.

Chapter 40

She blushes, the tiniest smile forming.
Reporters are still shouting questions.
The entire arena is buzzing.
But none of it matters right now.
Because she just took control of her story.
Of her job.
Of her life.
And I'm standing beside her, exactly where I want to be.

* * *

Fans are cheering.
Signs appear.
Someone screams:
"WE LOVE YOU, LIZZIE!"
"POWER COUPLE!"
"GOOD RIDDANCE, MADISON!"
Wintercrest has chosen a side.
And it's ours.
Lizzie squeezes my hand.
"You really okay?" I ask.
She exhales shakily.
"Yeah. I think I am."
I lean down, brushing my lips against her temple.
"Good," I whisper. "Because this? Us? The world can get loud, but I'm not going anywhere."
She melts just a little against me.
Ryan watches us, shaking his head.
"This is insane," he mutters.

Then he looks at me.
"If you ever hurt her—"
"I know," I say. "Six feet under."
He smirks.
"Glad we understand each other."
And just like that—
We're official.
We're public.
We're unstoppable.
We're choosing each other.
And Wintercrest is rooting for us.

Chapter 41

Lizzie

Outside the arena, cameras still flashing in the distance, Ethan's hand never leaves the small of my back. Not once. Not through the doors, not down the hallway, not while security shields us from the last of the reporters.

The moment we're out of sight, he exhales like he's been holding his breath all day.

"You held your ground today," he murmurs, thumb brushing my hip. "You were stronger than anyone in that room."

My chest tightens. "I was terrified."

"But you didn't look it."

He steps closer, heat rolling off him.

"You looked like someone I should kneel for."

My breath stutters.

The tension between us is no longer subtle — it's a physical pull, a gravitational force dragging me closer.

He leans down, lips barely grazing my ear.

"Come home with me."

It's not a question.
It's not an order.
It's a promise.
My voice comes out as a whisper. "Yes."
His jaw flexes — relief, hunger, restraint all fighting for space.
"You sure?" he asks softly. "Because if you walk through that door with me…"
His eyes darken.
"I won't be able to take it slow tonight."
A full-body shiver rolls through me.
"I don't want slow," I breathe.
That's all it takes.
His hand slides into mine, firm and certain, and he guides me to his truck with a look that says tonight will destroy us in the best way.

* * *

Ethan

By the time we make it up to my place, I'm hanging on by a thread.

The second the door shuts, the world goes quiet. No cameras. No reporters. No teammates. No Ryan pacing like he's two seconds away from homicide.

Just her.

Lizzie stands there in the soft lamplight of my loft, fingers still tangled with mine, hair a little messy from the wind, cheeks flushed from the cold and the chaos of the day.

Chapter 41

And she's looking at me like she's trying to decide whether to kiss me or climb me.

Please let it be both.

"You held it together today," I say, voice low. "You were fire in that press room."

She huffs out a shaky little laugh. "I thought my heart was going to explode."

I step closer, crowding her gently back against the door.

"Mine is exploding right now," I murmur.

Her eyes flick to my mouth.

I'm done pretending I don't see it.

I tilt her chin up with a knuckle. "Lizzie?"

"Yeah?" she whispers.

"If you want to change your mind, this is your last chance." My voice comes out rougher than I intend. "Because if I touch you the way I've been thinking about all day, I'm not going to be able to stop at one kiss."

Her breath stutters.

"Good," she says. "I don't want you to stop at one."

The last thread of my control snaps.

I kiss her.

Not careful.

Not slow.

Hungry.

She melts into it, hands fisting in the front of my hoodie, pulling me down, kissing me back like she's been starving too.

She presses closer, chest flush with mine, and then her hands slide under the hem of my hoodie, fingers against my bare skin.

I groan into her mouth.

"Oh, no," I rasp, breaking the kiss just enough to breathe. "You are absolutely playing with fire, Paperheart."

Her lips curve.

"Then burn me, Frozenfire."

Jesus Christ.

I slam my palms against the door on either side of her head, caging her in. Her breath catches, but she doesn't look away.

"I warned you," I growl.

Before she can respond, I grab her thighs and lift. She gasps and automatically wraps her legs around my waist, fingers clutching at my shoulders.

"Ethan—"

"I've got you," I murmur, voice rock-bottom low.

I kiss her again as I carry her through the loft, her fingers in my hair, her little noises going straight to my sanity.

By the time we reach my bedroom, I'm already gone.

I set her on her feet at the end of the bed, hands braced on her hips.

"Take this off," I say softly, tugging at the hem of her top.

She reaches for it, but I stop her, catching her wrists, bringing them up over her head and crossing them lightly.

"Slow," I murmur. "Let me watch."

Her pupils blow wide.

I release her wrists and step back half a step, chest heaving.

She does it—slowly, like I asked. Fingers sliding under the hem, inch by inch, pulling the fabric up, revealing skin that should be illegal.

My jaw tightens.

"You're going to kill me," I say, voice hoarse.

"You're a pro athlete," she whispers. "You'll survive."

"Debatable."

Chapter 41

When her shirt comes all the way off and hits the floor, I reach for her like I've been drowning.

My hands skim her sides, her waist, her back. I kiss her again, deeper, pushing her gently backward until the backs of her knees hit the mattress.

"Lie back," I say.

She does.

And everything in me snaps into focus.

She's here. In my bed. Officially mine. And no one in the world can argue with it now.

"Lizzie," I murmur, eyes dragging over her slowly, reverently. "You have no idea how long I've wanted this. How long I've wanted you."

She bites her lip, cheeks flushed.

"Show me," she whispers.

I intend to.

All night.

* * *

Lizzie

I don't think I've ever seen Ethan look like this.

Not on the ice.

Not at practice.

Not even the first time we were together.

This is… different.

Focused.

Dark.

Hungry and gentle at the same time.

His hands slide over me like he's mapping out his favorite place. My skin feels too tight, too hot. Every brush of his fingertips sends a shiver racing down my spine.

"You're staring," I breathe.

He huffs out something like a laugh. "Yeah. Get used to it."

He kisses a path down my throat, slow and claiming. Every time his mouth grazes a sensitive spot, a little sound escapes me, and every single time, he reacts like I just scored a winning goal for him.

"God, I love the way you sound," he rasps against my skin. "I want to hear every noise you make tonight."

My thighs press together.

He notices. Of course he notices.

"Move your legs," he murmurs. "Let me in."

I do, and he settles between them, solid and warm and too much and just enough all at once.

I hook a finger in the collar of his hoodie.

"This needs to go," I whisper.

He grins, slow and wicked.

"Yes, ma'am."

He pulls it off in one smooth motion, and for a second I just stare, because... yeah. That body really does exist.

"See something you like?" he teases.

"I plead the fifth."

His answering smile is lethal.

"Come here," he says.

He leans down, kissing me again, hands starting to roam with more purpose now. He kiss that tender spot behind my ear that makes me lose mind.

He doesn't rush it.

That's what ruins me.

Chapter 41

Ethan's hands slide slowly down my sides, thumbs brushing bare skin as if he's memorizing me. He kisses his way along my jaw, my throat, my collarbone—lingering just long enough at each place to make me ache for more before moving on. Every inch of exposed skin feels like a promise he's deliberately delaying.

"Patient," he murmurs against my skin, like he knows exactly what he's doing to me.

I shiver as his hands work lower, unhurried, coaxing instead of demanding. He lets fabric fall away piece by piece, punctuating each movement with another kiss, another slow drag of his mouth that makes my breath stutter. By the time I'm finally bare beneath his hands, I'm trembling—not from the cold, but from the way he's taken his time making me feel wanted.

His palms skim over me then, warm and sure, and I swear my body leans into his touch on instinct alone.

By the time he finally lets his hands go where I desperately want them, I'm already falling apart.

"Ethan," I gasp, fingers clutching at his shoulders. "I—"

"Breathe," he murmurs. "I've got you. Let me take care of you."

His voice is steady, anchoring. Something inside me loosens, even as everything else tightens.

I trust him.

Completely.

He moves with intention, reading every breath, every small reaction like it's a language only he understands. His touch is slow at first, exploratory, then surer—learning me, coaxing me open piece by piece. Every time I start to tense, he murmurs something low and calming, like he's keeping me tethered even as I drift higher.

"That's it," he whispers. "You're doing so good. I've got you."

The pressure builds in waves, overwhelming and sweet, until I can't tell where I end and he begins. My hands clutch at him, my breath breaking apart as he guides me through it, never rushing, never letting me feel lost.

And when I finally tip over that first edge, it's like everything shatters and reforms at once.

I come back to myself in pieces—his hands firm on my hips, his forehead pressed to mine, his voice still there, grounding me as the world slowly settles.

"You okay?" he asks quietly.

I nod, dazed. "Yeah. I... holy shit."

He laughs, low and proud. "That's the idea."

"I thought hockey was your job," I murmur weakly. "Pretty sure it's actually this."

"Don't tell my coach," he says. "He'll want tape."

Chapter 41

I swat his shoulder. "Gross."

He kisses me again.

And round one isn't over.

* * *

Ethan

She thinks I'm done.

I am absolutely not done.

I flip us carefully, pulling her on top of me. Her hair falls around her face, eyes still hazy, lips kiss-swollen, cheeks flushed.

"You're so beautiful," I say, no teasing in my tone now. "You know that, right?"

She swallows. "I... not like this."

"Especially like this," I correct, hands gliding up her thighs. "Especially when it's just us."

Her fingers slide down my chest, nails scratching lightly.

"You're wearing too many clothes," she murmurs.

"Fix it, then."

She does.

Slowly.

Painfully.

Deliberately.

She starts with my hoodie, fingers hooking into the fabric like she's testing how much I'll let her take. She drags it up inch by inch, her knuckles brushing my skin on purpose, eyes never leaving my face as if she's cataloging every reaction.

I hiss a breath when her nails skim my ribs.

"Jesus," I mutter, already losing the fight.

She smiles—small, satisfied—and keeps going. Palms flatten against my chest, thumbs tracing slow lines like she's learning me by touch alone. Every time she pauses, it's just long enough to make my patience snap.

"You're enjoying this way too much," I say, voice rough.

"Mm," she murmurs, leaning in just enough that I can feel her breath. "You told me to fix it."

Piece by piece, she strips me down, kisses following where her hands have been, never rushing, never letting me forget who's in control right now. I can feel my restraint fraying with every deliberate touch, every soft exhale she pulls from me.

By the time I'm down to nothing and she's straddling my hips, I am one second away from losing the last of my sanity.

"Lizzie…"

"Yeah?" she says softly, that shy-bold mix that kills me.

She moves against me again, slow and deliberate, like she knows exactly what it's doing to my control. My breath stutters, my hands tightening on her hips as I fight the urge to flip us immediately.

"Careful," I warn, voice already wrecked. "You keep moving like that and I won't be gentle."

Chapter 41

Her smile is all confidence and fire.

"I don't want gentle," she whispers, brushing her mouth along my jaw, my neck. "I want you."

That does it.

I roll us in one smooth motion, pinning her beneath me, the bed creaking softly as I slot myself between her thighs. Her gasp hits me straight in the chest, and I brace my forearms beside her head, holding her there while I look at her properly—flushed, breathless, eyes dark with want.

"Look at me," I murmur, thumb tracing along her jaw until she does. "Tell me who you're with."

"You," she breathes. "Only you."

Something fierce and possessive twists low in my gut.

"Good," I say quietly. "Because you're mine."

The world narrows to heat and movement and the sound of our breathing filling the room. I set the pace, slow at first, dragging it out until she's arching beneath me, fingers digging into my shoulders like she's holding on through a storm.

"That's it," I murmur against her ear. "I've got you. I'm not going anywhere."

Her answer is a broken sound that goes straight through me, and when she finally comes apart in my arms, it feels like winning something I've been chasing my whole life.

I follow not long after, the tension snapping all at once, leaving us both shaking and breathless.

When it's over, we're a tangled mess of limbs and heat, my chest heaving as she collapses against me, hair tickling my skin, heart racing just as fast as mine.

I wrap my arms around her.

"Round one," I say, kissing her temple. "You good?"

She laughs, breathless. "I can't feel my legs."

"That's a yes."

* * *

Lizzie

I'm pretty sure my bones melted.

I lie there, sprawled on his chest, listening to his heartbeat pound against my ear, feeling stupidly, ridiculously happy.

Safe.

Claimed.

Worshipped.

The world still knows my name now. There are still headlines and comments and pressure and playoffs.

But right here?

None of that exists.

Just us.

"Ethan?"

"Yeah?"

"I think my soul left my body."

Chapter 41

He snorts softly. "I'll bring it back in a minute."

"That was... a lot."

His hand strokes up and down my spine, soothing. "Too much?"

"No." I smile against his chest. "Perfect."

He's quiet for a second.

Then he shifts.

"Come shower with me."

I lift my head. "You're already planning round two?"

"Round two, three, and four," he says. "We're celebrating, remember? We're official. You destroyed Madison. My dad thinks you walk on water. Your dad literally gave you power to fire people."

My cheeks heat.

"I don't walk on water," I mutter.

He grins. "You did just now."

I hit him with a pillow. "You're impossible."

He grabs my wrist and pulls me back down, kissing me hard enough that my brain goes fuzzy again.

"Come shower," he says against my lips. "Let me worship you properly."

Heat curls low in my belly again.

"Okay," I whisper. "Yeah. Okay."

* * *

Ethan

The hot water hits our skin, steam filling the glass shower, fogging up the door as if the universe is giving us privacy.

She's in front of me, hair damp, water beading on her shoulders, eyes half-lidded as she tilts her face up into the spray.

I press her gently against the tile, one arm braced beside her head, the other skimming down her side.

"You know what the best part of today was?" I murmur.

"Firing Madison?" she says.

"That was a close second," I admit. "But no. Best part was watching you stand in front of the entire world and not flinch. Best part was realizing I get to be the one you come home with after."

Her eyes soften.

"Ethan…"

"You're mine," I say, voice low enough to vibrate between us over the hiss of the water. "Not a rumor. Not a secret. Not a scandal. Mine."

She shivers, water cascading over both of us.

"Say it," I murmur, stepping closer, chest to chest, heat to heat. "Tell me who you belong to."

Her breath catches.

"You," she whispers. "You, Ethan. I'm yours."

I close my eyes for a second, because that right there? That's everything.

"Good girl," I murmur.

Her knees almost buckle.

"What are you going to do to me?" she breathes.

I smile slowly.

"Round two."

He leans in, lips finding mine under the spray, slow and deliberate, like he's reminding me exactly who's in control.

Chapter 41

The kiss turns deeper, hungrier, water slicking between us as his hands roam with purpose—down my back, along my hips, steadying me when my legs wobble.

"Look at me," he murmurs, forehead resting against mine. "Stay with me."

I do, breathless, clinging to him as he lifts me just enough to pin me gently against the cool tile, the contrast stealing a gasp from my lungs. His mouth trails along my jaw, my throat, every kiss unhurried, like he's savoring the way I react to him.

"You feel so good," he murmurs, voice low and reverent. "So responsive. Like you were made for this."

For us.

My fingers dig into his shoulders as the water pours down, the heat between us building until it's impossible to tell where one of us ends and the other begins. He keeps me grounded with quiet words, with touches that say *I've got you* even as everything inside me starts to unravel again.

By the time we finally break apart, both of us are shaking—laughing breathlessly, foreheads pressed together, steam curling around us like a secret.

When we stagger out of the shower, wrapped in towels and clinging to each other, it feels less like we survived something and more like we earned it.

"That," she pants, "was dangerous."

"That was necessary," I correct, kissing her forehead. "And we're not done."

Her eyes widen. "We're not?"

"Oh no," I say. "I haven't even really tasted you yet."

Her face goes nuclear.

"Ethan!"

"What?" I ask, all innocence. "You think I'm stopping before I worship you properly?"

* * *

Lizzie

He lays me out on the bed like I'm something sacred.

Hands gentle.

Eyes dark.

Mouth soft at first, then hungry.

"Ethan…" I whisper, already feeling my pulse climb again.

"Relax," he murmurs, kissing down my stomach. "I'm going to make you forget your own name."

I choke on a laugh. "That's dramatic."

"Try me."

He slides lower.

My heart is going to explode.

"Look at me," he says softly.

I do.

His eyes lock on mine, and the intensity there is almost too much—devotion and heat and something that feels dangerous in how deeply it sees me.

Chapter 41

"You're mine," he says again, voice low and steady. "Let me show you how well I take care of what's mine."

The way he says it makes something inside me snap.

He moves slowly, deliberately, like he wants me to feel every second of it. His hands keep me grounded even as my thoughts scatter, his mouth tracing a path that steals my breath and leaves nothing but sensation behind. His voice follows me everywhere—soft, firm, unyielding.

"That's it," he murmurs. "I've got you. Don't fight it."

I try to stay quiet. I really do.

But the tension coils tighter and tighter until my body betrays me completely. My fingers twist into his hair, my back arching as the world narrows to heat and pressure and his voice saying my name like it belongs to him.

"Ethan—"

The sound rips out of me, sharp and broken, and I don't recognize myself anymore. I'm shaking, unraveling, coming undone in a way that feels dark and overwhelming and right all at once.

"Let go," he whispers. "That's it. I'm right here."

I do.

I break with his name on my lips, the sound echoing in the room as everything inside me gives way. When I come back to myself, it's in fragments—breathless, trembling, his hands firm on my hips like he never once considered letting me fall.

He kisses his way back up my body, slow and unhurried, mouth curved in a way that tells me he knew exactly how far he was pushing me.

And he'd do it again.

"Still alive?" he teases.

"Debatable," I gasp. "I—I think you killed me."

He grins.

"Your turn," I whisper.

His expression shutters, then heats.

"Are you sure?"

I nod, fingers trailing down his stomach.

"I'm not made of glass," I say softly. "I want to take care of you too."

He groans.

"Lizzie, you're going to be the death of me."

"Good," I say. "Then we'll match."

* * *

Ethan

She is… unexpectedly lethal.

Shy at first. Curious. Then bolder when she realizes she can make me swear under my breath with just a touch.

Chapter 41

"Tell me what you like," she whispers.

"Everything you're doing," I grind out.

"That's not helpful."

"Neither is you looking at me like that while you're touching me," I say through my teeth.

She smiles—sweet and wicked.

"Then don't look."

"Not a chance."

She starts slow.

Too slow.

Her touch is tentative at first, like she's learning me—watching my face, tracking every reaction. Every time I swear or inhale sharply, her confidence grows.

"Yeah," I breathe. "That's it… you're doing so good."

Her eyes flick up to mine, dark and focused, and something in my chest snaps.

"Fuck, Lizzie," I mutter. "You have no idea what you're doing to me."

She doesn't stop.

"Don't," I warn weakly. "If you keep going like that—"

She keeps going.

"Good girl," I rasp, losing the last of my control. "Just like that."

Secrets On Ice

She looks up at me then, eyes wide and focused, like she's memorizing the way I react to her. The sight alone nearly breaks me. I've been hit harder on the ice and kept my feet better than this.

"Tell me if it's too much," she whispers.

"It's not enough," I choke out. "Jesus—Lizzie—"

I try to warn her. I really do.

"Fuck—Lizzie—" My grip tightens in the sheets. "You need to stop or I'm—"

She doesn't.

She absolutely does not.

And that's it.

I lose it completely—every last shred of control gone, my breath tearing out of me as the world goes white around the edges. When it's over, I'm flat on my back, staring at the ceiling like I just saw God and he personally wrecked me.

She crawls up my chest, warm and flushed, eyes bright with that shy-proud look that makes my chest hurt in the best way.

"Was that… okay?" she asks softly.

I grab her face and kiss her hard, pouring everything I can't

Chapter 41

say into it.

"Okay?" I rasp against her mouth. "I'm going to be thinking about that in the middle of games, and it's going to ruin my career."

She laughs—light, delighted, completely unbothered.

"Worth it," she says.

"Completely," I agree.
Sometime after, we end up tangled in the sheets again, her draped over my chest, my hand tracing lazy patterns on her back.
I could sleep like this.
Live like this.
Die like this.
"I love you," I say, before I can stop it.
She stills.
I freeze.
Then she lifts her head, eyes shining.
"I love you too," she whispers.
That's it.
That's game over.

I roll us gently, pinning her to the mattress, kissing her like she just handed me the rest of my life. Like this moment is something sacred I don't want to rush or ruin.

"One more?" I murmur against her lips, brushing my thumb along her cheek.

She laughs softly, that sleepy, satisfied sound that still somehow wrecks me. "You're insatiable."

"For you?" I say quietly. "Always."

This time is different.

Slower.

I take my time with her like I'm memorizing her all over again — the warmth of her skin, the way her breath stutters when I kiss the corner of her mouth, the way she relaxes the second she realizes I'm not going anywhere. My hands move with intention, not hunger, and she feels it immediately.

Her fingers slide into my hair, not pulling, just holding — anchoring us together.

"Ethan," she whispers, like she's grounding herself.

"I've got you," I murmur back, resting my forehead against hers. "I'm right here."

We move together, unhurried, eyes locked like neither of us wants to miss a single second of this. Every kiss is softer, deeper, full of things we don't have words for yet. Every touch feels like a promise instead of a question.

"I love you," I say quietly, the words slipping out without fear this time.

Chapter 41

She stills for half a heartbeat — then her eyes soften, shining in the low light.

"I love you too," she whispers, pressing her lips to mine like it's the most natural thing in the world.

That's when it hits me — this isn't about wanting anymore.

It's about choosing.

We stay wrapped around each other until everything fades except the steady rhythm of our breathing and the warmth between us. Until the world quiets and all the noise that's ever lived in my head finally shuts up.
When we finally collapse for real, both of us done, the room dim and quiet and warm, I pull her into my chest and tuck the blankets around us.
She falls asleep like that, hand over my heart.
And for the first time in a long time, I fall asleep knowing:
No matter what the world says, no matter what the playoffs bring, no matter what anyone thinks—
She's mine.
And I'm hers.
And we are absolutely, undeniably, terrifyingly real.

Chapter 42

Lizzie

Morning light spills across the bed, warm and soft, and for a moment all I feel is the aftermath of last night — the closeness, the heat, the tenderness beneath all the intensity.

Ethan is wrapped around me from behind.

His arm is tight across my waist.

His breath is slow and warm against the back of my neck.

His legs are tangled with mine like he couldn't stand even an inch of space between us.

It's the most peaceful I've ever felt.

But then — slowly — his body changes.

Not the softness.

The tension.

A tiny shift in the way his arm tightens.

A slight hitch in his breath.

A tremor I might have missed if I didn't know him so well.

He's awake. And something old and frightened has surfaced.

Chapter 42

Just a little — but it's there.

I roll gently, turning in his arms. His eyes are open now, staring at the pillow like it offended him.

"Hey," I whisper softly. "Morning."

He tries to smile. It almost works.

"Mornin'."

Something twists in my chest.

I know this.

I've seen this — once, long ago.

Before he learned how to hide it.

When I was eight, I woke up thirsty in the middle of the night and wandered downstairs.

I heard Ethan crying in my kitchen.

Sobbing into my mom's sweater as she hugged him tight.

Trying to get the words out:

"Sh-she left. She… she left us. And she's not coming back."

He was ten.

Heartbroken.

Lost.

He never saw me.

I never told him.

I don't tell him now either.

Instead, I cup his cheek gently.

"What's wrong?" I murmur.

He flinches like he doesn't want to say.

"I'm fine."

"Ethan." My voice goes soft. "Talk to me."

And just like when he was ten — when all his walls were paper-thin — something in him cracks.

***

Ethan

I hate mornings.

I always have.

You'd think being older would change that — but every time I wake up with someone in my arms, full sunlight hitting the room, the first thought that hits me is:

What if she leaves too?

And that's pathetic. I know it is. I'm a grown man, not a scared kid. I have a career, friends, a life.

But trauma doesn't care about any of that.

My mom left in the morning.

No warning.

No explanation.

Just gone.

Lizzie strokes my cheek, and I feel my breath shake.

"I don't want to ruin this," I mutter. "But mornings… they mess with me."

She nods slowly, understanding flickering in her eyes in a way that makes my throat tighten.

"Do you want to tell me why?" she asks softly.

I swallow hard.

"When I was eleven, my mom walked out on us. She didn't say goodbye. Didn't even leave a note. Dad told me the next morning, and I—"

My voice cracks.

"I didn't take it well."

Her thumb rubs soothing circles on my skin.

Chapter 42

"And after she left," I continue, "Dad… shut down. Not in a cruel way. Just cold. Distant. Everything became about training and discipline and making sure I didn't fall apart."

Lizzie listens quietly, eyes gentle and patient.

"It felt like," I say quietly, "he was preparing me to live without anyone."

Her breath catches.

And then — so quietly I almost miss it — she whispers:

"I'm not going anywhere."

My whole chest tightens.

"You say that now," I breathe.

Her fingers slide into my hair.

"And I'll say it tomorrow," she replies softly. "And the next day. And every morning after."

A long, shaking exhale leaves me.

She means it.

God, she means it.

"I think," I murmur, "I need to talk to my dad."

She nods like she knew I'd say that.

"I'll come with you," she says. "If you want."

I lace my fingers with hers.

"Yeah," I whisper. "I want that."

* * *

Lizzie

His dad's house is literally next door to mine — a symbol of how intertwined our families have always been.

He answers the door wearing a Wintercrest Wolves sweatshirt and that familiar stern-but-warm expression he saves for me.

"Lizzie, sweetheart," he says immediately, pulling me into a hug.

Then he looks at Ethan.

A small smile softens his face.

"Son."

Ethan relaxes just a fraction.

We step inside.

His dad adores me — he always has. I've been at every Thanksgiving, every backyard barbecue, every Christmas Eve since I was little. He's never treated me as anything less than family.

He doesn't have an issue with me dating Ethan.

He never did.

The problem has always been the space between father and son.

We sit on the couch — Ethan on one end, his dad on the other. I sit nearby, quiet, supportive.

Ethan clears his throat.

"I don't want to fight," he says.

His dad nods. "Neither do I."

A long pause stretches.

Then Ethan speaks.

"When Mom left," he says quietly, "I think I blamed myself. And when you got harder with me… I thought that meant you blamed me too."

His dad straightens, eyes softening deeply.

"Ethan," he says, voice steady but emotional, "I never blamed you. Not for a second."

Chapter 42

Ethan swallows.

"I thought you were disappointed in me."

His dad shakes his head immediately.

"No. Never. I was disappointed in myself. I didn't know how to raise you without her. I didn't know how to be both parents at once. So I trained you hard because I thought strength would protect you when love couldn't."

Ethan looks down, breath unsteady.

His dad continues:

"And for the record, I'm proud of you. I always have been. I didn't say it enough — that's on me. But son..."

His voice cracks.

"You've become a better man than I ever taught you to be."

Lizzie's eyes fill with tears.

Ethan's do too — though he tries to blink them away.

Then his dad looks at me — and smiles.

"And Lizzie?" he says warmly. "She's been like a daughter to me since she was seven. If she makes you happy, then I approve."

Ethan's head drops forward — relief crushing him.

His dad stands first and pulls him into a hug — a long, real one.

Ethan slowly melts into it.

And something inside both of them finally heals.

When we walk back to Ethan's house, he's quiet — not the distant kind, but the peaceful kind.

His shoulders are lighter.

His breathing deeper.

His hand so steady in mine.

On his porch, he stops, turning to face me.

"You stayed," he says softly. "You always stay."

I smile.

"I always will."

He kisses me — not hungry like last night, not desperate — but slow and full of meaning.

A promise.

For the first time in Ethan's life, a morning doesn't feel like the moment someone leaves.

It feels like the moment everything begins.

Chapter 43

Lizzie

The morning after Ethan's emotional breakthrough with his dad feels different—steadier, quieter, like the whole world is holding its breath for something huge. Wintercrest buzzes with nervous anticipation, every storefront draped in Wolves colors, every street humming with talk of Game Seven. But inside Ethan's place, everything is soft and slow. He's calm in that dangerous, locked-in way athletes get before big games, but his hands are warm on my hips, his forehead pressed to mine like he's memorizing me before he steps into battle. When he whispers, "I'll find you in the stands," it sinks into my chest like a promise. By the time I leave to meet my family at the arena, my heart is pounding harder than the music already blasting blocks away. Tonight isn't just a game. It's history. It's the end of everything we've been fighting for—and the start of everything that comes next.

Secrets On Ice

* * *

Ethan

The sound of the arena is not a sound. It's a force. A living, rolling thing that presses against your chest and somehow makes your lungs work better.

Game Seven. The Stanley Cup. The kind of night that gets tattooed into a lifetime.

I stand in the tunnel with my helmet in my hands, feeling the cold sweat under my jersey. The boys are a mess of last-minute jokes and clipped focus. Coach's voice is calm; Matty's pacing like a caged animal. Ryan taps my shoulder twice with the kind of look that says everything we don't whisper in public.

"Play smart," he says. "Play ours."

I nod. Words are small here. Actions are big. Actions win Cups.

The lights dim. Spotlights slice the dark. A single, ripping cheer rises from the crowd and won't stop. The rink mouth opens and it's like stepping into a maw of noise and heat. The air hits me—hot and sharp—and for one breathless second I can't see past the helmet.

And then I see her.

Lizzie is pinned against the glass in the family section, scarf tight around her throat, hands fisted, lips moving around some unsaid prayer. She's not reading tonight. There's no book. Her eyes are on the ice like a blade. Like she knows where I'll be, even if I don't.

Everything else—roar, lights, music—drops the weight of a feather.

Chapter 43

I skate out to warmups and every part of me wakes to life. Blades bite, boards thrum, pucks ping. The bench banter is tighter than usual; everyone's breathing like they've been holding it for weeks.

First period is a war of inches. They come at us with everything they've got. Hits. Pucks thrown into the crease. Our goalie eats a scream-inducing rebound and makes a stop that makes the building lose its mind. We answer with speed, possession, the kind of patient play we practiced a thousand times.

Halfway through the period, I get tangled up on a forecheck with Matty. I spin, see a seam, and try the long pass across the slot. It's a risky thread through skates and sticks but Ace finds it. The puck slides, Ryan reads it like a map and rips a one-timer that folds into the net. The red light flashes. The arena detonates.

1–0 Wolves.

I look up at Lizzie—she's standing now, swinging like a pendulum between "no way" and "sobbing." She wraps her hands around Sasha, who's losing her mind with a grin so wide it's ridiculous. For a moment I let myself smile. The boy in me who grew up in these stands wants to throw his gloves into the crowd.

We finish the first 1–0. It's only the beginning, but it matters. Every shift matters.

* * *

Lizzie

I can't remember the last time my palms were this numb from cheering. It's not the cold; it's the pressure—my throat raw from yelling, my heart a drum behind my ribs.

He found Ryan for that first goal. My body launched before my brain did. I was standing, screaming, clapping until my hands stung. Sasha's voice is a tornado beside me—jokes, swears, tears—and for the first time since all the headlines, the attention, the noise, I feel alive instead of watched.

During intermission, Dad gives me a look—part pride, part father worry—and I squeeze his hand. I don't need to read my own journal tonight. Her blank page stays in my bag. Tonight, I'm not writing. I'm watching.

Back on the ice, the second period is where hockey lives. They come out like they want to take our souls. Hits so loud they feel personal. A power play against us means everyone on the bench mutters. I bite my lip as Ethan gets hammered into the boards and scrapes up, cursing, reaching for the puck like it's a lifeline.

It's late in the second when the other team claws one back—an odd bounce, a tip, our goalie left flat-footed. 1–1.

The building exhales. Fear slinks back into my stomach. I press my palms to the glass because it feels bigger than me otherwise.

Then Matty answers. We get another push. We keep trading hits and goals like a war of attrition: they score, we score; they get momentum, we ground it out. The scoreboard feels like a heartbeat I'm tapping to. 3–2. 3–3. Back and forth. Every goal is a gut punch and a salvation.

By the third period, everything is electricity. This is not just a game. This is the thing players dream about in hotel rooms

Chapter 43

and plane rides and childhood garages. All the stupid, costly choices and sacrifices and bruises and lonely fights—this is the moment that makes them worth it.

* * *

Ethan

The third period is chaos carved into precision. The other team's star is slick and mean; ours answers. We take a penalty and the crowd goes batshit until our kill line pulls it out like carved granite. I'm skating faster than I know, everything muscle and memory, and the clock thins like a held breath.

With five minutes left, Matty gets tripped on a rush and goes down in dramatic slow motion. Power play for them. The bench tightens. Faces harden. Coach's voice is a hum in my ear through the noise.

They press. They take the lead on a wrister from the point that skims through traffic 4–3 against us with 3:28 left on the clock.

A long, hot silence settles in my chest. My hands are clamps on my stick. I can hear my teammates breathing—sharp, steady. We skate like men cutting away regret.

"Push," Ryan says in that low voice. "Push and trust."

We trust each other. We push.

We win a turnover in the neutral zone—Matty battles, wins the board. I pick up the loose puck, cross the line, feel a shoulder at my hip, and the world narrows. Two on one. I look up. Time dilates.

Secrets On Ice

There's a seam between their defense and the goalie, a sliver of white. I see Ryan going to the net, his timing perfect, his stick ready. I could shoot. I could go for the angle. But something deeper than strategy nudges me. Everything funnels down to Lizzie standing in the family section, jaw set, hands clenched. Her eyes find mine for a fraction of a beat.

If this is for anything, it's for her. For the nights she sat alone in the stands, for the way she always, always loved the game even when it wasn't cool to, for the way she believed in the boys at twelve when nobody else did.

I pass.

Ryan takes it on his stick and—no, he doesn't. He fakes. He draws the defense. He slides a perfect feed back across, a blind-side pass to me who has cut to the slot. The window opens. I don't think. I shoot.

The puck is a bullet. It sings off the post and somehow, impossibly, slips in on the short side. The horn explodes. The red light screams. 4–4. Tie.

I don't remember skating back. I remember the sight of Lizzie's mouth open, the way Sasha is bawling next to her. For a second I can't breathe because the weight of it hits me like a wave: the season, the pain, all of it rolled into a small, bright moment.

We're headed to overtime.

* * *

Lizzie

Chapter 43

Overtime at a Game Seven is the kind of thing legends are made of. The arena sounds like a living thing waiting to be plucked. No one sits. No one breathes. Every face in the crowd is carved with the same terrible, beautiful intensity.

My heart is a drumbeat in my throat. Dad's grip on my hand is white-knuckle. Sasha has gone full hysteria and I let her because she's needed. I scan the ice like it's a church—our boys are on it, and everything I care about is sandwiched into thirty faithful minutes of sacrifice.

***

Ethan

OT is fast and clean. Muscle memory rules. We trade chances in a way that feels like flirting with disaster—one wrong touch and it's over. The puck is a comet: hit, deflect, glimpse, miss. A clatter at the boards. A whistle. A faceoff.

And then—late in the overtime—Matty wins a clean, beautiful faceoff back to me. The crowd hushes like a hand closing over a beating heart.

We cycle. We have speed. I carry in deep, I draw two defenders and slide a soft pass back to Matty at the top of the circle. He's got a second. He sees Ryan and—no—he sees me cutting in. It's all instinct. He feeds me.

My stick meets the puck. It's a thing of gravity, of muscle and will. I wind, I snap, and time... slows.

I watch the puck leave the blade, feel it kiss the air in a way that's almost tender, and then I see the goalie commit the tiniest fraction too far to the blocker side. The puck threads through the five-hole like it found a doorway.

Secrets On Ice

The red light explodes in a scream.

The arena forgets how to breathe.

We win.

The Stanley Cup is ours.

For a moment there is no sound in my head. Then the building erupts in a thunder that feels like the sky crashing down to hug us. My teammates are on me in a blur—Ryan first, eyes shining, voice breaking into the kind of laugh that's half-cry. Matty tackles me in a hug that knocks the air out of me. Coach is there, hollow and laughing and proud. I can't even find breath to form words.

Then I see her running.

No, not running—flying. Lizzie is out of the stands, vaulting the barrier, security momentarily stunned, Sasha shrieking like a banshee at her side. For a second I fear the refs will grab her, because this is the kind of move that gets you escorted out of arenas forever.

But Ryan's voice cuts across the chaos—sharp, commanding—and as if it's the green light, the security steps back. Ryan waves her on.

She crashes into me and everything is a fever of arms and faces and cameras. I bury my face in her hair because I can't look at her and not feel like the luckiest man alive.

"You did it," she breathes into my shoulder. "You did it."

"We did it," I say, because she's right. This is ours. Mine and the team's and hers, a braided thing that's bigger than any of us.

We climb toward the officials and the Cup ceremony like a pack of happy lunatics. The Cup is cold and heavy and stupidly bright. They put it in my hands for a heartbeat and I laugh because I can't do anything else. I taste salt—sweat,

Chapter 43

tears, champagne.

And when the camera finds us, when the world—suddenly relentless again—wants our faces, I find one face that matters and kiss her. Not the chaste, safe kiss of last night. This is a kiss that says: we survived, we fought, we are stubborn and stupid and brilliant, and you were there the whole time.

The cameras explode. Reporters push forward. The highlight shows loop on the jumbo screen. My dad is in the family box, eyes wet, proud. Ryan grabs my wrist and gives it the kind of brotherly squeeze that says everything from apology to love in one line.

Tonight, Wintercrest is a place where every street will be ringing with whistles. Tonight, we are champions.

Lizzie

I have been to games where I clapped politely. I have been to games where I cried in the stands because the team lost. I have been to games where the boys were good enough and we were only slightly hopeful.

This is everything.

I crash into him at ice level and his arms are the only place on earth that seem to make sense. He smells like sweat and cedar and victory and I am suddenly the most sentimental person alive. Sasha is leaping around us and security's yelling something about protocol, but Ryan's okay with it. Ryan is grinning like an idiot. My dad is laughing and hugging the nearest stranger.

He lifts me—no, he carries me—so the Cup is held between players and lovers and we're the stupidest, most glorious tableau ever broadcast for the world. I feel like falling apart from happiness. The cameras love us. The internet will melt. We are monumentally ridiculous and I don't care.

Ethan kisses me properly then—deep, fierce, the kind of kiss that makes you question gravity. It's a promise and a confession and a victory cry.

On the ice, in front of thousands and millions more, he whispers into my mouth: "Write the rest with me."

My heart stops. Then it breaks open in the best possible way.

"Yes," I say, voice small and big at once. "Yes."

We lift the Cup together. The team lifts us too. We are crying and laughing and everyone is chanting and the building is a heater of human joy.

For the first time, I know what it feels like to belong somewhere completely, to not be a footnote in someone else's life but the headline of my own story.

We skate off the ice holding hands, wet and wrapped in celebration. Cameras flash. Fans scream. It will be a week of interviews, of late-night shows, of our faces on every front page.

But right now, the only thing that matters is the weight of his hand in mine and the hum in my chest that says: this is home.

We go home that night with confetti in our hair and the taste of champagne on our lips. There will be more battles—press cycles, pissed-off rivals, the steady strain of fame—but at the center of it all is a little blank journal in my bag, a glowing heart on the ice, and the man beside me who looks like he was built for this, and who kisses me like he's been given a second life.

Chapter 43

"Tomorrow," he murmurs as he tucks me in, "we start writing."

"And the next day?" I ask.

"And the next day," he says, smiling into the soft dark. "Always the next day."

Outside, Wintercrest hums with victory. Inside, we are a small, perfect wreck, and the season ends the way everything in me had hoped it would: with love, with a Cup, and with a promise.

Chapter 44

Lizzie

Wintercrest still feels electrified from the championship parade, the city buzzing with Wolves merch, banners, and kids wearing Ethan's number. Everywhere I go, people are smiling, congratulating him—congratulating us.

But today?

Today isn't about Ethan.

Today is about me.

And he knows it.

Because the morning sunlight barely hits the curtains before Ethan rolls over, cups my face, and whispers:

"Today's your victory lap, Paperheart."

And the wild thing is…he means it more than he meant winning the Cup.

* * *

Chapter 44

It happens less than a week after the Cup.

It starts small.

A TikTok of someone finding my book on a local display table goes viral overnight.

Then a popular romance reviewer posts:

"How is this girl not already published traditionally? This is one of the most emotional debuts I've ever read."

Then an editor from a major publishing house reposts it.

Then two more.

Then five.

By noon, I've got eight unread emails from literary agents, five DMs from publishers, and a voicemail from Barnes & Noble corporate asking if I'd be open to a feature in their "Emerging Authors" spotlight.

I sit on the floor of my childhood bedroom, phone shaking in my hand, whispering:

"Oh my God…is this real?"

Sasha barges in without knocking, sees my face, and immediately screams like we won the lottery.

"YOU DID IT! YOU ACTUALLY DID IT! MY BEST FRIEND IS GOING TO BE A FAMOUS AUTHOR AND I CAN SAY I KNEW HER WHEN SHE ONLY HAD GOOGLE DOCS AND DREAMS!"

She tackles me into a hug.

We spin around.

We cry.

It's everything.

In the six days since the cup my manager calls me in.

I expect a "we're proud of you, now don't forget you're scheduled Saturday."

Instead, when I walk in, there's a whole table—my book

front and center, surrounded by candles, fake snow, and fairy lights. A sign reads:

LOCAL AUTHOR SPOTLIGHT: LIZZIE HARPER — WINTERCREST'S OWN

I cover my mouth.

"I—I didn't think—"

My manager smiles. "You earned this, Lizzie."

And for the first time in my life, I let myself believe that.

***

Ethan meets me outside the store after his morning workout.

Still sweaty, still in Wolves gear, still the hottest man on the continent.

He lifts me off the ground in one swoop.

"I saw your display inside," he murmurs into my neck. "You should've seen your face."

I shove him lightly.

"You weren't even in the store."

He taps his temple.

"I keep track of my girl. Especially when she's out here taking over the world."

My stomach erupts into butterflies.

He takes my hand.

Serious now.

"Lizzie... I'm so damn proud of you. I've dreamed of winning a Cup since I was a kid, but watching you chase what you love?"

He swallows.

"That's better than any win I've ever had."

Chapter 44

My throat tightens.

"And I want you to keep going," he says. "Write the next one. And the next. And the next after that. Don't let anything dim this."

I breathe out shakily.

Because for the first time, I actually believe I can.

That night, I open my laptop with my offer emails glowing like stars.

And for the first time ever...

I don't feel scared.

I draft my reply—an official query to one of the top literary agents in the country.

Right before I hit send, Ethan sits behind me, wraps his arms around my waist, and kisses my shoulder.

"Nervous?" he teases.

"Terrified."

"Send it anyway."

I click.

It sends.

And he whispers:

"There she goes... the woman who's going to own shelves across the country."

***

Later, we lie in bed—Ethan on his back, arm hooked behind his head, me tracing patterns on his chest.

He asks softly:

"So... what are you going to write next?"

I smile.

"A love story."

He smirks. "Based on anyone I know?"

I kiss him.

"Yeah," I whisper. "The man who forced his way into my heart with one anonymous message… and never left."

He pulls me onto his chest.

Breathes me in.

And murmurs:

"Then I'll make sure I stay impossible to forget."

Chapter 45

Lizzie

Wintercrest feels different now.

Not louder.

Not busier.

Just… mine.

The Wolves parade banners are still fluttering across main street. Kids still run around in little jerseys with Ethan's number. Barnes & Noble still has my book displayed under fairy lights.

And Ethan?

He's been glued to me like I'm his personal trophy he hasn't stopped celebrating.

But tonight… it's quiet.

We're sitting on the roof of his townhouse—his favorite spot—wrapped in one giant blanket he swears is "not pink" even though it's absolutely pink. The sky is clear, stars bright, and Wintercrest looks like it's breathing beneath us.

Ethan brushes his fingers over mine, slow and warm.

"You've been thinking all day," he murmurs.

"I always think."

"Not like this."

His thumb traces circles on my palm. "You look... settled."

I exhale, leaning my head on his shoulder.

"I feel settled," I admit. "For the first time in my life."

He goes still, listening without interrupting.

"I have my book career starting. I have the Wolves job I love. I'm not hiding our relationship anymore. And... I feel like everything is finally aligned."

Ethan turns his head, pressing a kiss into my hair.

"I want to talk about something," I say quietly.

His shoulders tense, just slightly. "Yeah?"

I smile.

Reassuring.

"Us. Our future."

His breath leaves him in one slow rush—relief, excitement, hope, all tangled.

"I want to move in with you," I whisper.

He freezes.

Then—slowly—he sets the blanket aside and shifts, facing me fully.

"Lizzie..."

His voice cracks.

He cups my jaw gently. "Are you sure? I don't want you to feel rushed. Or pressured. Or—"

"I'm sure," I cut in. "I want to fall asleep with you every night. Drink coffee on your counter. Trip over your hockey gear. And... be part of your everyday life."

His throat works as he swallows.

"You already are," he says, voice rough. "But having you live

Chapter 45

with me? That's—fuck, Lizzie, that's everything I've wanted for months."

I grin.

"Then say it."

He tugs me into his lap, forehead pressed to mine, hearts lined up like magnets.

"Move in with me," he says softly. "Not someday. Not eventually. Now."

My smile is instant, unstoppable.

"Yes."

He breathes out a shaky laugh, burying his face in my neck.

"I'm gonna treat you so damn good," he mutters. "I swear to God, you'll never regret this."

I kiss him, slow and certain.

"I know."

* * *

Ethan

I'm not thinking about marriage.

Not because I don't want it—not even close.

It's because she's young.

She's building a career.

She deserves time. Freedom. Choice.

But moving in together?

Being part of her daily life?

Sharing a home?

That feels right.

Real.
Perfect.

So later that night, when she's curled against me on my couch, wearing my hoodie and doodling her next book cover in her journal, I say:

"When you move in… you should keep your own office."

She looks up.

"Office?"

I nod.

"You're going to need one. For writing. For your Wolves schedules. For… all your author things I don't understand but pretend to."

She laughs, hitting my thigh with the journal.

"You're ridiculous."

"I'm right."

She bites her lip. "And where will your office be?"

"Wherever you are," I say simply.

She blushes.

Every time she does that I fall a little deeper.

* * *

Lizzie

"What about marriage?" I joke.

Half-teasing.

Half-curious.

Ethan stills.

Then smiles—slow, sure, devastating.

Chapter 45

"I'm not going anywhere," he says. "But I want to do this right. Not rushed. Not because Wintercrest is watching us. When I propose…"

He lifts my hand, kissing my palm.

"It'll be at a time when you're ready. When I'm ready. When life feels like ours, not the world's."

I melt against him.

"Okay," I whisper.

He cups my cheek.

"But don't worry," he adds softly. "I already know the answer."

My heart flips.

"You think so?"

"I know so."

He tucks a strand of hair behind my ear.

"You love me. I love you. And I want a life with you that lasts longer than a hockey career."

I kiss him again, longer this time.

"I want that too," I whisper.

* * *

Ethan

She falls asleep on my chest around midnight, breathing slow and even, holding onto me like she always does—like she trusts me completely.

I tighten my arm around her.

Moving in together.

Building a home.
Writing.
Hockey.
Our families.
Our dreams.
A quiet, steady future.
Ours.
And for the first time in my life…
I don't feel like I'm waiting for something to go wrong.
I feel like I'm finally where I'm meant to be.
With her.
In Wintercrest, finally starting the next chapter together.

Epilogue 1

Lizzie

If someone had told me a year ago that my life would look like this, I would've laughed.
Or hidden under a blanket. Or both.
But here I am:
Living with Ethan Walker.
The love of my life.
The man who still can't keep his hands off me.
(And absolutely doesn't try to.)
My second romance book sits half-finished on my laptop, my publisher waiting patiently—well, impatiently—for the next chapter. Barnes & Noble has already asked if I'll do another signing. And the Wolves... they finally treat me like I'm more than Ryan's little sister. I'm the Assistant GM. Officially. Actually. Confidently.
All of it feels surreal.
But my favorite part?
Coming home.

Tonight Ethan returns from practice early, dropping his bag by the door with a tired groan that goes straight to my heart. He's wearing sweatpants and one of my old bookstore shirts because he refuses to stop stealing them.

"Baby," he calls, voice warm and low. "Where are you?"

"Office!" I shout back.

He appears in the doorway a second later, hair damp, cheeks flushed, eyes locked on me like I'm the only thing that matters.

"You look hot when you're focused," he says, walking straight over.

"You look sweaty," I tease.

He smirks, leans down, and kisses me until I forget my own name.

***

Ethan

I still get butterflies.

Actual butterflies.

Me. Ethan Walker.

A grown-ass, six-foot-two professional hockey player.

Because she's here.

Mine.

Every night.

Every morning.

When I pull away, she giggles—soft, breathy, completely destroy-me adorable.

"How was practice?" she asks.

Epilogue 1

"Good." I lean my forehead against hers. "Missed you."

"You saw me this morning."

"And?" I shrug. "Still missed you."

She rolls her eyes but she's smiling—bright and shy, like it hits her every time that I mean it.

I sit on the edge of her desk, glancing at her laptop. "Is that the new book?"

She groans dramatically. "It's chaos."

"Hot chaos?" I ask.

She throws a pencil at me.

But then her face softens. "You're my muse, you know."

I swear my heart actually stutters.

"Good," I say quietly. "I like being that."

* * *

Lizzie

Later that night, Sasha comes over for dinner.

She's wearing lip gloss.

And a dress.

And she keeps glancing out the window.

Which can only mean one thing.

Ryan.

When he finally walks in—loud and dramatic as ever—her whole face lights up before she can stop it. She pretends to be annoyed. He pretends not to stare at her legs. Ethan nudges me and whispers:

"They're next. Calling it now."

I elbow him because absolutely not.

But also… absolutely yes.

Sasha flushes every time Ryan laughs.

Ryan glances at her every two minutes like he's checking she's still there.

It's painfully, deliciously obvious.

A spark waiting for its book.

* * *

Ethan

Dinner is loud, chaotic, comfortable—exactly how Wintercrest always is.

Lizzie sits curled against my side, my hand on her thigh, her hair falling over my shoulder. My parents love her. Her parents love me. Ryan tolerates me.

Okay, fine. Ryan still threatens me twice a week.

But it's progress.

After dessert, I lift Lizzie into my arms and carry her upstairs while Sasha and Ryan bicker in the kitchen like an old married couple.

In our bedroom, she wraps her arms around my neck.

"One year," she whispers.

"One year," I echo, kissing her forehead. "And I'm still obsessed with you."

She blushes—soft and pink, like she doesn't realize I mean it every single day.

"We have a good life," she murmurs.

"We have the best life," I correct. "And we're just getting started."

Epilogue 1

***

Lizzie

Later, when he's asleep beside me, arm wrapped tight around my waist, breath slow and even against my neck, I look around our room.

My books on the shelves.

His jerseys on the wall.

Our future everywhere.

Wintercrest is still small.

Still snowy.

Still loud with hockey fans.

But it's also the place where I found myself.

Where Ethan found me.

Where we found each other.

One year later…

I'm still choosing him.

He's still choosing me.

And we're only turning the first page of everything we're going to be.

Epilogue 2

Three Years Later

Lizzie

Wintercrest hasn't changed much.

The snow still falls heavier here than anywhere else.

The Wolves banners still line Main Street.

The arena still glows wolf-blue every night.

But I have changed.

I'm twenty-nine now, married, writing my fourth book, assistant GM of the Wolves, and finally living the life that used to only exist in my journals.

And Ethan?

He still looks at me like he did the night everything began.

Tonight, we walk hand-in-hand down Main Street after dinner, bundled in coats. My wedding ring catches the light from the Christmas lanterns lining the sidewalks. Ethan's thumb brushes over it like he still can't believe it's there.

"Three years," he murmurs.

"Three years," I echo.

"And I'm still obsessed with you."

I smile. "Good."

Epilogue 2

We stop in front of the bookstore—my bookstore—and there in the window is my newest novel, displayed under fairy lights… right beside a cardboard cutout of Ethan smirking like he owns the place.

Ethan loves it.
Ryan claims it haunts him.
Sasha says it's "peak unhinged boyfriend energy."
It's perfect.
"Ready?" Ethan asks softly.
"For the ceremony?"
"For everything," he says.
And I am.

* * *

Ethan

Walking into the arena with Lizzie on my arm feels exactly right—like this building, this city, this life… all of it led me to her.

The Wolves' newest championship banner hangs from the rafters. Our second Stanley Cup in five years.

She squeezes my hand.
I squeeze back.

At the tunnel entrance, Ryan is waiting—smirking like an idiot—and Sasha stands beside him looking too pretty for someone who "didn't dress up on purpose."

Lizzie waves. "Hey!"
Ryan hugs her first.

Sasha does too, a little too quickly.

And then it starts.

The weirdness.

Sasha keeps glancing at Ryan.

Ryan keeps glancing at Sasha.

But every time they make eye contact, they jerk their attention away like someone hit them with a spotlight.

Lizzie notices immediately.

"Are you two... okay?"

Ryan snorts. "We're fine. Totally fine. Absolutely fine."

Sasha nods aggressively. "So fine. The finerest. I mean—finest."

They flinch after speaking in unison.

"Okayyy..." Lizzie whispers.

Ryan clears his throat. "I'm gonna... go check on something."

Sasha blurts, "Yes! I mean—me too! But separately! In opposite directions!"

They both march off... in the same direction.

Lizzie turns to me slowly.

"What is happening?"

I shrug.

"Whatever it is, they're not admitting it yet."

She hums, eyes narrowing.

Seeds planted.

Perfectly.

***

Epilogue 2

Lizzie

The ceremony begins with the usual Wintercrest magic—fireworks on the roof, confetti in Wolves colors, a crowd packed into the arena like it's their church.

When Ethan's name is announced, the stadium erupts.

But when the announcer adds:

"And a special acknowledgment to Assistant GM and best-selling romance author, Lizzie Harper-Walker…"

I want to sink straight through the ice.

The crowd screams.

Ryan wolf-howls.

Sasha giggles.

Ethan beams.

I try to hide my face in my scarf, but Ethan catches me and pulls me gently to the stage.

He takes the microphone, looks out at the thousands of people… and then at me.

"My wife," he says, voice steady and warm, "is the reason I'm standing here today. If you've read her books… you know she writes about the kind of love people dream of that I get to live it every day."

The arena goes wild.

I go breathless.

And for a moment, it's just him and me.

The crowd fades.

The lights soften.

The world narrows.

I fall in love with him all over again.

***

Ethan

After the ceremony ends, I take Lizzie's hand and lead her onto the empty rink.

Center ice.

Where everything started.

Where everything changed.

She steps onto the wolf-logo and smiles up at me.

"Still happy?" I whisper.

She looks around the arena—our arena—then back at me.

"I'm more than happy," she says. "I'm home."

I slip a small velvet box from my coat pocket.

She gasps. "Ethan—"

"Not what you think." I open it.

Inside is a silver charm: a tiny wolf pup curled against its parent.

Lizzie's eyes fill instantly.

"It isn't a hint," I say softly. "Not pressure. Just a reminder. That when you're ready—when we're ready—I want that future. A family. With you."

She throws her arms around my neck, tears warm against my skin.

"Someday," she whispers. "Yes. Someday."

I exhale shakily against her neck.

"That's all I need."

I clip the charm onto her bracelet, next to the tiny wolf from years ago and the miniature book charm we added after her first signing.

Our story.

Epilogue 2

On her wrist.
Forever.

***

Lizzie

We stand there on center ice, holding each other, the arena glowing around us. Wintercrest hums outside—alive, loud, loving.

I look at Ethan.

My husband.

My muse.

My once-impossible dream.

"Ready to go home?" he asks.

I lace my fingers with his.

"I already am."

And just like that…

standing in the place where everything began…

we take our next step toward everything still waiting for us.

Our forever.

WINTERCREST WOLVES — OFFICIAL TEAM ROSTER + PLAYER CARDS

TOP LINE — STARS OF WINTERCREST
ETHAN WALKER (28)
Position: Center • Role: Co-Captain
Broody. Strategic. Scary on the ice, soft for one girl off the ice.
The man you want in overtime and in your bed.

RYAN HARPER (28)
Position: Right Wing • Role: Co-Captain
Charming trash-talker with a lethal shot.
Best friend's sister? Off limits. (For now.)

WINTERCREST WOLVES — OFFICIAL TEAM ROSTER + PLAYER CARDS

LUCAS "ACE" MADDOX (27)
Position: Left Wing • Role: Alt Captain
Cocky flirt. Camera loves him. So do fans.
Future book boyfriend material.

SECOND LINE — THE HEART OF THE PACK
MATTEO "MATTY" ROJAS (26)
Defenseman • Quiet. Brilliant. Slow-burn king energy.
TYLER BROOKS (23)
Defenseman • Chaotic menace. Needs supervision.
NICO ALVAREZ (25)
Utility Center • Loyal. Private. Future mystery romance hero.

THIRD LINE — THE WARRIORS
BRANDON "BRICK" CARTER (29)
Defenseman • 6'5", 240 lbs of softie. Calls everyone "kid."
CODY JENSEN (24)
Left Wing • Fast. Goofy. Team baby.
JACK SULLIVAN (30)
Center • Veteran leader with dad-vibes.

GOALIES
JAXON REID (27)
Starting Goalie • Cold, calm, cocky.

A future dark romance waiting to happen.
THEO GALLAGHER (23)
Backup Goalie • Hyper, unhinged, always chirping.

COACHING & STAFF
  Head Coach: Mark Leighton
  Assistant Coach: Dani Kovac
  Team Therapist: Dr. Avery Lin

LOCKER ROOM CONFESSIONS

Wintercrest Wolves Official Magazine Quiz

Who is your fictional hockey boyfriend?
  Circle your answers, tally your points, and claim your man.

1. How do you like your romance heroes?
   A — Broody, loyal, protective
   B — Charming, cocky, loves attention
   C — Quiet, steady, secretly soft
   D — Flirty menace, talks too much
   E — Gentle giant with a soft heart
   Points:
   A = 5 | B = 4 | C = 3 | D = 2 | E = 1

2. What kind of kiss makes you weak?
   A — The "grab your jaw and kiss you stupid" one

B — A playful, teasing, crowd-watching kiss
C — A slow forehead kiss that ruins you emotionally
D — A wall-pin, breath-stealing kiss
E — A shy, blushing, "can I kiss you?" kiss
Points:
A = 5 | B = 4 | C = 3 | D = 2 | E = 1

3. Pick your favorite trope:
A — Brother's Best Friend
B — Enemies to Lovers
C — Slow Burn
D — Friends With Benefits
E — Sunshine × Grumpy
Points:
A = 5 | B = 4 | C = 3 | D = 2 | E = 1

4. Your ideal date night?
A — Being held tight at a hockey game
B — A rooftop kiss after dinner
C — A quiet bookstore moment
D — A dangerous amount of flirting at a party
E — A cozy movie night in sweatpants
Points:
A = 5 | B = 4 | C = 3 | D = 2 | E = 1

LOCKER ROOM CONFESSIONS

5. How should your man confess his love?
  A — In a grand emotional gesture that makes you cry
  B — Accidentally in public after a win
  C — Whispering "it's always been you"
  D — During an argument that turns into a kiss
  E — By hugging you and saying "I'm not going anywhere"
  Points:
  A = 5 | B = 4 | C = 3 | D = 2 | E = 1

SCORING

Add up all your points:

25–21 points → ETHAN WALKER

Your fictional boyfriend is the intense, jaw-clenching, protective center who would burn the world down for you.

He loves hard, kisses harder, and if you sigh too loud he'll pick you up like it's nothing.

Congratulations — you've pulled the co-captain of your dreams.

🔥 Bonus: He reads your favorite books.

20–16 points → RYAN HARPER

Your fictional boyfriend is the cocky, charming right wing who jokes his way through feelings—until he falls for you.

Playful, competitive, secretly soft for one girl only.

He'll chirp you, kiss you, and fight anyone who looks at you too long.

🔥 Warning: Brother's best friend vibes included.

15–11 points → LUCAS "ACE" MADDOX
You want a flirt.
A show-off.
A man who thrives in the spotlight and makes you feel like the only girl in the arena.
He'll ruin you with one smirk and take you home smiling.
🔥 Future series star.

10–6 points → JAXON REID
You're into quiet danger.
Your fictional boyfriend is the dark, cold goalie with a heart that only melts for you.
He's chaos controlled, eyes like storms, and lips that say very little but mean everything.
🔥 Your book will be spicy.

5–0 points → BRICK CARTER
You want the gentle giant.
The warm hug.
The soft protector.
He'll lift heavy things for you, defend you without blinking, and worship the ground you walk on.
🔥 Warning: May buy you a puppy.

WHAT KIND OF WINTERCREST GIRLFRIEND ARE YOU?

Take this quiz and find out where you'd fit in the Wolves world...

Circle your answers and tally your points at the end!

1. Your game-day vibe is...
   A — Full glam, nails done, Wolves jersey cropped just right
   B — Cozy hoodie, messy bun, yelling louder than the superfans
   C — Cute boots, notebook in hand, analyzing plays like a coach
   D — VIP suite energy — champagne, lip gloss, chaos
   E — Quiet pride — you're there for him, not for the cameras
   Points
   A = 4 | B = 3 | C = 5 | D = 2 | E = 1

Secrets On Ice

2. Pick your courtside snack:
   A — Nachos loaded with everything
   B — A pretzel the size of your head
   C — Hot chocolate with extra whipped cream
   D — A charcuterie plate you snuck in yourself
   E — Whatever he hands you with a smile
   Points
   A = 3 | B = 4 | C = 5 | D = 2 | E = 1

3. What do you do when the ref makes a bad call?
   A — Stand up and yell (politely...)
   B — Boo so loud the mascot looks nervous
   C — Pull up stats to prove he's wrong
   D — Flip your hair and say "he's blind, it's fine"
   E — Grab your man's jersey and hope he's okay
   Points
   A = 4 | B = 5 | C = 3 | D = 2 | E = 1

4. What's your ideal post-game moment?
   A — A kiss behind the locker room
   B — Him lifting you after a win
   C — Talking strategy on the drive home
   D — A spicy shower together
   E — Cuddling in sweatpants and ordering takeout
   Points
   A = 4 | B = 5 | C = 3 | D = 2 | E = 1

WHAT KIND OF WINTERCREST GIRLFRIEND ARE YOU?

5. How do you handle the attention that comes with dating a pro athlete?
A — With confidence — you're THAT girl
B — You don't care what anyone thinks
C — You'd rather stay low-key
D — You love the glamour
E — You just want him happy
Points
A = 4 | B = 5 | C = 3 | D = 2 | E = 1

SCORING

Add up your points → then find your girlfriend role below:

21–25 POINTS: THE FIRECRACKER

You're loud, loyal, and full of passion.

You hype your man like he's the entire NHL.

You'll fight a ref, scream from the first row, then kiss your boyfriend senseless after he scores.

Perfect match: Ryan Harper (he needs someone who matches his chaos)

16–20 POINTS: THE STRATEGIST

You're smart, observant, steady — the brains of the arena.
Players secretly call you "Coach Jr."
You know every stat, every play, every shift.

Perfect match: Ethan Walker (captains fall for women who make them better)

11–15 POINTS: THE SWEETHEART

Warm, cozy, loving — you're the emotional core.
You don't need spotlight.
You're his peace after a stormy game.
Perfect match: Brick Carter (he would adore you endlessly)

6–10 POINTS: THE SIREN

You're all confidence and flirting.
A little dangerous.
A lot irresistible.
You make hearts melt—and players stumble.
Perfect match: Lucas "Ace" Maddox (your future series troublemaker)

0–5 POINTS: THE QUIET STORM

Soft on the outside, feral when necessary.
You stay silent… until someone talks trash.
Then they'll meet God.
Perfect match: Jaxon Reid (goalie soulmates always choose each other)

Acknowledgements

To my best friend, Elizabeth (Lizzie) —
My muse, my ride-or-die, my forever safe place. Thank you for being the heartbeat behind this story, for inspiring a heroine as brave and soft and strong as you. For every late-night talk, every chaotic conversation, every moment you believed in me even when I didn't believe in myself — this book carries your fingerprints on every page.
To my dad, my biggest supporter and wisest adviser —
Thank you for cheering me on through every chapter, every doubt, and every dream. Your belief in me has been the foundation I've built my courage on. I'm forever grateful.
To my family, who support me quietly but fiercely in the background —
Your love gives me space to grow, to write, and to chase this crazy passion of mine. I feel you rooting for me with every word.
And finally, to my readers —
You are the reason I write. Your excitement, your messages, your devotion to these characters… It keeps my heart beating in this world of stories. Thank you for letting my

imagination live on your shelves, in your hearts, and in your hands. I write for you as much as I write for myself — and I'm honored you're here.
This book exists because all of you exist in my life.
Thank you, truly, for everything. This is only the beginning.
Thank you, truly, for everything.

Book 2 Teaser

Ryan & Sasha
Enemies to lovers. Friends with benefits. No strings. Big feelings.

* * *

Sasha

Ryan Harper is the one man I should never want—and the only one I can't stop thinking about. He's arrogant, smug and infuriatingly handsome in that "I know you want me" way.

And worst of all?

My best friend's older brother.

But the problem is…

I see him every damn day.

At the arena.

At Harper family dinners.

In Lizzie and Ethan's house like he lives there.

And every time our eyes meet, it feels like we're two seconds away from either killing each other or ripping each other's clothes off.

Usually both.

Tonight, after a team celebration, he corners me in the hallway behind the VIP lounge — stupidly gorgeous in his Wolves jacket, smelling like victory and trouble.

"We need to talk," he says.

I cross my arms. "About what? Your ego? Because that might take a while."

His jaw ticks.

"My ego is not the problem."

"Oh?" I smirk. "Then what is?"

He steps closer. Too close.

"This."

His eyes drag down my body, slow enough to make my pulse trip.

"This thing between us."

"There is no 'thing,' Ryan."

He laughs — low, deep, annoyingly sexy.

"Sure there is. And it's driving both of us insane."

My stomach flips so hard it hurts.

I hate that he's right.

"So what do you suggest?" I ask, trying to sound bored when my throat is dry.

Ryan leans in, lips almost brushing my ear.

"We get it out of our system."

I freeze.

He pulls back, eyes dark.

"No strings. No feelings. Just… stress relief."

My mouth goes dry.

My heart pounds.

"And when we're done," he adds, "we go back to hating each other like normal."

I swallow. "You really think that would work?"

His smirk is lethal.

"I think we want each other enough that it's worth a shot."

God help me…

He's right.

And that's exactly why I should say no.

But instead…

I whisper, "Fine. One rule."

"Anything you want." His voice is smoke.

"No falling in love," I say.

And for the first time… he doesn't look smug.

His smile fades just a little — like the idea hits deeper than he expected.

"Deal," he says.

We shake on it.

His hand is warm.

His touch lingers.

And I already know we're both in trouble.

Major trouble.

* * *

Ryan

This is a terrible idea.

A catastrophic, career-ending, family-exploding idea.

Sasha Brooks is off limits.
She always has been.
My little sister's best friend.
The girl who knows exactly how to piss me off.
The girl I've been trying — and failing — not to touch for years.
But when she agreed to my stupid proposal…
No strings.
No feelings.
Just… us…
Something inside me cracked open.
I'm screwed.
We're both screwed.
Because I know one thing for sure:
Once I have her…
I'm not letting her go.
Not even if it ruins everything.

www.ingramcontent.com/pod-product-compliance
Lightning Source LLC
LaVergne TN
LVHW091701070526
838199LV00050B/2246